ORDINARY ANGELS

INDIA DRUMMOND

TRINDLEMOSS
PUBLISHING

Ordinary Angels

Copyright © 2011, India Drummond

Published in the United Kingdom 2011 by
Trindlemoss Publishing

e-ISBN: 978-1-908436-04-7
ISBN: 978-1-908436-05-4

To Colin, who understands my artistic temperament and loves me anyway. My very own angel.

To Colin, who understands my artistic temperament and loves me anyway. My very own angel.

Acknowledgements

Warm, heartfelt thanks to: Marsha Moore and Mollie Bryan for helping me through those early drafts, Jill Watt for letting me borrow her car and her mailman, and Daniel Mahgerefteh for showing me the secret life of a Tuesday dancer. To John Ponderoyn, Ute-Christine Klehe, and Rhonda Kurz: You were there at the beginning of this writer's journey, before this story was even a twinkle in my eye. Thank you.

Most of all I owe deep gratitude to Kate McIntire. Your never-failing faith and encouragement made so many things possible, including this book.

CHAPTER 1

ALL BUT ONE OF ZOË PENDERGRAFT'S friends were dead. This didn't bother her, because most had died long before she met them. Henry, for example, died in 1883. Not in the Fiskers building itself, obviously, since the Fiskers building wasn't constructed until 1924. Of all the spirits she saw living their afterlives, she only called a few friends, and Henry topped that list.

She looked up and down the corridor once more to make sure no one could see her. "Henry?" she called as she stepped into the company's vast, dank boiler room and closed the scuffed, dirty door behind her. "It's me. Zoë." She'd had to avoid several co-workers on the way to the maintenance area, but she had a special reason to visit Henry today.

"I know it's you, Miss Zoë. I always can tell." Henry appeared from behind a series of pipes along the north wall. He must have been handsome when he was alive. She saw the appeal, even though he wore the overalls of a railway worker from the nineteenth century. Henry's wide, dark face broke into a grin, showing a full set of gleaming teeth.

"I brought you a present," Zoë said, matching his smile with her own.

"Now, you didn't have to do that. You know it's enough that you come see Old Henry and chat once in a while."

With a dip into her jacket pocket, she closed her hand around the small metal object. "Guess what it is," she said.

"Why I couldn't begin to guess, Miss Zoë. You're always full of surprises."

She held out her hand and revealed an antique key. The decorative top, or bow as Henry had taught her to call it, had blackened with age, but she could still see the intricate scrollwork forming the cloverleaf design. The post had two identical bits on either side. Viewed together, they looked like two capital Fs back to back.

"I found it at a shop on Union Street. Isn't it great?" One of the things she loved about San Francisco was the fantastic antique stores dotted all over the city.

Henry towered over her and peered at the key in her hand. "That's just fine, Miss Zoë. The finest one I've ever seen." His weathered face glowed for a second as he placed a hand over the key.

Zoë could have sworn the key shimmered blue

when he got closer, but the effect passed so quickly she dismissed the thought. "Shall I put it with the others then?" She crossed to the farthest, darkest corner of the boiler room where a pegboard hung in front of a forbidding and disused metal door. On the pegboard was a mismatched collection of odds and ends from a century past with a few things even older than Henry. She placed the new key on an empty peg somewhere in the middle, above a line of trinkets that included a pocket watch, a small knife, and a carved piece of ivory. Nothing was particularly valuable, but they had each caught her eye, and she knew Henry loved old keys. "There."

When she turned around, Henry looked teary. He pulled an old hanky out of his pocket and wiped his nose.

"Oh, Henry, I'd give anything to be able to give you a hug right now."

Henry smiled. "You sit yourself down, Miss Zoë, and I'll tell you a story."

About nine months ago, shortly after she had started coming to see Henry, she'd smuggled down an old quilt to cover a long metal box. It wasn't enough to make the seat soft, but it did protect her from the worst of the grime. She made herself comfortable on it now, settling in for a chat. Henry put his hand over hers. It went right through, and a deep chill made her bones ache. She tried to suppress the shiver that sliced through her body, because she wouldn't want to offend her dear friend.

"In 1878 I worked for Southern Pacific as a stake driver," Henry began and then interrupted himself.

"Have I told you this before?"

"Don't think so," Zoë said, although he had. Dead people, she noticed, had a horrible sense of anything that happened after they quit living. Time got fuzzy and days, weeks, even years ran together into an insignificant blur.

Henry had a gift for storytelling though, so she didn't mind the repetition. The images of the men working in the hot sun floated in her mind as if she'd blistered her back alongside them. Painting scenes of life in another age, he often talked about the "China House" where he'd bunked with the Chinese railway workers, and sometimes touched on his time in the gold mines in Lament, California. She'd noticed spirits rarely talked about how they died. Although she was curious, it seemed rude to ask, and Henry was such an old gentleman that she didn't want to offend him. She'd been able to see ghosts for all her twenty-five years, and she'd learned which topics to avoid.

When her watch beeped once, Zoë couldn't believe how the hour had sped by. She looked up at Henry, who hadn't noticed the sound. He was in full swing, talking about his foreman, Bill Bradshaw, and the argument one day over water that nearly got him and his friend Li killed.

"I'm sorry, Henry. It's time to go back to work."

"Time," he said and shook his head sadly. "I thank you for the key, Miss Zoë. It's a real beauty."

"It's nothing," she said as she stood to straighten her skirt and slip her shoes on.

"I met a lot of people in my life, Miss Zoë, and I've met even more after it." He smiled and his eyes glistened. "It's not nothing when a young, pretty girl takes the time for an old man like me. You should be out doing whatever it is girls do nowadays. Going to the shows or something."

"I do, Henry. Just not at lunch time." She made her way to the door, wanting to leave before he got to fussing about her social life and telling her to find some man to settle down with and have babies. There was no way a spirit could understand what it meant to be able to see him and the others, and how it made talking with regular people painful at times, and finding that special someone a distant dream. She waved when she got to the door, wiggling her fingers and grinning. "Bye, Henry. See you tomorrow."

"Bye, Miss Zoë. Don't you worry about me. I'll be here."

Zoë breathed easier after her visit with Henry. Tension and work headaches melted. She happily took the stairs two at a time back to the main floor. On the way, one or two guys in gray jumpsuits with bright yellow reflective stripes across their torsos waved and smiled. They'd gotten used to her coming into their domain nearly every day. As far as she could tell, they didn't think anything of it, except maybe they thought she was on the odd side for taking her lunch hour in the boiler room.

Before she returned to her desk, she ducked into the ladies room to dust herself off. It was always wise to check if her brown curls had gotten unruly while she lounged below. She pondered her reflection, considering getting highlights, and then dismissed the thought.

While she applied some lip-gloss, a wisp of light reflected in the bathroom mirror caught her eye. The wisp shuddered for a moment as a small girl flickered into the room.

"Have you seen my mommy?"

Zoë turned around and did her best to smile at the child spirit. "No, honey. I haven't."

"My house shook, and I got stuck. After I got loose, I couldn't find her."

Without thinking, Zoë bent down and reached toward her. The spirit extended a tiny hand. As the cold chill of her touch bored through Zoë's fingers, the girl vanished.

The bathroom door swung open as Zoë straightened up, and Marilyn Baker walked in. Marched was more like it. Zoë fought not to roll her eyes. "Hi, Marilyn," she said.

"Are you all right?" Marilyn made everything sound like criticism. Today she wore her short black hair tight around her face, making her look even more severe than usual. Her black vest showed too much cleavage, and her high heels made her at least five foot ten, tall enough to tower over Zoë's petite frame.

"Yeah," Zoë said, walked to the trash receptacle on the wall and pretended to throw something in it. "Just dropped something."

"Where have you been? I've been looking for you."

Zoë fought the rising annoyance. She was entitled to her lunch hour, and she was at most two minutes late back to her desk. "Um, just popped down to maintenance. Light bulbs."

"Again? Look, I've told you to call extension five-three-one and they will send someone around. And tell them to bring you a new desk lamp. It's ridiculous how often that one burns out."

Zoë shrugged. "Okay." She found it best to agree with Marilyn as often as possible.

"It's not as though you don't have enough to do without doing maintenance's job for them."

She realized she'd better leave before Marilyn noticed she wasn't carrying any light bulbs, so she chirped, "Back to work," and slipped out the door.

As she stepped into the corridor Zoë collided with her best friend, in truth her only *living* friend, Simone Wallace. Simone nearly dropped the manila folder she clutched in her arms. Her long hair perfectly framed her dark oval face.

"There you are," Simone said, flicking her red nails with a gesture of annoyed impatience. "I've been looking for you."

"I had lunch with Henry."

"Do you know Dustin Bittner?" Simone asked, her coal-black eyelashes fluttering.

Zoë grinned. She loved that she could tell Simone things, like how she'd had lunch with a dead man, and Simone wouldn't notice, much less call her a nut. Too much of Zoë's life had been occupied with making certain no one found out about her peculiar abilities, so having someone with whom she could be herself was a relief. "Sure," she said as they walked toward her desk. "Second floor. Engineer, I'm pretty sure."

"Married?" Simone sounded eager, like she'd picked up a scent.

"I dunno. I take him mail sometimes if it comes through the project office, but I don't really talk to him."

"He's not wearing a ring, I don't think. It was hard to tell without staring." Simone looked thoughtful. "You should do your psychic thing on him."

Zoë sat down in her chair and chuckled. "It would only work if he were dead, Simone. And maybe not even then. You know how it is."

Simone eyed her, obviously not knowing how it was. But Zoë wouldn't bother once again explaining the difference between a medium and a psychic.

"Why don't you do an internet search? Isn't stalking potential boyfriends the reason God gave us Google?" Zoë pulled a file folder out of her desk and shifted through a pile of expense receipts.

"I did, but I didn't find much. You gotta help me."

"Okay. I'll see what I can find out. Maybe there will be a letter for him soon, and I'll call you to take it to him. Give you an excuse to say hello."

"Me?" Simone said, "You have to be kidding. I can't do that. You do it, and ask him if he knows me."

Zoë laughed. "That's the dumbest plan I've ever heard."

"Say whatever you want. You're good with people." Simone looked toward the door, and her tone changed. "Mmm, mmm. Special delivery."

Zoë started to argue about being good with people and amend it to say she was good with *dead* people, which wasn't the same thing, but her friend's slack-jawed expression distracted her. She turned to follow Simone's line of sight when she saw him.

"He's radiant," Zoë said absently, staring at something her brain could not quite process. A man walked toward them, but even that wasn't right. Although every part of her body told her this was indeed a man, the word didn't come close. Not a spirit. Too solid. Her eyes scanned him up and down. Very solid.

"He's something," Simone agreed, nearly dropping her folder again.

The oddest thing about this person, Zoë realized, was that he wore blue shorts. Mailman shorts. Glancing at his tanned legs, she indulged in a momentary fantasy, and swallowed hard. All of a sudden, she noticed he stood in front of her desk, smiling down at her. "You're the mailman," she said, not yet in complete control of her powers of speech.

"I am," he said in a tone that was unbelievably sexy, considering the brevity of the statement. "I am supposed to give you this," he said and handed her a bundle of letters. "And these," he continued, and produced a few small padded envelopes out of his blue mailman's bag.

"Aren't you going to ask me for my phone number?" Zoë blurted out and then blushed all the way to her hairline.

"Does Ronald do that?"

"Oh, yes," she said, not adding that she never gave it to the regular postman who flirted with her daily. If Zoë was honest, which she nearly always strove to be, she didn't mind that Ronald persisted. It had become a game, but one she didn't particularly want to follow through.

"Why does he ask for your phone number?" the new mailman asked, leaning forward as though expecting to hear something important and secret.

"To ask her out. Are you stupid or something?" Simone's uncharacteristic sharpness snapped Zoë back to reality.

"Simone," she whispered harshly.

"Well, really. What kind of dumb question is that?" Simone mumbled.

The mailman burst into delicious, warm laughter. He ran his hand over his choppy, light brown hair. "I am not sure what kind of dumb question it is. How many kinds are there?" He squeezed his eyes together in what could only be described as a two-eyed wink. Not a blink, but the sort of thing a child does when he doesn't know how to close only one eye.

Marilyn burst into the cluster of three with a loud clacking walk. She leaned over to straighten her strappy high heel, and showed her deep cleavage. She had mastered overt sexuality without being sexy in the least. Marilyn's eyes instantly locked on the mailman, devouring every inch of him.

"I'm not paying you to stand around gossiping," she said with her usual sharp tone, although she hadn't managed to peel her gaze off the new arrival.

He grinned. "Are you paying me?"

Simone snorted a laugh. "No," she said, "But I, for one, *am* getting paid to be here, so I'm going back to work." She took her folder and sashayed away, giving her hips an extra wiggle as she did. "Goodbye, M.B.," she said to Marilyn.

"Erm, goodbye," Marilyn said. Poor thing didn't know M.B. stood for Mega-Bitch and not Marilyn Baker, however, Zoë could tell her instincts had kicked in and told her something was up. It didn't take any special powers of deduction to know Simone didn't like her.

Zoë suppressed a smile. "I should get back to work too," she said to the postman.

"Okay," he said. "May I have your phone number?"

"Um, yeah. Okay," Zoë said, wrote down her mobile and handed it to him.

"I do not have a phone though," he said, which might have annoyed her coming from anyone else, but from him, it sounded adorable and charming.

"And I don't know your name," she replied, surprised at herself. She never gave her number to strange men, and this one had a quality she couldn't call anything but strange.

"Alexander," he said, "but I am not really a postman."

Marilyn stood, still staring. "But you brought the mail."

Zoë feared Marilyn was going to hear something she wasn't ready for. "Thank you, Marilyn," she said, hoping she wouldn't pay too dearly for it later. Zoë knew Alexander wasn't a spirit, but he wasn't human either. The possibilities made her edgy. The unknown unsettled her.

Marilyn walked away without another comment, to Zoë's surprise, but she did it reluctantly, as though she wanted to find an excuse to stay, but couldn't.

"I'm Zoë Pendergraft. So, what are you, Alexander? You're not human."

"I am an angel." Something in his tone convinced her Alexander was telling the absolute truth. "And what are *you*?" The question could have sounded simple or stupid, but he was neither. His green eyes radiated something magnificent and beautiful. The way his tousled hair stuck out around his face seemed artful and perfect.

Zoë didn't know how to answer. Several thoughts presented themselves, but none fit. So she did what any woman would: she ignored the question. "I guess if you don't have a phone, you're not going to call me." She stopped herself before adding "for a date", but she needn't have bothered.

"I could come to your house after work, and we could go on a date," he said. "I have never been on a date."

"Okay. I'd like that," she said and then wondered at her inability to control what came out of her mouth, as though someone had given her truth serum.

"I will see you later then," he said and turned to go. When he reached the door, he waved and then left. Zoë could breathe again. The ordinariness of her gray half-cubicle closed in on her, dull and lifeless with Alexander gone. Only then did she realize he hadn't asked for her address.

CHAPTER 2

THE GRAY AFTERNOON DRAGGED, and Zoë couldn't wait to leave. She begged off when Simone came by for a coffee break and told her friend a flat lie, saying there wasn't any mail for Dustin, which would mean she had no pretense to check out the newest object of Simone's office obsessions.

At four o'clock, Zoë stuck her head into Marilyn's office. "Hey, I'm taking off early. I have a killer headache. I'll come in at seven tomorrow." The words came in one long flow and she scurried away before Marilyn could argue. Marilyn wasn't even technically her boss. Zoë was more of an area support person, but since no one seemed to know what an area support person did, or who they were supposed to report to, Marilyn had co-opted Zoë as she believed was her right. No one minded the arrangement, so Zoë went with it without too many issues.

Zoë's world didn't quite come back into alignment after her strange encounter with Alexander until she made it out the doors of Fiskers Technology Group and into the parking lot's far corner. She plopped into the driver's seat of her new Mini Cooper. Oh, how she loved that little thing. It was small and perfect and sexy and hers, all hers. She bought it as a gift for her twenty-fifth birthday three months ago and ordered every detail exactly the way she wanted, from the distinctive viper stripes to the sat-nav. Like a kid waiting for Christmas, she'd counted off the days off one by one as she waited for delivery from the Oxford factory. It still smelled like a new car. Zoë breathed in and closed her eyes, savoring the scent of new leather. Finally she decided she'd better get going before other people started filtering out of the office, so she started the car and made her way toward Highway 101.

She drove confidently and zoomed in and out of traffic, stopping forty-five minutes later at a Starbucks drive-thru four blocks from her house to grab a mocha. When she arrived at her house, a three-bedroom townhouse in San Francisco's Mission District, which she'd inherited from her grandmother, she realized she was out of food. Sighing, she parked in the driveway rather than pulling into the garage and locked her car. Half-way up the path, she noticed Alexander sitting on Mrs. Paez's steps, chatting with the old dear next door. Still wearing blue mailman shorts. A flash of annoyance disappeared before it had a chance to take root. He looked sweet, and she'd never seen

Mrs. Paez beam before. *A real angel*, Zoë thought, and shook her head, uncertain what this would lead to. It wasn't that she didn't believe his explanation. She did, and that was what gave her a twinge of a headache.

"There she is," Mrs. Paez called out when she spotted Zoë. "Alexander was telling me you two have a date." She pronounced it *Allisander*. "And I was saying that my Hector, may he rest in peace, always wanted you to find a nice man."

Zoë smiled politely. She doubted very much Hector Paez had said anything of the kind. "Alexander," she called, "Could you come here a minute?"

Alexander jumped up, took Mrs. Paez's hand and bowed over it. "Señora," he said and then bounded to Zoë. He stood close and smiled into her eyes. She had to fight the urge to reach up and twirl her fingers in his messy brown hair, which stuck out in teasing wisps. "Yes?" he said, his voice low and sensual.

"Alexander," Zoë began, but wasn't quite sure where to start. "For one, you're early."

"Am I?" He grinned, as though seeing her made him happier than anything.

Zoë lowered her voice when she noticed Mrs. Paez still peered at them from her porch swing. "Are you really an angel? I mean I can tell you're... different. But, well..."

"You are different too," he said.

"Am I?" Zoë thought about that for a moment.

"Wait, no I'm not. I'm human, and you're not. You're..." She waved her hands up and down at him. "Glowy on the inside."

"That makes you different," Alexander countered. "Nobody else can see my true nature."

"That's nothing," Zoë said and dug in her purse for her key. Mrs. Paez was still watching. "It probably comes from being able to see dead people, although that's not the same thing, is it, since you're not dead." She paused as she inserted her key in the lock and turned it. "Are you?"

Swinging the door open wide, she put her purse and the paper cup from the drive-thru on the kitchen bar and punched in her alarm code. When she turned around, Alexander was still standing over the threshold. "Aren't you coming in?"

"You can see spirits of departed humans?" Alexander asked, his voice barely above a whisper.

"And another thing. Why are you still dressed in that mailman outfit?" She waved him inside, and he stepped after her. "I'm not even sure I want to know why you were wearing it in the first place, because I can't imagine it's part of your normal routine."

"I did not know what I should wear, so I thought I would ask where you wanted to go. Do you like to dance?"

Despite feeling tired from her dull, gray afternoon, cheerful energy surged into her. "I love to dance. That sounds perfect." She couldn't help but smile. Zoë also hadn't anticipated that he would change clothes in front of her, or the manner in which he would do it. In a matter of a few seconds, his uniform vanished and new clothes appeared, but not before she'd gotten a startlingly good view of his naked body. She fought the urge to fan herself. She felt as though the temperature of the room had gone up several degrees in an instant. Alexander definitely had the attributes of a human male and in delightful abundance. She cleared her throat.

"You do not like this," he said, indicating the dark jeans and black button-down shirt he now wore. He ran his hands through his hair as though perplexed, and Zoë thought this a charmingly human affection. Then a vision of his naked body darted into her mind and she mused that he certainly did have other human characteristics in spades.

She shook her head. "No, gosh, no, Alexander. It's fine." Then, flustered and looking for something to do she said, "Listen why don't you sit with my grandmother while I shower and change. I can't do the quick presto thing."

He laughed. "Very well. When will she be home?"

"Oh, she's upstairs."

"No. There is no one else here."

Uncertain of the wisdom of arguing with an angel, Zoë shrugged. She could detect the faint flutter of her Gran's presence, since her Gran was, like Henry, not among the living. She took Alexander's hand and led him to Gran's sewing room. "She's up here."

When they wound up the stairs and around a laundry basket Zoë left in the hallway, she became acutely aware of the warmth of his hand, and the pleasant tingling she felt from touching his skin. She wondered if it happened because he was an angel or because she'd gotten an unexpected view of his incredible body.

At the end of the corridor, she tapped on a door and went in. "Hi, Gran," she said. The old lady sat in a rocking chair next to the window, as always wearing a lilac pant-suit, a necklace with large drooping beads, and perfectly round pearl earrings. Her white hair curled around her pale face. When Zoë entered, she put her needlework in her lap and pulled off her tiny glasses, letting them rest on a gold chain around her neck. "Gran," Zoë said, "this is Alexander. Can you talk to him while I go shower? We have a date, and he was a bit early."

If it was possible for a spirit to go pale, Gran did just that. "Sweet Lord, what have you done, child?"

"Oh, yes. I met Alexander at work. He's, um, a mailman, but you know, not our regular one."

"Ha," Gran said, but without humor, "I can see that right enough. Honey, you can't go bringing home angels. They aren't stray dogs. Their kind ain't nothing but trouble." The old spirit snorted and picked up her needlework again, as though her pronouncement ended the conversation.

Zoë blushed again, but this time pure mortification drowned out any fantasy she might have entertained earlier in the evening. "I'm sorry, Alexander." Under her breath she added, "She's sort of set in her ways."

Gran snorted.

Alexander looked distinctly uncomfortable. "I take it she said she does not want me here."

"You can't see her?"

He shook his head. "I can sense the emotional disturbance, but that is all."

"Disturbance!" Gran chortled. "I'll show him a disturbance."

The temperature in the room dropped a couple of degrees. Zoë shivered. Torn, she glanced from Alexander to Gran. "I'm sorry about this, Gran. I didn't mean to upset you." She took Alexander by the hand and led him downstairs and out the front door. "This is awkward," she said. She'd assumed spirits and angels would have a lot in common and was surprised Alexander couldn't even see Gran.

"You want me to go," he said.

"No, Alexander. It's not that. The last time she didn't like someone I was dating, she hid all my earrings and slammed cabinet doors all night for a month. Maybe she'll change her mind. Once she gets to know you."

"I do not think so." Although his words were gentle, his tone was final. "It is complex," he said and then added with a smile, "I do not want to be the cause of you not wearing earrings ever again." He reached up and brushed her curls away from her ear and tapped the heart-shaped stud she wore. A tingling jolt shot through her, and her breathing quickened.

"Alexander, I'll talk to her. I do want to go out. Let me shower and change. Wait here, okay? I promise I'll be back before you know it."

Although she thought it unconscionably rude to dump him on the front step, Alexander looked happy enough. "Okay," he said and sat down on the steps.

Zoë dashed inside, straight up to her bedroom where she stripped naked, her mind carelessly returning to the sight of Alexander's perfectly formed body. Moments later in the shower, she lingered a few minutes as she soaped up her soft skin and smiled to herself. The only thing keeping her from indulging in an even more decadent moment was the knowledge that the object of her fantasy sat outside.

After rinsing and drying, she grabbed lacy black panties and bra from her dresser and pulled them on, then went to her closet and tossed hanger after hanger aside, trying to decide what to wear.

She nearly screamed when Gran shot out of the closet and went right through Zoë, leaving Zoë's skin frosty cold where she'd touched it.

"You don't know anything about angels, child," Gran began.

Zoë pulled out a pair of low-slung pair black trousers. Trousers? she asked herself. Not really sexy dance-wear, but safe for a first date. But did she want to be safe? She dismissed the trousers and picked out a black skirt that draped to her knees and a wrap-around wine colored top. She adjusted it to cover her bra, and hoped she wouldn't spend the whole night messing with it. "Gran," Zoë said as she began to rummage for shoes with the right amount of sexy straps, but not so high she'd have purple feet for a week. "This isn't like you. It's no big deal."

"No big deal? It couldn't be a bigger deal, Zoë Pendergraft. What if he's one of the Fallen?"

"Fallen," Zoë said, and stopped fussing with her curls in the mirror. "Like a demon?"

Gran rolled her eyes. "That right there shows you don't know diddly."

Just as Zoë was bracing herself for a ding-dong of an argument, Gran faded. Zoë reached out, but it was like trying to embrace a cloud. She was alone. Exhaling a sigh, she couldn't understand Gran's behavior. Normally the old spirit was sweet and gentle.

Annoyed and slightly concerned, Zoë checked her reflection again and then headed downstairs. She pulled the front door closed behind her and locked it. When she turned, she found Alexander sitting exactly as she had left him. He stood and smiled.

"Alexander," she said, hoping her next question wouldn't sound inexcusably rude, "Are you one of the Fallen?"

"No," he said, not losing even a fraction of his lovely smile.

"My Gran wanted to know."

"Ah, yes." He paused for a moment as though choosing his words carefully. "Not all angels are the same. Maybe she has had some dealings with us before. Some are not tolerant of those who do not cross over when they die. They think it is rude."

Zoë laughed. "Rude? Now that's funny."

"Ready?" he asked.

"You know what I just realized. I don't know where we can dance on a Tuesday night. I wasn't thinking."

"I know the perfect spot," Alexander said. Once in her car, he directed her to Clandestine, a club in SoMa she drove by from time to time, but never gone into. Tuesday night, it seemed, was Salsa Night, and she could hear the music as soon as they got out of the car. It grew more intense as they approached on foot, hand in hand.

The atmosphere was overwhelming, and Zoë had no choice but to get into the spirit of the evening. Neon pink, green, and blue shone from overhead lights and played across a black bar. Even the towering potted palm next to the bar had colorful lanterns hanging from it, swaying as the crowd of people milled in chattering anticipation of the live band beginning their set.

Alexander led her to a low, high-backed red booth that faced the crowd. She watched him watching people, enjoying the happiness on his face. For a being she knew absolutely nothing about, she felt drawn to his simplicity and innocent face.

When a harried waitress in a short black skirt spotted them, she smiled at Alexander and squeezed through the crowd to approach. Her dark brown eyes sparkled at him. "What can I get you two?" she shouted over the rambunctious Latin music.

Alexander smiled at the server in a way that gave Zoë a jealous pang. She cleared her throat, trying to bury the irrational emotions and smiled brightly, hoping she didn't look like a maniac with a fake grin plastered on her face. "I'll have a Coke please."

Alexander chuckled as though he could see right through her, and she blushed. He ordered a beer, and then as soon as the server was out of sight he said, "Dance with me."

He led her to the dance floor, his hips swaying with the beat. With a deft flick, he spun her around and they twirled together amongst a throng of enthusiastic dancers. Zoë hadn't danced a salsa in ages, and she stared at Alexander's feet, desperate to keep up with his elegant moves. She cringed as she flubbed every sixth step. Alexander took her chin in his hand, and turned it up. "Look at my eyes," he said. It didn't improve her footwork, but when he put his hand on the small of her back she relaxed and moved in sync with him.

Campy disco balls sparkled overhead, and Zoë became lost in a rush of swirling skirts, twisting legs, and couples rhythmically pushed around the floor by the salsa beat. They danced until her feet ached, even switching partners now and again with the thrumming crowd. Most of the men were gracious about her careless steps, and with less skilled partners than Alexander, she missed more steps than she nailed, but nobody seemed to care.

Back in Alexander's sight, she made her way to him, and they danced together for a final time, though weariness had begun to creep up on her. She'd forgotten to eat anything, and the drink she'd ordered hadn't lasted long in her empty stomach. The pleasure of his presence melted her discomfort, and she forgot her complaints.

The band took a break and encouraged everyone to visit the bar. Zoë gasped for air and laughed with sheer delight. Tumbling away from the dance floor with the rest of the crowd, Alexander spun her once and pulled her into an embrace. Zoë's heart fluttered. "Let's go somewhere we can talk," she said.

"Sure," he said and led her outside, past the line of people waiting to get into the now-bustling club. A warm breeze scuttled leaves and bits of paper down the pavement. They meandered together, heading in the direction of her car, but in an indirect route. She'd never felt so safe wandering the streets.

"Alexander," she began after a while, "why did you ask me out?"

"You wanted me to," he said.

"Yes, but did you want to?"

"Of course." He slid his hand into hers as they crossed the street at a signal.

"But you don't know anything about me. And, well, you're an angel. I saw how women react to you. Why pick me? Why would an angel date a human? Is it sex? You can have sex, right?" A wave of embarrassment crashed over her. "What I mean is… is that what you're after?"

"Are you asking me to have sex with you?" His

eyes sparkled and his lips curved into a playful smile. He stopped walking and faced her.

"No!" Zoë wanted to crawl into a hole.

"So, you do not want to have sex?"

"No! I mean, it's not that I don't. Goodness, Alexander!"

He laughed and tugged at one of her curls playfully. "There is something in you that keeps you apart from others. I understand that. I am apart too."

Remarkably, she understood. She felt distant from other people because of her ability. It was hard to pretend she was normal, and some spirits wouldn't take no for an answer when they approached her. Even worse, sometimes they insisted on telling her things they knew about her boyfriend of the moment, which could be surprisingly often for people who rarely left whatever spot they decided to roost.

For a time she tried dating spiritualists and so-called mediums. The two mediums she'd met, she instantly recognized as fakes. Perhaps, when she had told them she spoke to spirits, they assumed she was faking too. Last year she'd dated a particularly understanding warlock, but she soon discovered he had wanted to use her gift to impress his coven, and they wanted her to contact their Uncle Bob or dear cousin Charlene.

Zoë shook her head to clear her thoughts. "Tell me about being an angel. Are there lots of you? I've never seen one before."

He nodded. "Three or four thousand."

"All over the world?"

"In San Francisco. But yes, we live and work everywhere humans do."

"Hmm," she said, trying to decide what to ask. "Why don't you have wings?"

"My human form is just human, at least in appearance. I have what any man would." He waggled his eyebrows at her, and she blushed obligingly.

Zoë cleared her throat and moved on before the imagery that had plagued her all night could resurface. "Can you eat?"

"Can, but do not have to."

She wanted to ask if he used the toilet, but decided that would be rude by any standard. "Are you immortal?"

He furrowed his brow. "When you die, you will still exist, but in another form. Like your Gran." He waited for her to nod. "Does that not make you immortal?"

Zoë shrugged, mostly because she didn't know what else to do. "Can you feel pain?"

His eyes turned serious. "There are all sorts of pain."

"You're being evasive."

He brushed her cheek with the back of his hand. "Not on purpose. It is difficult to fit my world inside of yours." After a pause he said, "If you were to drop a stone on my head I would not be crushed, and the things that would end you will not end me. However, there are perils for me, things which are beyond humanity."

Zoë flirted with the idea of being insulted, but as she was making up her mind, he leaned forward and planted his lips on hers. They were warm and soft, and tasted sweet, like a decadent treat from a baker's window.

He pulled back and said, "I should take you home. Humans need to sleep at night." He made it as a pronouncement, something he'd been instructed to memorize, as though to him sleeping seemed a bizarre practice by some strange foreign culture.

"Will you allow me to take you back to the car?" he asked.

Only then did she notice they'd wandered into an area she didn't recognize. She looked around for a street sign. "Sure," she said.

With a blur of motion, he wrapped his arms around her. They turned together and when he released her, they stood next to her car. *Well*, she thought, and her mind stayed blank with shock. They didn't talk on the drive home, her mind turning over the strange and improbable evening. But she had to confess she'd had a wonderful time.

When she parked in the driveway, Alexander got out and opened her door. Before she had a chance to speak, he'd lowered his lips to hers and kissed her softly. She leaned into him and put her hand on his chest, noticing the rhythm of a heartbeat. It gave her immense comfort. She wanted him to kiss her again. She longed for it in a way that she'd never done before. Was it some angel mojo, she wondered, or was this something real?

She could see his smile in the darkness. He whispered, "Goodnight, Zoë Pendergraft."

"Goodnight," she said.

He stepped away. She got her key out of her purse and wandered to the front door. When she turned around, he waved. Once inside she went to the window, but Alexander had gone.

CHAPTER 3

WEDNESDAY MORNING ZOË'S foul mood wouldn't let her enjoy the drive to work in her zippy little car or that arriving early had allowed her to find a parking space much closer to the front door than usual. She should have been elated after such a lovely night with Alexander. She could still feel the gentle pressure of his kisses on her lips, and she recalled with delicious clarity the faint taste of warm blueberry muffins, or was it crumpets, on his lips.

Grabbing her purse from the backseat, she locked up and headed inside, clipping on her ID badge as she walked. A co-worker joined her as she entered the building. "Morning, Luis," she said.

"You all right, Zoë?" he asked, his expression burrowing into a frown.

"Yeah. Just didn't sleep well." She put on her best fake smile and plopped herself behind her desk.

He nodded sympathetically without stopping,

and she was grateful he didn't pause for a chat. She should have been in a good mood. She deserved a wonderfully yummy mood. But Gran spent the entire night rattling around the house, creaking floorboards and shifting boxes in the attic. Zoë called out to her, hoping to talk, but the old woman refused to appear, and instead groaned and scraped like a Hollywood horror movie all night.

Zoë shuffled through the pile of undelivered mail and decided now was as good a time as any to get moving on it. She started with her department, tossing mail into inboxes without paying attention. Her mind wandered, and she couldn't help but think about Alexander. He was an extremely graceful dancer. Surely angels didn't take dance lessons. But then, how did they learn things? Were they somehow born knowing how to dance? No, that wasn't right either, because angels weren't born. *Were they?* Zoë grumbled to herself. She'd spent the evening asking the wrong questions and still didn't know anything important about him.

She looked down at the fat envelope in her hand. Dustin Bittner. Simone's new...whatever. Stalkee. When Zoë walked upstairs to his office to plop it on his desk, his chair spun around. She shrieked.

"Oh my God." Her heart raced. "You scared me," she said. "I didn't expect you to be here."

Dustin sat in his chair, looking startled and puzzled. "This is my office," he said.

"Right. I know that. I didn't know you came in this early." Zoë straightened a curl that fell in front of her eyes. She held up the delivery. "Mail for you." She handed it to him.

He accepted the package, turned it over and examined both sides before carefully opening the end. Zoë could see why Simone was interested. Probably close to forty, he had a good face, open and friendly. He wore his thick, silvering hair combed back and his blue eyes, although pale, showed intelligence and humor. Not pretty, but something in his look appealed to Zoë.

"Thanks," he said, and she realized she'd been staring.

"Sorry. I was thinking." Zoë turned to leave, but then a whim took her. "Are you married?"

His eyebrows shot up. "Erm, not anymore." Then slowly he turned his head, as though he'd just figured something out.

"Oh," Zoë said. "Not for me. I mean, I'm sure you're very nice. Simone. You know her? In Purchasing?" Since he continued to stare, she rambled on, "Anyway, she mentioned you the other day and seemed to think you were...well, and anyway, she's my friend, so I thought I'd ask. You know?" *Shut up, Zoë*, she told herself, willing her mouth to close and the words to stop falling out. "Right, so I must get back." She smiled and left his office with little grace.

When she made it to the corridor and down the stairs, she rolled her eyes and smacked herself on top of the head with the few remaining envelopes in her hand. "I should have called in stupid today," she muttered, but she didn't mean it, because she couldn't stay home with Gran in such a mood.

By the time she arrived at her desk, the office had bounded to life with the couple dozen bodies that worked in her department. Before she could even sit down, Marilyn came from nowhere and planted herself in front of Zoë's desk. "I thought you were coming in early today."

"I—"

"You can't just take off whenever you like and show up at all hours. We pay you for a full week's work, and we expect you to work it." A scowl darkened her features.

Zoë's head throbbed. She felt like crap when she didn't get enough sleep, and Marilyn's pointless tirade didn't help. It wouldn't make any difference to point out that she wasn't *really* Zoë's boss, that she was paid by the hour so it didn't hurt anyone else if she didn't work a full day, and that she *had* come in early.

"And furthermore, I don't like your friends coming up here and hanging around. This is a place of business."

"He was the *mailman*, Marilyn. Remember? I can't tell the *mailman* to stay away." One of these days, Zoë told herself, she should get clarification from personnel about who she reported to.

"Just because he has to be here doesn't mean you have jabber." Without awaiting a response, Marilyn turned on her heel and marched into her office.

"Nice dramatic exit," Zoë muttered.

When Zoë looked up, she jumped. An obnoxiously beautiful man stood in front of her desk. As with Alexander, she could tell he was—alive but not human. He had a similar presence, so she guessed he was an angel too. He had straight blond hair and the type of tan one could only get from spending countless afternoons lounging by the pool. Did angels take holidays? She could see quite a bit of his tan. His short-sleeved shirt barely had any buttons fastened, and his cargo shorts hung low around his hips revealing with certainty that he wasn't wearing underwear. He held out an ecru envelope. When she took it, she read her own name on the front.

Her bad mood completely overtook her civility and her curiosity. "Are all of you people delivery men? That does rather explain the state of the universe, you know."

His eyes met hers, and he looked at her strangely, as though no one had ever been rude to him before. With his good looks, it was possible no one had. "What's this?"

"Letter from Thomas," the messenger said.

"Thomas who?" Zoë tore the back of the envelope.

"Thomas of San Francisco." He looked bored and not at all as though he was joking.

"Right." Zoë glanced over the letter but didn't take in what it said. The stiff, expensive paper had a slight woodsy scent, as though she could smell the tree it came from. The handwriting curled gracefully in archaic loops that made it difficult to read. "What's this about? Is this even English?" Her vision blurred slightly as she tried once again to make it out. He shrugged. She couldn't help but admire the way his shoulders carelessly rose and fell. "You're a witness, aren't you?"

"A witness? To what?"

"In Alexander's case? You're going to testify before the Celestial High Court?"

"Alexander? His case?" Zoë's patience was about at an end. She waved the paper in front of the messenger. "I don't know what any of this means."

"Here," he said, slipping her a business card. "Thomas." When he leaned in close, she noticed he smelled like freshly baked bread.

Sure enough, the card read "Thomas" and below it, a local phone number. Zoë turned it over, thinking some explanation might be inscribed on the back, but she found it blank.

As if she had been lying in wait, Marilyn came out of her office to confront Zoë. "See," she said and pointed at the angel. "This is exactly the kind of thing I'm talking about."

"He's a messenger, Marilyn. I'm being called to testify in court."

"Uh huh. So he brought a subpoena?" Then glancing up and down at him, Marilyn added, "He doesn't look like a law clerk."

"No, a letter, and I never said he was a law clerk. He looks exactly like a messenger, which is what he is." Zoë said.

"Yeah, sure," Marilyn began, and took a breath as though planning to begin a long-winded rant.

Before she got a chance, the angel leaned over. Marilyn eyed him suspiciously at first, but she didn't back away. He took her hand and whispered into her ear. Zoë couldn't overhear what he said, but Marilyn relaxed, starting with the knotted muscles in her face. Her shoulders loosened, and her posture softened.

The messenger guided her back toward her office and let go of her hand at the door. Marilyn followed helplessly.

"What did you do to her?" Zoë asked.

"I told her to chill out a little," he said and winked before turning toward the office door.

He left before Zoë could think of a response. She looked down at the business card in her hand before tossing it down by the phone next to the letter from this Thomas of San Francisco. "I'm starting to think Gran was right about them," she muttered. "Nothing but trouble."

Zoë did her best to get through the morning by burying herself in work. She forced her way through a sheaf of expense reports she'd been avoiding and organized a particularly nasty pile of papers in her "I don't want to think about these right now" stack.

For the last fifteen minutes before her lunch break, she watched the clock hands, dusted her desk, and refilled a bowl of peppermint candies that had disappeared overnight. Finally when the big hand reached the six, she jumped out of her chair. Often, she'd discovered, walking with a sense of purpose discouraged comment, and she made her way down the maintenance stairwell to Henry's room, striding like she had a mission from above.

"Henry?" she called once she was down in the boiler room. "Henry, are you here?"

For some reason Zoë hadn't quite figured out, Henry always seemed to appear behind her. "I'm here, Miss Zoë. And you're right on time."

Zoë grinned. She knew as well as Henry did that time didn't matter to him, but he still wore that old pocket watch of his, and he'd pull it out and look at it as though it still ticked. "Henry, I need your help."

"Why, sure. Anything for you." He grinned at her, revealing a gleaming smile.

Zoë hesitated. Henry seemed the perfect person to ask, but then, what if he reacted the same way Gran had? She perched herself on her usual spot in the back of the boiler room and paused. "It's delicate, Henry," she began.

"I've always found, Miss Zoë, when you have something that needs saying, the best thing is to get it on out there and done with. No worries. Old Henry's heard it all. You haven't gone and gotten yourself in trouble, have you?" He sat down in front of her, close enough that a chill came off his wispy form. She found his presence comforting, despite his lack of physical warmth.

"No," Zoë said, knowing that "trouble" in his day

meant a girl getting herself pregnant. "The problem is with Gran. Sort of."

Henry nodded but didn't interrupt.

"You see, I met someone, only she doesn't approve of him, and I was wondering if you could help." She paused but went on when she realized there wasn't anything to do but say it. "Well, Alexander isn't precisely human."

"And what *precisely* is he?" Henry asked, in a serious tone that reminded Zoë far too much of her father.

"He's...I suppose you might say he's an angel." She braced herself for Henry to react, but he didn't.

Henry leaned back and watched her for a moment, and rubbed his chin. "Where'd you go and find yourself an angel?" Then as though something horrible had occurred to him, he said, "He's not your Guardian, is he?"

"Oh." She hadn't thought of that. "I don't know. He brought the mail yesterday, and then he invited me on a date. I think he only did it because I sort of asked him to ask me. I'm not sure why I did, actually."

"Hmm," Henry said. "He might be a messenger then. Did he bring anything special?"

"No, another one did today though. This one definitely had a messenger vibe. Brought some letter or something, but I couldn't read it. The script was too loopy and it made my eyes go funny."

"Two angels?" Henry laughed. "Now that's quite a

thing, Miss Zoë. Quite a thing. Most people go their whole lives without seeing any angels, and you get two in as many days."

"But then most people don't see spirits either, Henry. No offense, of course."

"None taken." Henry smiled. "I do know what I am. Always have. That's the secret, you know. You got to know what you are." He leaned forward, as though he'd told her something very important, and he searched her face to see if she understood. Then, without giving any indication if he had found what he had hoped for in her eyes, he said, "What did he want, this mailman who could be but maybe isn't your Guardian? It would help, you understand, if you knew what sort of angel he is."

"I don't think he wanted anything but to deliver mail. Then we got talking, and he asked for my phone number. Only, he didn't have a phone." Zoë shoved her curls back with her fingers while she tried to puzzle why Alexander would have been delivering the mail in the first place. "What sorts of angels are there?"

"Well, now, we don't exactly mix in the same crowd, you see. But I hear things from time to time. There's all kind of angels, and there's all kinds that might say they are, even if they aren't. Angels aren't the only things out there, you know. And even if he is what he says, it don't mean he's the good kind."

"The Fallen, you mean. I asked him already, and he said he's not."

"No, and I wouldn't call them that to their faces.

They like to be called the Free, not the Fallen, because they don't see as how they've fallen from anything. Not all the stories you've been told are the right ones, and writing something down don't make it so. Like us, angels have free will, and they choose their own path. And also like us, and this is the important part, what they call themselves isn't the best way to tell what their intentions might be. But you know all about people calling themselves one thing and being another, don't you?"

Zoë knew Henry meant her father. Until the day he died, he'd considered himself a good, Christian man. She nodded, holding back tears that came from an old familiar place. "So, how do I know? I really like Alexander, Henry. He's different, but at the same time we're a lot alike."

"Trust your eyes, Miss Zoë. You'll see the truth."

"But appearances can be deceiving," she shot back, hidden doubts bubbling to the surface. "What if he somehow dazzled me like that messenger did to Marilyn earlier. He whispered in her ear, and she went funny and calmed right down."

"No. Not with you. You're a seer, and that means something. You think it's an accident you happened to see me? And I'll bet when you laid eyes on him you didn't think he was just the new mailman. Didn't you ever ask yourself *why* you can see me, your Gran and the others?"

"I don't think it's that uncommon. They've even got TV shows now about people like me, seeing spirits and helping them resolve their issues."

"Resolve their issues," Henry repeated with a whooping laugh, as though that was the funniest thing he'd heard in a long time.

"Yeah, I guess some people think those who stay here after they, you know, don't know how to get to heaven. Or they have some reason for not going yet, some thing they want to do before they move on." Zoë looked at Henry's shimmering face. "How come you are still here, Henry? Don't you want to go to heaven?"

"That's just stories," he said, his tone firm. "I already had my heaven, and there ain't no going back to it." Henry stood and looked down at her. "You trust your eyes. What you got in yours ain't common. You're a good girl, Zoë."

She sat, her eyes downcast, unable to look at him. "Henry, why hasn't my father ever come to visit me?"

The softness returned to Henry's voice. "He can't get here from where he is, Miss Zoë."

"He's in..." Zoë couldn't bring herself to say "hell." She'd told her father to go to hell more than once, but now the thought horrified her. Visions of lava and three-headed dogs and swarms of stinging bees filled her head.

"No," Henry said quickly. "Heaven and hell, they aren't what you think. All them books about what happens once you cross that threshold were written by people who hadn't done it. It's wishes and nightmares, but what's real—that's something else altogether."

"Can you go where he is, Henry? To maybe give

him a message for me?"

"What message would you give him, if you could?" Henry shook his head, pity etched deep in his eyes. "What do you want to say?"

"I don't know. I always thought he stayed away because..." She paused and finished the statement silently. *Because he didn't want to see me.*

"There's lots of places I can't go, and if I tried, I couldn't get out again." Then seeing the startled expression on her face, he added, "Don't you worry about your father, Miss Zoë. Now is a time for you to be living your life."

"Don't you dare do anything to hurt yourself, Henry. I couldn't stand it if I didn't have you. You're one of my best friends." Zoë stood up and wiped her eyes. The day hadn't turned out like she thought it would.

"Why, Miss Zoë, that's the kindest thing I think anyone has ever said to old Henry. Things sure have changed since my day." He leaned over and planted a kiss on her cheek. It tingled against her skin. She closed her eyes and put her hand to her face. Times had changed since Henry was alive, an era when black men and white women would hardly have become friends and shared a lunch hour telling stories. It saddened her, this thing they never talked about, but at the same time she was glad it didn't come between them now. Death improved some things more quickly than time ever could. She struggled for the right words, but when she opened her eyes seconds later, Henry had gone.

Zoë made her way up the stairs slowly, the weight of the things she needed to think about pushing her shoulders toward the ground. Simone was standing at her desk when Zoë arrived. "You have got to quit spending your lunch hour with dead people. It's not right. You're never going to find yourself a man if you don't go into the real world sometimes."

"I had a date with a man last night, in fact." Zoë sounded more defensive than she wanted to. When Simone's eyebrows shot up she said, "You know. Alexander. The mailman."

"Didn't waste any time, did he?" Simone said.

"Simone, you can't be annoyed that I don't go out and then be critical because I do."

Just then, Ronald approached through the main entrance, and Zoë couldn't help but feel disappointed to see the ordinary human postman.

"Are my ears burning?" he said. His blond hair stuck out around the edges of his US Postal Service baseball cap.

"Not you," Zoë said. "We were talking about the guy who took your route yesterday. Alexander." Then she added, "Do you know him?"

"No." Ronald's expression looked vague and confused, as though he was trying hard to piece the story together in his head.

Zoë sighed. She didn't even know how to get in touch with Alexander, and he didn't have a phone. She looked down at the business card the messenger had left. Thomas. Hmm, she thought. Then his words sank in. Testify? A panic filled her. Was Alexander in some sort of trouble? *Why wasn't I listening before?*

While she'd been lost in her own world, Ronald had dropped the mail on her desk and headed to the door. Simone started to ask about Zoë's date with Alexander when people began filing back in from lunch in twos and threes. Zoë mouthed "later," and sat down.

"Simone, right?" Dustin Bittner had come in with a couple of colleagues. They kept walking while he hesitated at Zoë's desk.

Simone froze in place with her mouth open awkwardly.

"Yes," Zoë said in a far-too-cheerful voice. Poor Simone and her stage fright. She was absolutely gorgeous and smarter than Zoë would ever hope to be, yet the sight of a normal, successful guy locked her brain up so tight Zoë expected to hear sirens.

"Umm, hi," Dustin said, suddenly floundering as badly as Simone.

Zoë rolled her eyes.

Then as though he'd come back to his senses after a couple of long moments, he guided the stunned Simone aside. "I was thinking," he said.

Zoë strained to hear the actual invitation, but he'd taken Simone out of earshot. *Damn.* Now she'd have to wait for the inevitable text message.

With no more distractions to tempt her away, Zoë dug into her reports. She tuned out the world and worked. Tension and worries lost their grip as she focused on the mundane.

Somewhere toward late afternoon, she came out of her industrious trance, lulled back to the bright florescent lights of reality by a dull buzz. Knowing it would be Simone sending a text with details of her conversation with Dustin, she grinned and touched the smudged screen of her phone with her fingertips, selecting "Read Messages" from the pop-up. Instead of the expected "Squee" however, the incoming message read "Call Thomas." The "Sender" line was blank, which shouldn't be possible.

"How did you get this number?" she wondered aloud and then laughed at herself for repeating such a phony Hollywood line. She recognized it wasn't the first time she'd wasted her time recently with the wrong questions.

She dialed the number on the odd business card. A woman answered in a warm, purring voice. "Thomas' office. How can I help?" Zoë paused, lost in thought for a moment. The tone evoked the feeling of a memory long forgotten, but just out of reach. "Hello?" the woman said patiently.

Zoë shook herself. "This is Zoë Pendergraft. I'm calling for Thomas?" The phone clicked twice, and she thought they'd been disconnected, but a few moments later a man's voice came on the line.

"Zoë, thank you for getting back to me. Is tomorrow morning good for you?" Like the woman before him, his voice was rich, but stronger, like dark chocolate. Why did angels always remind her of food?

"Tomorrow morning for what?"

"We need to go over your testimony before the hearing, of course. I explained in my letter."

Zoë picked up the letter and looked at the looping calligraphy Once again she could hear Henry's voice telling her to trust her eyes. Must not always be applicable, since her eyes didn't seem to want to focus enough to let her understand what it said. "I have to work," she said.

"No problem," Thomas said. "We'll make it afternoon. I'll send someone to pick you up. One second," he said, and Zoë heard a muffled sound as though he'd put his hand over the phone's mouthpiece. When he came back he said, "Thanks again, Zoë. I'll see you tomorrow." The phone went dead.

Zoë held it away from her ear, staring at it. "I don't care if you do smell like chocolate, you're an ass." She looked around for a moment, hoping no one heard her swearing at inanimate objects. Besides, one couldn't actually smell people over the phone, which was probably a very good thing.

As soon as she put down her cellphone, her desk phone rang and the "Line One" button lit up. She punched it. "Good afternoon. Fiskers Technology Group."

"Hi, Zoë! Caroline from Personnel here."

"Hi, Caroline. Hey, I've been meaning to ask you. Who exactly am I supposed to report to?"

"Haven't you been here for over a year?" Caroline

sounded startled.

"Something like that. I just wanted to make sure." Zoë felt stupid for asking, but this situation with Marilyn was getting on her nerves.

"Who do you usually check in with?"

Zoë had to stop herself from saying "Mega-Bitch." She cleared her throat. "Marilyn Baker, but—"

Caroline cut her off with a cheerful squeak. "That's fine. You keep doing that."

"Right." That wasn't what she'd wanted to hear, but she couldn't think of any way around it.

"Great," Caroline said, bringing perkiness to an entirely new level. "I'm calling about your court dates."

Zoë pulled the phone away from her ear, stared at it a second and then brought it back. "Umm, yeah. I just heard about that myself."

"Listen, Zoë, I know it's tempting to want to get out of it, but it's our civic duty, and Fiskers always encourages employees to vote, sit jury duty, and gives the necessary time for reserve duty or other military service and the like." She sounded like she was reading out of the Fiskers Terms of Employment Reference Manual, or F-TERM as Zoë remembered it being called the one and only time she ever laid eyes on it. "So you take the time you need to comply fully," Caroline said. "It's been cleared with our office. We'll get a temp to cover your desk tomorrow. Don't worry about it."

"Thanks, Caroline, that's great." *Great*, Zoë

thought with more than a little dread. She didn't even want to know how Thomas had managed it. She was beginning to have an idea of the reach angels had, and she suspected it went much further than she'd first imagined.

"No, problem. See you!" Caroline signed off, sounding like nothing could make her happier, as though Fiskers was strengthened by Zoë's civic-minded and selfless deeds.

Zoë reached for her phone and keyed in a text one-handed, holding the device below the surface of her desk so no nosy passers-by would read it. *Off-tmrow. Call u later.* Then she picked Simone's name off her very short call list and hit send.

She didn't know which she was more depressed about: that Gran hated her new boyfriend, that her new boyfriend wasn't even human and she had no clue what he wanted from her, or even worse, that she wasn't sure if he *was* her boyfriend. *One date and I'm using the 'b' word?* To make it worse, the aforementioned "not-her-boyfriend" seemed to be in legal trouble and some guy named Thomas with squirrelly ancient handwriting wanted her to testify.

Zoë folded the letter from Thomas, stuffed it into her purse, and tidied her desk. It seemed strange, knowing a temp would sit here tomorrow, go through her papers, answer her phone and eat her peppermints. With that uncomfortable thought, Zoë popped a candy into her mouth before heading to her car.

She felt somewhat better that since she'd arrived early, she'd been able to park close to the front door today. Not that it mattered much. It was a difference between a fifteen second walk and a two minute walk. *Oh, well*, she thought and reminded herself little things did matter. Now all she had to do was drive home and make nice with Gran. She couldn't cope with another sleepless night.

When she arrived home, though, Gran was nowhere around, and Zoë felt guilty, but incredibly relieved. She spent the evening watching a two-hour special episode of a trashy medical television show about twenty-something interns who couldn't seem to stay out of each other's pants. On commercial breaks, she ran back and forth to the laundry room, throwing clothes in the machines and then taking them out so she could fold during the next decadently drama-laden segment. When her show finished, she wiped tears from her eyes. It annoyed her that such a stupid show made her cry every single episode. She was powerless to stop herself, but she watched without fail. If it wasn't on, she moped and wandered aimlessly like her best friend had stood her up.

The clock had rolled toward midnight by the time Zoë realized she'd forgotten to call Simone, so she tucked herself into bed with her electronic book reader, another gift-to-self. The house felt empty and quiet without Gran. Zoë rolled her eyes. The old lady was probably trying to teach her a lesson about respecting her elder spirits or something.

Unable to get into her book, and knowing it was going to be at least a couple more chapters before she got to the smutty bits, she put it down on the bedside table and turned out the light.

CHAPTER 4

WHEN FAINT MEDITATION MUSIC started playing in Zoë's bedroom, she reached over and whacked the short, fat CD player without opening her eyes. She disliked waking to loud noises, and she'd gotten the CD free at a housewares store with a purchase of bath salts. Using it in her alarm player, she'd heard the first three seconds of that song at least five hundred times, but none of it beyond the first minute.

It took her a moment to remember she had the morning off. Caroline had told her to take the day, and she didn't have to worry about getting to see this Thomas of San Francisco until some unstated point in the afternoon. The sheer pleasure of not having to do anything washed over her. It was like found money, winning a day in the lottery. She ordinarily stacked her time with to-dos and shoulds, but this morning was genuinely free. A purr rumbled in her throat and she snuggled down into the feather duvet.

The yearning piano notes started to play again, and she had the presence of mind to hit the off button rather than the snooze, but she had to open one eye to do it. That was the only reason she discovered Alexander sitting in the small, overstuffed peach chair in the corner. She went through shock and anger at breakneck speed, and then the mortification set in. He'd apparently moved the jeans, blouse, bra and panties she'd slung on the chair the night before. She lay back and stared at the ceiling.

"Alexander," she said, trying to maintain her calm. "Out."

"Out?" He looked adorable. She had noticed that much. Why, oh why did he have to be completely deficient in some areas, like common sense, while being utterly appealing in others? He looked innocent and like raw sex at the same time.

She sat up, taking care to discreetly ensure her naked body didn't show from under the huge mound of crumpled duvet. She pointed to her bedroom door. "Out. I'm going to get up, and I want some privacy. Make some coffee or something."

"But— "

"There's coffee beans in the left-hand cabinet. Now, out." She left no room for discussion or argument. He stood and walked out the door, closing it quietly behind him, a forlorn expression on his face. She wondered if he really had to use doors, or if he was being polite. She reached out with her senses, scanning the house. Gran wasn't home. Relief washed over her. Zoë genuinely hoped Alexander would never waltz into the house with Gran in it, because who knew what might happen. "Alexander, Alexander. The things I don't know about you and the things you don't know about *anything* could fill... well, an entire library."

It surprised her that she could sense Alexander. He had a presence unlike a spirit's, and she couldn't think of a way to put it into words. At least this strange, newfound ability told her he was in the kitchen as she'd asked, and not waiting outside her door.

With regret at being denied a languid sprawl among the sheets, she slipped out of bed and put on some clean undies and a bra. She tossed the ones Alexander had folded into the wicker laundry basket. Padding to her closet, she threw on a pair of jeans and a sleeveless emerald shirt.

Although she could still sense his presence in the kitchen, Zoë looked both ways outside her bedroom door before tiptoeing to the bathroom. She felt like an idiot. Why should she sneak? It was her house. Technically, Gran had owned it long before she had, but it was Zoë's name on the paperwork, and meant something. Zoë sighed. It didn't mean anything. Only living humans seemed to care about things such as whose name was on a piece of paper. All the other citizens of time and space didn't give a crap.

Her curly hair stuck in wild directions, and refused to behave until she got it damp and applied some miracle goop she'd gotten from her hairdresser. She couldn't really afford the expensive stuff from salons, but it was either that or look like a startled poodle.

When Zoë arrived in the kitchen, she saw that Alexander had found the coffee beans and poured them into her cup-sized mortar. He began to grind them with a pestle. She leaned in the doorway and laughed, her reaction ranging from delight to dismay. The whole morning was so strange, and she should be annoyed and confused, but instead a warm happiness spread over her.

Alexander turned and said, "How many do I need to do?"

She was tempted to leave him to it for the perverse pleasure of seeing what he would come up with, but in the end, sparing herself the task of cleaning up whatever mess he might make conquered curiosity. "Umm, let's do them in the grinder. It's faster."

She slid up beside him, took the beans from the mortar and poured them and a few more into the compact grinder on her counter top. Alexander watched with dedicated interest. "So, Alexander," she said after the whirring machine had finished. "I should say it's not particularly polite to show up in a girl's bedroom. You might have frightened me, or caught me, erm, indisposed or with someone." She blushed. Why had she said that? She didn't want him thinking she might at any moment have a man in her bed, but still the point needed making.

"I checked before I came in," Alexander said. "I like seeing you sleeping. You looked happy."

"People value their privacy. We have boundaries. The front door is a big one. You knock, or ring the bell, and we answer it and invite you in."

Alexander nodded. Zoë put the coffee into the empty filter in the coffee maker, filled the machine with water and pushed the "Brew" button.

"Are you hungry?" she asked automatically and then stopped. "Sorry, I forget..."

"I am not human?" he offered with a boyish smile.

Best to keep going, she told herself. "So, why are you here anyway?"

Alexander leaned against the counter in a relaxed pose that made him look as though he belonged in her kitchen. "Thomas said to bring you today."

"Yeah, about that," Zoë said. "Alexander, I don't understand what's going on. I meet you, and we had such a lovely time the other night, and now I've got angels coming out of my ears." Then not being certain he would get the metaphor, she decided to press on. "Who is Thomas, and what's this meeting about?"

"How much do you know about angels?"

"About as much as you know about making coffee." Zoë grinned. She couldn't believe she was enjoying herself so much, considering she kept her life under such tight control, making plans, considering options, weighing choices. Flying by the seat of her pants wasn't her style. She had to admit the freedom intoxicated her. "Why don't we sit down, and you tell me what I need to know." She grabbed a mug from the cupboard and poured coffee into it even though the gurgling machine had not yet finished filling the carafe. It splashed coffee on her counter, but she left it for later.

Zoë led the way to the living room. She gathered up the pens, receipts, magazines and a candy bar wrapper she'd left there last night. "Sorry," she said. "I wasn't expecting company today."

Alexander sat on the soft couch. "I do not care where you keep your magazines, Zoë."

The way he said her name sent a shiver over her body. She wasn't convinced he didn't understand her embarrassment and suspected somewhere down in her socks he was making fun of her. She decided to play it straight until something convinced her otherwise. "Another time I'll explain more about why this matters, Alexander, but for right now can you tell me about Thomas and this court thing?"

"It is a kind of custody case."

"Custody? You have children?" She didn't know anything about Alexander specifically, or about angels in general, but this idea shocked her.

"No, my custody."

Zoë lowered herself into an easy chair. She leaned back and rubbed her hands along the fabric arms, taking in what he said. "You're not an adult?" She swallowed hard.

"Zoë, I am not human."

"I understand that. So, tell me why you are in

someone else's custody. Is this like parole?"

"You are angry now."

"I'm frustrated." She motioned with her hand for him to continue. "Just, please explain."

"We do not age, so when I say I am not human, it is because you keep asking human questions. I am not an adult, I am not a child, and I will never be old. Do you see? We appear as human adults from the moment we enter the mortal timeline more out of tradition than necessity."

Zoë nodded, not speaking because she hoped he would eventually get to something that would make her understand.

"I have a custodian. Celion. He was entrusted with teaching me, and the Higher Angels have brought a charge of negligence against him. In tandem with that, I have been accused of interfering with mortality to the detriment of the timeline progression plan." Alexander frowned.

In tandem? This from someone who couldn't grind coffee beans. Okay. "This Celion is your mentor, and not your father."

"No, my father is Duncan of Edinburgh."

"Duncan." Zoë thought that was possibly the least angelic name she could think of. Except maybe Vince. Or Roger.

"Yes. I was brought into this world by Duncan of Edinburgh and Aemilia of North Uist two hundred and seventeen years ago."

"You had parents?" Zoë hadn't exactly paid the

closest attention on Sunday morning. She'd much rather read a lurid romance than dig up the Bible she'd gotten from Grandma Jean in grade-school, but this wasn't anything she'd heard before. "You're telling me you were born?"

Alexander grinned. "Close enough."

Zoë was tempted to ask about angelic procreation, but the time wasn't right. She didn't want it to sound like a proposition. She'd save it for later. "Right, so Thomas is your lawyer?"

"Advocate, yes."

"And these Higher Angels are what?"

"Hmm, think of them like the celestial civil service. And then some."

"And they're saying you interfered with… something?"

"Mortality. Humans, in other words. To the detriment of the timeline progression plan."

Someone has a plan? This is interesting news. "Timeline progression plan. Alexander, what did you do?"

"Ronald was having a very bad day."

"Ronald. My postman?" She took a drink of her coffee and wrinkled her nose when she realized it had gotten cold. She made a disgruntled noise and put the mug down.

"Two nights ago, that would be Monday, Ronald's girlfriend learned he had been having a sexual relationship with another woman. This vexed her."

Vexed? Zoë held her mouth as straight as she could. "I can imagine." Suddenly she was glad she'd never given Ronald her phone number and felt guilty for enjoying the way he'd asked for it on a near-daily basis.

"I have never quite understood the complex relationships between human beings and their various sexual partners," Alexander said.

"Focus, Alexander," Zoë said. "The timeline?"

He sighed. "I discovered that Valerie, the girlfriend—"

"Valerie the Vexed." Zoë fought hard to keep back the giggles threatening to burst out.

"Quite. She hired an ex-boyfriend to break Ronald's legs on Tuesday. I should say she hired him on Saturday. The breaking was planned for Tuesday."

"That's why you took his route? So he wouldn't get hurt?"

"I discovered that the ex-boyfriend, someone called Spider, wanted to be restored from the ex-boyfriend category, and therefore planned to remove Ronald from the timeline."

"You mean kill him?" Zoë couldn't help it. She was shocked. Just because several of her friends were dead didn't mean she liked the idea of any more of them *becoming* dead. She chided herself for the melodramatic thought. Ronald wasn't a friend. He was the postman. But still, one couldn't go around murdering postmen. "Of course you did the right thing."

Alexander looked forlorn. "I did not. He was supposed to die. It was his time."

"Says who?"

"The Higher Angels. Not only that, Spider and Valerie were supposed to go to jail, and a witness to the crime should have met her future husband on jury duty. The list goes on."

"Ah, so you can't go push him off a bridge now to make things right." Zoë found it incredibly difficult to take this seriously, even though they were talking about someone she quite liked, and his untimely un-demise.

Alexander looked horrified. "No. We do not do that."

"Uh huh. You don't kill people, but you're not supposed to protect them either?" She was getting annoyed. "So you're a guardian angel then, I take it?"

"An apprentice. Until yesterday, anyway."

"You got fired?"

"Suspended, yes."

"Okay, so how can we get you your job back?"

"I do not think we can. Thomas is going to try."

"This just happened two days ago. They sure don't waste time on red tape, do they?" Zoë looked at Alexander and felt a mixture of things, but mostly proud. "It was a good thing you did, Alexander, no matter what anyone says. You can't let thugs named things like Spider go around killing perfectly good postmen. It isn't right. And besides, what's the point of being a guardian angel if you can't actually do anything when it counts the most? I'm proud of you. It takes courage to do something you think is right even when you know it's going to get you into trouble."

They paused for a moment in silence. It was a nice quiet, where they could sit and think without worrying about having to be clever or entertaining. Zoë felt happy, and then a thought occurred to her.

"You aren't *my* guardian angel, are you?"

Alexander grinned. "I am nobody's Guardian anymore, but no, you are Briony's concern."

"Can I meet her?"

Alexander shook his head. "I should not even have told you about her. I think I had better try to stay out of trouble for today, do you not agree?"

Zoë nodded, though she couldn't help but wonder what help this Briony had been in her life, and if she were going to get her legs broken or worse by some character named Spider, whether Briony would step in. She thought it unlikely, considering what Alexander had said about the rules concerning interfering with mortality. Although she'd never expected anyone to jump out and save her should the need arise, it made her sad to know there was someone who could, but wouldn't.

Now seemed the perfect time to change the subject. "I was talking to a friend," Zoë said, "who told me I should find out what you wanted with me."

Alexander looked at Zoë curiously. "Unless you

have told your living friends I am not human, I would assume this friend is among the departed." He said the last three words as though he had wished there was a way to put them even more delicately, as though death was somehow offensive. In some ways it was, she supposed, as she considered the drama surrounding Ronald and Valerie the Vexed and the death that didn't happen.

Zoë nodded.

"I would like to be your friend." The intensity in his warm voice made Zoë's temperature rise.

She wasn't offended by the use of the word "friend," not when he said it that way. "There aren't any rules about angels and humans, erm, spending time in one another's company?" *God*, she thought, *why am I talking like Scarlet O'Hara? Why can't I say "screwing," since that's what I truly want to know?*

He shrugged. "We live in the same world." As if that explained anything. Alexander stood. "Thomas wants us now. We should go."

"Sure." Apprehension surged. Meeting Alexander was one thing, but she could always imagine he was one of a kind, a fluke, just someone a bit different, like her. Something inside told her she was about to wade into waters deeper than she'd ever swum before.

Alexander offered her his hand. She took it and stood beside him. "Maybe I should ask what you want from me, Zoë Pendergraft." He kissed her hand tenderly.

A flash of flushing, throbbing, hormone-driven

ideas flowed through her brain, and she caught her breath. At that moment, she wanted to taste his lips again and feel him press up against her. Unbidden, the memory of his naked body popped into her mind, and she blushed furiously. Why did that keep happening? It made her feel like a teenager. "I want..." She'd started to say she wanted to be his friend too, but it seemed cheesy, and she couldn't bring herself to say it when the truth was much more.

Alexander chuckled, and she wondered briefly if he could read her mind. He touched her cheek. "Do you know how different you are?"

Zoë couldn't stop staring into his sparkling green eyes. She shook her head slowly. Words wouldn't come. "I'm nothing special," she finally choked out.

He leaned forward until he was so close she couldn't focus her eyes. He whispered, "I believe the truth to be otherwise." She closed her eyes, and then his lips touched hers. A tingling current went through her body, her nipples hardened and her groin tightened.

She put her hands on his chest, ran them up and wrapped them around his neck, returning his kisses with deep intensity she was not accustomed to. Quite a few kisses had crossed her lips before, and they seemed pale and dead in comparison to the pure silky warmth that flooded her senses now.

When his tongue touched hers, Zoë nearly cried out from pure delight. Her body responded with juicy, yet aching desire. It was the longest, fullest, most perfect kiss she'd ever received or given in her life.

His hands rested lightly on her hips and she let her body slowly fall toward his. He was hard and solid, and as she leaned into him, she felt fragile, as though he could break her with a thought, but at the same time she had a sensation they were floating together, and gravity seemed to mean a whole lot less than it had a few moments before.

Slipping one hand to the small of her back, Alexander embraced her with such tenderness that she couldn't remember what it felt like to be afraid. Out of nowhere, a doubt appeared. These sensations were new. Never before had a man made her feel like this. Could it be a response to his angel nature? Could he be mesmerizing her? Her mind told her she needed to slow down, but her body didn't agree.

Finally, her mind won out, and she pulled back. Alexander didn't let her go, and although she was shocked at first, she was grateful when she realized they had floated several inches off the ground. They descended together and she couldn't help but smile wide. "Wow," she said.

He gave her another quick kiss before letting her go. "Very." He paused as though listening. "We should go. Thomas does not like waiting."

Zoë considered saying something cheeky, like Thomas would have to wait, but she decided that as long as he was helping Alexander with this legal stuff, she'd best hold her attitude in check. "Right. Let me get my things."

Alexander seemed amused, but didn't say

anything more. "Shall we take your car? I like your car."

She beamed with pleasure. Loving her car was a sure way to her heart. "Okay." Then as they came to the front door she said, "Hey, can't you whoosh us there?"

Alexander laughed, and she couldn't help but go all gushy when she heard it. "I could whoosh, but it is probably better to keep a low profile where we are going."

"And where's that?"

"Civic Center Station."

The BART Station? Zoë nodded, but wondered why they couldn't drive to Thomas' office, because as politically incorrect as it was, she hated public transportation, particularly Bay Area Rapid Transit. She figured she was personally responsible for the ice caps melting. "No problem," she said. "Hey, if it doesn't take too long, I'd like to stop on the way back. There's this antique store over in the Marina District that's always worth a rummage."

She wasn't sure what Alexander would think about antique stores, being technically an antique himself, although celestial beings wouldn't fit into the same category as an old teapot. Then she reminded herself what he'd told her earlier: *Alexander isn't young and he isn't old. He just is.* That suited her fine. More people, she mused, should quit worrying and just be.

CHAPTER 5

THEY DROVE IN A COMPANIONABLE silence. Alexander seemed to enjoy watching the people who milled around the streets, shopping, walking, waiting for buses. When she pulled her car into a parking lot near the Civic Center BART station, Zoë said, "Okay, why won't you tell me where we're going?" So much for serenity and not dwelling on the uncertainty of their destination, and more importantly, everything that would happen there.

Alexander looked puzzled. "We are here." They walked inside the station, but instead of going toward the platforms, he led her down a long corridor where the crushing crowd thinned. Up ahead, a blue wall blocked their way. Wall, perhaps, was overstating, but the only word that came to mind was 'force field', and she dismissed that obviously ridiculous concept. But then she noticed people walking right through it. She squinted. They glowed. Well, most of them. A few were plainly human. Zoë felt light-headed for a moment, but then told herself to pull it together. *Okay. Force-field. Check.*

It took Zoë a second to realize she'd quit walking. Alexander took her hand gently. "An invisible wall repels humans, but if you hold my hand, it makes it easier."

Invisible? She almost said it aloud, but decided to keep her trap shut. *When you don't know what to do, shut up and pay attention.* That's what Gran taught her. Thank you, Gran. Instead she nodded and took Alexander's warm and muscular hand. Holding onto him bolstered her confidence.

"Ready?" he asked, and when she nodded, they proceeded. She'd expected to tingle or sparkle when she passed through the barrier, but instead the desire to run the other direction melted away. Then...nothing. Just ordinariness again.

Zoë didn't want to stare like a tourist, but being surrounded by angels would make anyone gawk. What surprised her was that most of them wore business clothes. She hadn't realized until that moment she'd hoped for long white robes and maybe, even though Alexander had told her they didn't need them, a few pairs of white fluffy goose wings. *Well, damn.* Zoë thought if she could look like anything she wanted to, she'd have long, silky blond hair and full, pouty lips. And bigger boobs. And pretty feet. She grinned. Angels must all have pretty feet. Why would anyone have ordinary feet if they didn't have to? She'd never understood foot fetishes, simply because feet were odd. *And penises aren't?*

Zoë snorted a laugh at the unbidden visual and then stopped herself short when she noticed Alexander watching her out of the corner of his eye.

"Here we are," he said and took her to an unmarked door. "Do not worry. It only seems weird the first time." Considering her train of thought about penises, it was all Zoë could do to not make some crack like, "*How many times have I heard that before?*" Alexander opened the door, oblivious to her wandering mind, and for that she was grateful. She smiled at him when he stood aside to let her enter first.

When she stepped through the door, a peculiar thing happened. Suddenly his comment didn't seem funny anymore. What had looked like a plain, empty white room changed the second she walked through. They definitely weren't in a BART station anymore.

It took Zoë's eyes a moment to adjust to the dim light in the bar. An angel bar? She didn't know where to begin to process the place. And it didn't look particularly angelic either. To her right was a long polished wood bar. Behind it hung a mirror that reflected several rows of bottles of varying sizes and colors. Patrons sat in groups of two and three at scattered wooden tables, listening to a piano player on a low stage.

The patrons, the bartender—none of them were human. Eyes narrowed, she checked out two men sitting together at a back table. They were the only humans in the place, besides herself, of course, but they didn't seem completely human. What else could they be? Her brain ticked with their presence, and she tried to place them, but couldn't. They looked as uncomfortable as she felt. They kept their heads down and refused to look at anyone else. They didn't even talk to one another. Even stranger, a spirit hovered behind them. It wasn't fully formed, as though it had trouble holding on. Zoë had difficulty making out its features. "Who is that?"

Alexander followed her gaze. "I do not know. Possibly clients of Thomas."

"He represents, um, other races?" She didn't know how to take it in.

"It would not be like him to discriminate." Alexander indicated a chair and pulled it out for her. She sat, wondering when they were going to get to the point, but not feeling particularly rushed. She relaxed as she listened to the music.

The piano player was quite good, although she supposed that shouldn't surprise her, since he was super-human. He was gorgeous too, with coal black hair and the deep gray eyes that made her wonder what the world looked like when he looked out of them. But again, none of these people were exactly ugly. The unfamiliar tune had a sexy, jazzy sound, and he played with feeling. It reminded her of something she couldn't quite place, and she lost herself in memories of a trip she must have taken with her parents, before her father died and her mother walked out. She had few memories of her mother. Some hotel restaurant, somewhere, more like a bar, but she was so young, it couldn't have been. In the South, she thought, but maybe she thought that because of the jazz. It took her a second to realize the music had stopped.

She looked up and saw the piano player nod at Alexander.

"Time to go," Alexander said. They stood and walked toward the stage, following the piano player through a curtain in the back, which led through a dark corridor. At the end of it, he opened a door, and they entered a beautiful office with high ceilings and leather furniture arranged in a small seating area. In the back stood a huge wooden desk, and the far wall was lined with hundreds of leather-bound books. It smelled like paper and ink.

The piano player turned to her, and she noticed he was tall. He smiled. "You must be Zoë." His faint accent carried a hint of something she couldn't place. "I'm Thomas."

She stuck her hand out. "Zoë Pendergraft." Did angels even shake hands? She wasn't left hanging because even if they didn't, Thomas was polite enough to take it. It pleased her that touching Thomas didn't have the same gushy effect on her that contact with Alexander did. So maybe it wasn't some kind of generic angel influence after all.

"Alexander has filled you in?" Thomas said and indicated one of the chairs to his right.

Zoë settled herself in one and put her purse beside her feet. "I think so. This is all, um, very new to me."

Thomas grinned. "Don't worry about that. It's supposed to be. Humans are generally kept in the dark about us and what we're doing, unless they choose to involve themselves."

"You're not interfering with the timeline by telling me this? It seems to me, Thomas, simply existing anywhere humans can see you is, in itself, interference. How can these Higher Angels expect Alexander to interact with humans, do his job, and yet not have any influence on them? Isn't that the nature of his work? I figure if you don't want to influence something, you stay the hell away from it. If, erm, you'll pardon the expression."

Thomas grinned. "It's a duality we can't ever completely get away from. What I need from you is to hear about Tuesday. Go through it in your own words. Don't leave anything out."

"Starting from when Alexander walked in?"

"Let's take it back a bit further to get a feel for the day. Did anything happen that morning? Something unusual you can't attribute to routine?"

Zoë considered, and wondered if he was trying to figure out if Alexander had influenced her before they even met?

"Before we start, Alexander, why don't you go ask Nicholas about the writ for me. We need to go over that in a little while."

"Sure," Alexander said and stood. "You are all right, Zoë?"

She smiled. What choice did she have but to be all right? "Yeah, I'm fine." She watched him go, sorry when his presence faded. Even Thomas' office seemed to lose some of its color.

She blushed when she realized Thomas watched her closely. "How long have you felt like that?" he asked.

"From the beginning, I think." Warmth crept over her skin.

He nodded and gestured for her to continue. "So, Tuesday?"

"Tuesday was pretty normal. I went to work, and everything was what I'd expect. I did paperwork in the morning. I had lunch with my friend Henry Dawkins. I'd gotten him a present, and was looking forward to giving it to him. He collects keys. Well, not exactly. I collect keys and give them to him. You know how it is, being dead. You can't really pick things up well. I mean he can, but Henry doesn't steal. Plus, not all of them seem to hold on to physical objects easily, if you know what I mean. But Henry is quite strong, for a spirit." When she looked at Thomas, she realized he hadn't known about her. *Oh, crap.* "Then, um, let's see, I saw a little girl I didn't know in the bathroom."

"Alone?"

"Yeah, um, she was dead too, you see."

"That happens to you a lot?"

"Always. They like it when they find someone they can talk to, usually. It's not like in the movies." Feeling dumber by the moment, she wondered if Thomas had ever even seen a movie. "I'm only friends with a few though. More than with living people, though, now that I think about it." She cleared her throat, wishing she had a glass of water so she'd have something to do with her hands.

"This didn't start Tuesday?"

"Heavens, no. All my life. Alexander is my first angel though." She smiled nervously, hoping she wasn't saying anything offensive.

Thomas walked her through her meeting with Alexander, taking her over everything she could remember. The worst part was his asking whether she had any unusual emotional reactions. How could she answer that? Flushed and horny was pretty normal, wasn't it, when confronted with a drop-dead gorgeous guy who wanted to take you dancing?

"What does this have to do with Ronald?" she asked finally, when he got to Tuesday night's date. She really didn't want to describe that.

"Nothing," he said.

"Then why—"

"The Higher Angles will question Alexander about the humans he comes in contact with, how he interacts, if he interferes with human lives as a matter of course. Because you met him on the day of the primary incident, they'll want to know about your relationship."

"Okay. Anyway, I think we said goodbye to Mrs. Paez next door, and I took him inside to meet Gran, since he'd shown up early. I thought she could keep him company while I took a shower. But it didn't go well. She doesn't have much truck with angels, apparently. I'd have thought the dead would like you people." Realizing that might sound bigoted she said,

"You see what I mean. They're dead, you're...well, not human." The supposed connection now seemed more tenuous than when it had first occurred to her.

"Your Gran is dead?"

"Yeah." Fidgeting with the trim on the couch, Zoë said, "Gran warned me about Alexander. Said to make sure he wasn't one of the Fallen." She stole a glance at Thomas.

She read nothing in his expression. Zoë figured this would mean he was a very good advocate, because it wouldn't be smart for an attorney to scowl every time he heard something he didn't expect, or to give away his plan by telegraphing it all over his face.

"I know it might seem rude to ask, but seeing as how some angels don't have much time for the, erm, not-so-departed, and nearly all of my friends are of that persuasion, I'm wondering if you are, well, that type, because if it means you wouldn't be fair about Alexander, knowing about me, it's something we might want to know." We. Like she and Alexander were an item and not two virtual strangers of different species who had gone out exactly one time. If she hadn't been waiting intently for Thomas' answer, she would have rolled her eyes at herself. So what? So what if she was being selfish and asking for herself?

"It isn't the Free that dictate to human spirits. My religion doesn't mandate where a person should or shouldn't go after he dies."

Okay, angels had religion. Zoë always thought

angels *were* religion, but today was a day for learning new things. Like discovering Alexander's advocate was a "Free Angel". Great. Whatever that meant.

"I also wondered because of the spirit in the bar. He doesn't seem very happy."

Thomas sat forward. "There's a spirit in the bar?"

"Yeah, and that's another thing. Why can't you guys see them? I thought maybe it was just Alexander who couldn't, because he seems to be... new."

Thomas grinned. "New," he said. "Yes, I suppose that's one way to put it." He sat back and spread his arms along the back of the couch. "The Higher Angels have certain abilities we do not. Angels are varied in power and ability." Thomas turned his head for a moment as though thinking.

"Zoë, would you mind helping me? I realize this is unusual, but the two men you saw in the bar are my clients. I'm not entirely sure if they're aware they brought a spirit with them. But we'll be faced with the Higher Angels at trial, and *they* certainly will be able to tell. I would like you to help me question it. Would you do that for me?"

She didn't have a reason to say no, but she sort of wanted to. But then, somebody had to speak up for dead people, and as strange as this one looked, it might need her help. Could this be a way of using her gift for something useful? On the other hand, she had a funny feeling about Thomas. Maybe it was some prejudice against the Fallen, rather, the "Free."

Another thought for another time, she told herself.

"Okay, yeah. I don't mind. If it's okay with him, I mean."

Thomas smiled. "Thanks, Zoë. I think that's all I need to know about you and Alexander. If you would wait in the bar for a few minutes?"

A gentle tap came from the door, and a rather remarkable angel peeked in. She had stark, raven black hair around a pale, heart-shaped face, and muddy green eyes that seemed both gloriously deep and troubled. "Ready?" she asked Thomas. She wore tragedy like a cloak wrapped around her shoulders. Zoë fought the urge to cry. Instead, she cleared her throat and stood.

"Yes," Thomas said, again his eyes fastened intently on Zoë. "Please show Miss Pendergraft back to the bar and offer her refreshment." To Zoë he said, "Have you had lunch?"

It wasn't until then she realized exactly how hungry she had become. "I would kill for a sandwich," she said, and then laughed. "Sorry, that was inappropriate. I don't know what's wrong with me today. It's a little overwhelming."

The sad angel touched Zoë's arm and led her out the door. She passed the two characters from the bar, and they refused to meet her eyes. The spirit followed them, clinging like a sticky spider web.

The female angel shut the door and smiled at Zoë, sorrow seeping from her being. "This way, Miss Pendergraft."

The sad angel told Zoë her name was Camille and brought her a tofu and avocado sandwich that turned out to taste a lot better than it sounded. Zoë asked for a Coke, and she listened to a new piano player who had taken Thomas' place after they left. Camille came and asked her if she wanted anything else. Zoë declined politely.

"He's really good," she said, indicating the man on stage.

Camille glanced up. "Yes. That's Marc." She smiled at Zoë and then went through the dark curtain leading to the offices. The other patrons had left, so the only people left were Marc and the bartender.

Zoë relaxed into the music, the notes swirling around her, leeching weariness and tension from her bones. The bartender smiled in a guileless and honest way, his bald head reflecting the light from above. She wondered if it was wise to trust these creatures she knew little about. Could they engender trust?

Zoë was relieved when Alexander returned.

"Sorry," he said. "I had something to take care of." He absently put his hand over hers and watched Marc for a moment. "How did it go with Thomas?" he asked after a while.

"Oh, fine. He wanted to know basically everything you've ever said to me."

Alexander turned and raised an eyebrow. "What did you tell him?"

Zoë shrugged. "I told him pretty much everything

you've ever said to me as best I could remember. He seemed a lot more interested in my spirit friends than in me."

"Did he?"

"Yeah, even asked me if I'd interview one for him. For a case he has. That's why I'm waiting." Then thinking it sounded like she otherwise would have ducked out the back, she added, "Besides waiting for you, of course."

Alexander squeezed her hand. "Of course."

"Umm, why does Thomas work out of a bar?"

"Oh," Alexander said, as though he'd never considered it. "I think he likes the place like this. I do not think there is a real reason, Zoë."

What was it about the way he said her name that made her melt? "Oh?" She resisted the temptation to bat her eyelashes.

"We are not prone to being logical all the time. I think being mortal makes you think you have to organize and be practical."

"I dunno," Zoë said. "These Higher Angels seem pretty organized to me."

Alexander nodded. "That is true as well. But then they are not like us ordinary angels."

She opened her mouth to make a comment about ordinariness and Alexander's complete lack of understanding of the word when Camille returned.

"Thomas would like to see you now," she said.

When Zoë stood, she saw Alexander wasn't

coming with her. She pondered that, and then thought if she was going to act as translator for the dead, there wasn't any excuse for her to invite her maybe-boyfriend to come along. That's when she understood Thomas scared her a little. He had an aura of power, something raw and, well, she didn't have words for it. Not animalistic, because he also seemed ethereal. No, maybe primeval. She decided to chew on the idea.

When she returned to Thomas' office, the two men she'd seen in the bar sat on one of the couches, and Thomas sat opposite, exactly as when she had left. He motioned to the two others. "I'd like you to meet Josh Grieve and Ren Jones."

Zoë nodded to them, since they didn't seem inclined to shake hands.

"Gentlemen, this is Zoë Pendergraft. She's going to act as our translator."

The "gentlemen" didn't seem pleased by the prospect. Zoë might not have been psychic in the least, but she could tell when people didn't want her around. Josh, with his intense pale eyes, seemed the more volatile of the two. He twitched and his leg jumped as though he was antsy. Ren sat back and stroked his ratty goatee. "Sure thing. Whatever." He smirked. Zoë could tell that whatever they were, and whatever they had done, they certainly didn't believe it was a big deal. Judging from the serious look on Thomas' face, however, he disagreed.

"Sit, please, Zoë." He stood and dragged over a chair from the other side of the room. It was straight-backed, but surprisingly comfortable.

"Zoë, is the spirit you saw in the bar here now?"

She nodded. It hovered around Ren's shoulder.

Thomas looked satisfied. "Do you need anything to proceed?" he asked her.

She smiled. A lot of people thought being a medium was some kind of hocus-pocus to do with energy or channeling or ritual. She didn't need to do a routine to talk to the dead any more than she needed to perform a rite to talk with the three people seated in front of her. She shook her head for politeness' sake, and kept her comments to herself.

"He's sick," she observed.

"Sick?" Thomas sat forward. "Sick how?"

The smirks on the faces of the other two faded, but only slightly.

"I don't know. It's hard to put into words." The spirit clung to Ren, like an eerie mist coming out of the collar of his dirty jacket.

To his credit, Thomas didn't interrupt. He just waited.

"I'm Zoë," she said to the spirit. "Can you understand me?"

A face coalesced briefly in the mist. It looked at her with hollow eyes before receding.

"He does, but he's not...whole somehow," Zoë whispered. Not that it would mean the spirit wouldn't hear her. It just seemed polite. To the spirit, she said, "What's your name?"

The sound like a wooden chair being dragged

across a worn hardwood floor filled her ears. "Jackson Burly."

She relayed the name to Thomas, and Josh went pale.

"Holy Christ," he muttered. That seemed particularly inappropriate to Zoë, but she ignored him.

"It's very difficult for him to speak, Thomas, so we'd best keep it brief. What specifically do you want to know?" The spirit snaked away from Ren slightly, and then snapped back, as though chained. "I've never seen anything like this." Zoë said, mostly to herself.

"Please ask him why he's still here. Why he's following my clients?"

This hardly seemed the most pertinent question, but he was the lawyer and she was just the translator. "Did you hear that, Jackson? Thomas of San Francisco..." She paused because she felt like an idiot calling him that. "...wants to know why you cling to Ren."

Strings of misty goo dribbled from the spirit's mouth. "Bound," it rasped.

Ren eyed her as she sucked in her breath. It should have been obvious to her, because spirits just did not wisp out of people's pockets, but it was at this moment Zoë understood something horrible had happened to Jackson Burly. She'd known it was possible to bind a human spirit using black magic, but she'd never imagined she'd see it for real. Fear tickled her skin as she looked at the men seated in front of her.

Ren's more-than-human glare dripped with malevolence, as though warning her not to say a word. She shook her head. "No," she said, her voice caught in her throat. How could anyone do something like this to a sentient entity? Tears threatened to fall as the spirit wailed in pain.

"Zoë," Thomas asked quietly, as though he didn't want to break a spell. "Zoë, what is wrong?"

Fury overcame fear. "What have you done?" she spat at Ren. She couldn't keep the bitter accusation out of her voice. Zoë wanted to get as far away from this place as she could, but she couldn't, no, she wouldn't, leave Jackson Burly supernaturally bound to this awful, evil creature.

Ren seethed, but he gave no answer. He pointedly turned his head away and refused to meet her eyes. Josh looked scared.

She looked again at Jackson's writhing spirit form. "Jackson, what has he done to you?"

"Zoë." Thomas' voice held a warning. He was their lawyer, she guessed, and maybe he didn't want to know, but at that moment she didn't care.

"Bound with a ring," Jackson wailed. He spiraled around Ren's head and pointed long, misty fingers into his coat pocket.

Without thinking, and certainly without planning, Zoë jumped out of her seat and threw herself at Ren. He flung his hands up to defend himself, as though he expected blows.

Thomas stood, and power rolled off him.

"Zoë!" This time it wasn't a plea, but a low, rumbling command that blazed. One she had tremendous difficulty ignoring. It pulled at the very fiber of her. Every cell in her body vibrated, demanding obedience.

Ren struck her hard across the face, then when she didn't let go, he began pushing at her with meaty hands. His strength astounded her. "You crazy bitch," he said and shoved her hard.

Anger seared her. She held onto his jacket, reaching inside, not caring about the pain vibrating through her.

Thomas roared. Zoë trembled and fell backward, no longer able to refuse to obey. When she looked up, her shaking intensified. Her teeth clenched involuntarily and her muscles spasmed. Thomas towered over them. Zoë noticed, as she was thrown to the ground, that Ren and Josh cowered in front of Thomas. He had changed. He no longer bore any resemblance to anything human. Sparkling green and red scales covered his large square face and his teeth glistened in his mouth. He had six arms, each bearing long knob-jointed claws. She laughed hysterically, no longer able to control her reaction.

Her prize fell from her hand. She'd never seen a real fetish before. She'd heard about Vodoun gris-gris, but had no experience to tell her what one would look like. But this was certainly a talisman of a black practice. A length of rope, doubled several times, crusted with dried blood and in the middle of it all was a wide golden wedding band. When it hit the ground, Thomas' power abated only slightly. He reached down with one of his lower hands.

"Don't touch it," Zoë screamed. "It's evil."

A deep laugh came from Thomas' scaly chest. The air thinned enough to allow her to breathe again. She gasped for air and said, "We must free Jackson."

Ren and Josh seemed to have recovered as well. They glared at Zoë, but when Ren looked up at Thomas, he must have thought better of anything that involved lashing out at her. Thomas reached down, and touched the thing with a claw. He easily slashed the twisted rope, and the ring fell to the ground.

The second it hit the carpet, Jackson's spirit flashed, then shattered. "Jackson," Zoë cried out, but she hoped he had merely escaped his prison. She had no way of knowing if he was all right, or if she had actually just witnessed the final destruction of a spirit.

She quivered weakly before the looming monster. "He's gone. He can't help you anymore." She tried to stand, rallying every mote of strength she had. "So neither can I."

Ren lunged toward the ring, and without even taking a moment to consider, Zoë fell back into a crouch and kicked him in the teeth. He made a horrible noise, and she felt sick when blood dripped from the corner of his mouth. The impact hurt her foot, but she would be damned if she was going to let it show. Well, she might be damned anyway.

Before anyone else could move, she scooped up

the ring, as careful as she could be not to touch the bloody rope. She glanced up at Thomas, afraid, and hating it. "What are you?" she asked.

"I am Thomas," came the growling reply.

She turned to him and shouted, "What are you?"

His yellow eyes blinked once, but he only said, "I am Thomas." She wasn't certain if he was angry, or if the fact that he looked like a cross between a dragon and, she had no idea what, made him appear less than cordial.

Zoë grabbed her purse and hugged it. "They are guilty." She didn't know of what, specifically, and it didn't matter. They deserved to burn for what they'd done to Jackson, even if she had no idea how they'd done it.

"Who isn't?" Thomas said. He looked at her intently, waiting.

She was sick, and furious, and more frightened than she knew she could be. Zoë leaped to the door, and stumbled through it, rushing down the corridor to the bar. When she staggered through the curtain, Alexander stood, and he too seemed bigger, more powerful than before, although he hadn't changed form. "Zoë?" he said, but she ran past him.

"Leave me alone," she shouted. "You stay away from me. All of you." She stumbled to the outside corridor, and headed for the plain, ordinary, cement reality of the Civic Center BART station.

Trembling all the way to her car, reality soon hit her. She stood there in broad daylight and threw up in the parking lot. People passed, but they hurried on their way, their eyes averted. It took a long time of sitting in her car before she managed to turn the key and make her way home. Suddenly, she was grateful to be alone.

CHAPTER 6

ZOË PACED HER LIVING ROOM FLOOR, sorry she had come home. But where else could she go? When her cellphone rang and she recognized Simone's number, she hit the 'ignore' button, not feeling fit company for anyone and not wanting to explain her ordeal. Sure, Simone knew about Henry and Gran, but there was a limit to what she could expect her friend to overlook, and she couldn't help but think morphing angels was a bridge too far.

Gran still hadn't shown up, so Zoë was alone. She laughed bitterly, trying hard to hold back tears that threatened to break free. She must be the only person who felt more at ease with dead people around than alone in a creaky shell of wood and stone. An empty house made her feel lonely and exposed, as though hiding in a tent while a tornado sped in her direction.

She ground coffee beans, but the aroma that usually soothed her made her stomach twist. She put the grounds in the coffee maker but left the machine turned off. She flipped through TV channels for five minutes before hitting the 'off' switch and throwing the remote onto the sofa cushions. Zoë wanted not to think, to be oblivious, and she envied people who found solace in getting drunk. Alcohol had a terrible effect on her, probably due to her abilities, and the few times she had indulged with so much as one beer, she faced walking nightmares. Her casual acquaintances probably thought she was an alcoholic because she refused even a sip. She wouldn't use mouthwash with alcohol in it and had refused a boozy trifle served at a potluck dinner once.

No, she was left to face stark reality, and for the first time ever, she wasn't sure what life had dumped in her lap. Unable to stand the contemplation, Zoë went to the distraction of last resort. She donned rubber gloves, found a spray can of Scrubbing Bubbles and a sponge, and headed for the bathroom.

After an hour, the tiles sparkled like they hadn't in a very long time. The toilet and basin were clean enough to drink from, although Zoë couldn't imagine a circumstance under which anyone would. Maybe if an earthquake shook the house and she was trapped, she would drink out of the toilet while waiting for rescue workers. She shuddered when she remembered the tiny spirit she'd seen in the ladies' room at Fiskers and wondered why her thoughts had taken such a morbid turn. *Oh yeah, angels turning into monsters. Check.*

Zoë's muscles ached from the effort, but she felt pleasantly tired. She peeled off the yellow rubber gloves, continued undressing until all her clothing lay in a pile on the bathroom floor, and stepped into the shower. Hot water flowed over her skin, washing away the tension. Tiredness crept through her limbs, and she felt more emotionally drained than she had in a long time, maybe since her father died.

For a little while, the horrors of the day left her. Zoë emerged from the bathroom in a white fluffy bathrobe, scrunching her curly hair dry with a towel. The clock told her it was only now coming up on six o'clock, but exhaustion plagued her, so she went to her bedroom, dropped the robe on her chair, and climbed under the covers, barely caring that going to bed with wet hair would leave her with a disaster to contend with in the morning.

A fierce chill and a tugging sensation woke her some time later. Groping in the pitch black, it took her a moment to recognize the here and now. She sat up and looked around her room. Squinting into the night she said, "Who's there?"

Gran looked nervous, something Zoë hadn't ever seen her do before. "There's some people here to see you," Gran said.

She broke into a wide smile. "Gran, I've missed you! Where have you been?"

The old spirit looked pleased. "You did? I thought maybe with that new beau of yours..."

"Don't be silly, Gran." There was nothing silly about it, but she didn't want to think about their falling out. Slowly her brain started to function. "Who's here?" She automatically reached out, scanning the house with her senses. Spirits. And lots of them. Their presence hit her like sounds of a near neighbor having a cocktail party.

"People have been hearing about what you did. I told them you needed to sleep, but there's so many now." And by "people" Gran obviously meant *dead* people.

"Okay," Zoë said. "I'd better get dressed if we have company."

Gran seemed happy with the pronouncement, and said she'd go tell everyone Zoë was coming down. Spirits, as a rule, didn't mind much what living people wore, since they themselves never changed clothes. Displays of wealth meant less and less when one couldn't actually possess anything anymore. On the other hand, some of the departed did concern themselves with manners. The least she could do was not greet her guests naked.

Zoë threw on jeans and a USC sweatshirt and ran her fingers through the tangles in her hair. When she was as presentable as she could be in the middle of the night, she made her way down to her living room, flicking on lights as she went.

Unlike TV ghosts, real spirits didn't particularly notice if it was daytime or night, and didn't care if the lights were on or off, at least in her experience. Zoë did admit, however, she wasn't an expert on spirits any more than someone who visited an aquarium was automatically a marine biologist.

When she went down the stairs, she was stunned to find nearly a hundred spirits in her living room.

Some were just sparks, which was what Zoë called those who didn't have the strength to show themselves as fully-fledged embodiments. Some of the stronger ones present could have sent a chill through any human with the slightest spiritual sensitivity. These hardly even looked misty, merely pale, although they wavered faintly when she looked straight at them.

Zoë sought out Gran's face, and found the old woman standing to the side of the crowd, facing her. "Gran?" she asked uncertainly.

"They've come to pay their respects," Gran said.

Zoë nodded, at a loss for what to do. "But why?"

A man's voice piped up from the back. "We heard about what you did for Jackson Burly," he said.

Zoë walked among the spirits, who swished around her. When she reached her easy chair, she sat on its edge, stunned beyond speech. Pockets of cool air wafted as the spirits surrounded her.

They waited with palpable anticipation, but Zoë had no idea what they expected. She gave Gran a pleading look. "I don't know what to say," she said. "I did what anybody would have done. And, Thomas of San Francisco, a Free Angel, protected me." She didn't know why she said that. Maybe he was protecting her, and maybe he had threatened her. She still didn't know for certain, but it didn't seem right to take credit for something that wasn't all that big a deal. It had been awful and nauseating and horrifying, but she'd done the only thing she could.

A collective shiver went through the room at the

mention of the angel's name. A gaunt young woman glistened brightly as she said, "Not everyone, Zoë Pendergraft, would have taken the risk. You showed great courage and compassion."

"Has anyone seen Jackson Burly? Did he...make it? I saw his image shatter, and he vanished. I was afraid he was..." What? Dead? In truth, she didn't want to think about the possibilities.

A young Native American man billowed in front of Zoë. His dark eyes pulled at her. "He will recover in time. We have taken him to a place of protection. We do not know if he will return to the other side."

Zoë sighed with relief. "Please tell him how pleased I am he's all right."

Two little girls stepped forward: twins, as best she could tell. They dipped into a curtsy in front of Zoë and laid identical roses on her lap. She ran her fingers over the soft petals. Moving objects was a struggle for some spirits, and she smiled graciously. "They're lovely. Thank you." The twins looked at each other, giggled, and curtsied again. Then suddenly they dissolved in a glittery flash.

Spirits approached one by one. Some gave her tokens: a few more flowers, a button, an earring. One boy gave her a tiny toy soldier, and another spirit left a grainy brown photograph, and another a strange green stone. One dropped something heavy at her feet. The human-looking spirits who didn't bring tokens bowed in front of her, and then only a few sparkling flashes of light remained. They danced around Zoë's head a few times before flickering out.

"I...I don't know what to say," Zoë said when all but Gran had gone.

"You don't have to say anything, child. You did just the right thing. Most people want something from the dead. You're one of the few who give without expecting anything in return. Hardly anybody would risk themselves for someone they didn't know, especially if that somebody was so different."

Different. What a charming way to describe "dead." Zoë smiled. "Thank you, Gran. This was very sweet. I...I needed that, I think. It helps, knowing it matters."

"Of course it matters, Zoë. This is a man's soul. Nothing matters more."

Zoë nodded and stifled a yawn. "You're right. I'm sorry. I'm still so tired."

Gran said, "You sleep. I'll watch over you."

Zoë didn't know why Gran planned to sit vigil, but it made her feel better. She didn't want to admit she was still shaken by her encounter with Thomas, not to mention the evil she'd glimpsed today. With Gran around, at least she'd get some warning if one of them showed up while she slept.

"Thanks, Gran," she said. She shuffled upstairs to her bedroom and put her treasures on the dresser. The flowers and trinkets touched her more than she could say. Each of these things meant something to the spirit who offered it to her. She was certain of that.

This time when she climbed into bed, she felt safe, and instead of falling into an exhausted sleep of emotional turmoil, she found a comfortable place in her mind, and drifted away. During the night, when flashes of frightening, but nameless images came to her mind, Gran's comforting presence soothed her.

CHAPTER 7

WHEN THE TINKLING PIANO MUSIC started, alerting her the day was about to begin, Zoë reached out and hit the alarm clock's 'off' button with only a hint of reluctance. In truth, she needed to work and be around humans again. Gran still sat in the chair beside the bed, but she had her eyes closed, as though sleeping. Zoë knew this to be an affectation, since spirits didn't sleep, at least not in the "shut your physical eyes" sense, but if Gran didn't want to talk, that was fine with her.

She gathered the flowers the spirits had brought, took them into the kitchen, and put them in a short, round vase. They each looked as fresh as if they'd been cut moments before. They were an odd hodge-podge of colors and shapes, but they looked sweet together, as though someone had gone through a garden plucking the prettiest flowers, one from each type of plant.

As Zoë went toward the front door, her foot

caught on something, and a metal object slid across the carpet. Kneeling down to search for it, she pulled back when she finally found it. It was a knife, not a kitchen knife either, but a hunting knife. It glowed.

With care, Zoë reached out to touch it, tapping it with one finger at first, almost afraid it would jump up at her. When her hand closed around it, a thrumming reverberated through her palm and up her arm. The sensation was not unpleasant, but unexpected. She turned the small, fixed blade knife, examining it. She slid it out of its sheath, and it hummed as she exposed the beveled blade. The sharp side curved upward, bringing it to a vicious point. The metal gleamed, but not from a reflective polish. Instead, it shone from within, as though constructed of blue ice. She balanced it and felt its weight. It snuggled into her palm as though it had been custom made for her.

She didn't know why, but Zoë did not want to leave the knife behind, so she tucked it into an inner pocket of her handbag. She couldn't remember which of the previous night's guests had dropped it. Which one? The question niggled. The blurred memory brought back her fear. She still found herself perplexed when she thought of the strange ceremony. She'd never heard of spirits doing anything like that.

It occurred to her she should find some other mediums. Real ones, not those fake TV people, and definitely not the idiot ghost hunters. The genuine sensitives in that crowd just wanted to scare themselves stupid. It reminded her of thrill-seekers who dove with sharks. Not that spirits were predatory. They could be, she supposed, but then anyone could.

By the time Zoë got to the Fiskers' San Mateo parking lot, she felt better. Still uneasy about the previous day, the passing of hours made the horror fade. The tedious, ordinary nature of her job helped. As much as she had wanted to be around people, Zoë buried her thoughts in work, and she tuned out the world as much as she could. The phone hardly rang, and she was glad for that. Of course, it was Friday and a beautiful summer day when those who could, played hooky.

She wasn't surprised when she learned Simone would come in a couple hours late. She guessed her friend had a date this weekend, possibly with Dustin Bittner, and had decided to spend the day shopping for a new dress rather than sitting through pointless meetings about strategy and synergy. Who wouldn't prefer that?

When lunchtime rolled around, Zoë waited until most everyone had gone, grabbed an apple from a break-room vending machine, and headed down to see Henry. She took her purse, thinking she would ask him about the strange knife. Although she could have asked Gran, Henry seemed more open to questions like that. Maybe he seemed worldlier than Gran, which was hardly surprising. It fit with what she knew of their mortal lives.

As she approached the door to the maintenance corridor, it flew open, and someone burst out, knocking Zoë into a crouch. "Hey!" she shouted after him. Startled, she picked herself up and straightened her clothes. With a grouchy mutter, she made her way down to the stairs.

A sense of wrongness swept over her. "Henry," she whispered, and dread filled her bones, holding her in place, while urgency swept her forward. The two conflicting impulses caused her to stumble to the boiler room. When she swung open the door, she knew Henry wouldn't be there. Something terrible had happened. The apple dropped from her hand and bounced on the cement floor.

Zoë didn't grasp what she saw at first. Her eyes scanned the body on the floor, her brain not wanting to register it. She stood in the open doorway and stared. A dozen, ordinary explanations flitted through her mind, but she summarily dismissed each one. She recognized dead when she saw dead, and the pile of flesh and bones lying in the center of the boiler room floor had no life in them. A flicker, undoubtedly a fresh spirit, sparkled in the corner. Zoë didn't bother to call Henry. He wouldn't be coming back. She accepted it without understanding it.

"Zoë?" a voice asked softly. "Zoë, what's wrong?"

She turned and saw a maintenance man watching her from halfway up the corridor. The body drew her gaze back. Her throat closed, and she couldn't speak.

The man approached with cautious steps, as though he too was encompassed by the dread that had held Zoë in place. When he got to the doorway, he rushed forward. "Kent?" he called out. "Kent, are you okay?" He turned the body over. Glassy eyes stared at the ceiling.

The maintenance worker—for some reason Zoë couldn't remember his name—whipped his head around and stared at her. "Call 911," he shouted. When she didn't move, he ran past her and headed toward the control room. She heard him pick up a landline.

The spirit in the corner quivered. She wondered momentarily if he would stay. Sometimes spirits did that, stayed in the place they'd died. But not always. "Kent?" she said to the spark. "Kent?"

Sid came back to her side. Sid. Relief washed over her. His name was Sid. She wasn't sure why it seemed important, but it did. "He can't hear you, honey." He put a hand on her shoulder. "Look, let's go sit in the office and wait for the ambulance, okay?"

Zoë stepped forward, unable to stop staring at the quavering spirit. "Kent?"

Sid tugged her arm again. "Come on, Zoë, there's nothing you can do for him now."

When the second being came into the room, pressure built in Zoë's chest. What this strange thing was, she couldn't imagine, but it wasn't human. It coalesced out of darkness, as though made of shadows. It stood about eight feet tall, robed in flowing gloom that snaked around its thin body like an executioner's robe.

Zoë trembled. Its presence filled the room with such force it pulled breath from her lungs. "What are you?" she whispered, unable to stop looking at the black holes where its eyes should be.

"Zoë?" Sid said uncertainly.

The figure produced something like a jar and guided Kent's spirit into it.

Zoë pushed forward, stepping out of Sid's reach. "Don't you touch him! No, no, no!" She screamed the words over and over.

The thing stopped and looked at her. Its empty gaze bored into her. When it approached, every sense within her, both physical and spiritual, sent such overwhelming signals that she lost control. She screamed and put her hands over her ears.

Sid grabbed her from behind and pulled her into an embrace. She buried her head in his chest, and he held her while she cried helplessly. Her sobs didn't stop for a long time. The next thing she knew, she was sitting in the maintenance control room, and a man she didn't know was flashing a penlight into her eyes.

"Ma'am, can you hear me?"

Zoë blinked hard. Even the pale light made her wince. "Yes," she said, but she wasn't sure if she made any sound at all. She couldn't get enough air, and the world swam around her.

"Ma'am, you're going to be all right. You've had a shock. We're going to take you to the hospital."

"No," Zoë said weakly. Sounds buzzed in her ears, and she went numb all over. "No, I just need to lie down."

She realized Sid was holding her hand. *I must be in bad shape. Why can't I clear my head?*

"Can I call someone to come get you?" Sid asked. "Would that be okay?" She wasn't clear if he asked the second question of her or this other guy. Who was he, anyway?

"Simone," she said. "Simone Wallace can drive me home."

"Sure, Zoë, I'll call her now."

Zoë heard the two men talking, and then she heard other voices. The police? There seemed to be some slight disagreement about something, but she couldn't care, not even a little bit. Her mind was completely blank. She couldn't even remember why she'd come down today.

She felt better when she heard Simone's voice. When her friend approached, she said, "Henry's gone."

It was Sid who replied. "His name was Kent, Zoë. You remember Kent?"

Right. *Kent.* Zoë's mind went back to the body on the floor and the figure that had taken his spirit, and put it in a jar like a glowing firefly. It was at that moment the world went black.

When she came around, a policeman asked her a couple of questions before the paramedic took her to the hospital, but she wasn't yet coherent enough to say anything particularly helpful. A doctor at the hospital wanted her to see a psychologist, and when she refused, saying she wanted to go home, a nurse gave her a brochure about Post Traumatic Stress Syndrome.

Simone stayed with her at the hospital and then drove Zoë home. By the time they pulled up and got inside, weariness overwhelmed her, but at least she had regained some presence of mind. Zoë shivered and hugged herself. "I feel so stupid," she finally said.

"You shouldn't." Simone went to the hallway cupboard and found a blanket. She came back to the living room and wrapped it around Zoë's shoulders. "It's not your fault."

That must be something people always said to someone who had been through a shock.

"It's not like it's every day you see a dead person," Simone said and then stopped cold. Because, of course, Zoë did see dead people every day, just not the fleshy parts. Zoë looked up and grinned, and Simone giggled, apparently relieved at the response.

"Simone, you can go. I really will be okay. I'm a lot better now." She didn't feel numb like before, but she was exhausted. "I just want to sleep."

"Okay. Want some help getting settled?" Simone's dark forehead crinkled into a pretty frown. Zoë could tell she wasn't sure if she should leave or not.

"Nah, I am going to throw some sweats on and crash. I appreciate you bringing me home though."

Simone nodded. "I understand. You call me if you need anything or if you just don't want to be alone."

"Don't you have a date with Dustin tonight?" Zoë could tell Simone was blushing from the expression on her face, though her dark skin barely showed the effect.

"Don't worry about that. He'll understand." Simone waved her hand, brushing the idea aside. Then she stopped. "How did you know? He asked me last night. Sorta last minute, but you know."

Zoë laughed. It felt cleansing to talk about something pleasant. "You were late to work today. Figured you went shopping. That's what you always do before a first date."

Simone rolled her eyes. "God, am I that predictable?"

"Yes. Now go fuss with your hair and have a good time. Call me first thing and give me all the naughty details." Zoë made her voice as strong as she could, willing Simone to go with a clear conscience.

Simone gave her a hug before she left and made sure the door was locked behind her. The warmth of the conversation held Zoë in check long enough for her snuggle down on the couch with the remote.

Drowsiness weighed on her body like gravity, pulling her down into sleep. She drifted somewhere between waking and sleeping, not able to let herself relax completely, as though unconsciousness held a horror she couldn't face.

CHAPTER 8

AFTER A SLEEPLESS WHILE, Zoë sat up and stretched, feeling less rested than when she'd started. The sun still shone brightly outside, even though it seemed an eternity had passed since she'd left for work that morning. Zoë sighed, knowing she had to talk to Alexander. She needed to tell him about the thing that took Kent's soul. Gran wasn't home, and it didn't seem right to ask her. Zoë knew with certainty it would upset Gran to hear about this creature, so Alexander was the best option.

Problem was, she didn't know how to find him. He didn't have a phone, and they didn't have any mutual friends. She considered calling Ronald at the Delaware Street Post Office in San Mateo, the one closest to Fiskers Technology Group, but Ronald had already told her he didn't know Alexander. Besides, he likely would be still on his route anyway, and there was a good chance he honestly didn't know what happened to him the day Alexander took his route.

Alexander might have conked him out and stuffed him in a closet while he took Ronald's place Tuesday. Zoë hadn't asked for specifics. On top of that, she didn't know anything about where Ronald went when he delivered mail or how long it took him. Their conversations had never been detailed or personal, just filled with flirtation and innuendo barely this side of workplace-acceptable.

Zoë found her purse and retrieved the white business card bearing Thomas' name. Images of Thomas as the beautiful piano-playing human-like being fought valiantly with the memory of the towering scaly dragon he'd become.

On one hand, he could have hurt her if he'd wanted to. She had no doubt of that. He could have stopped her from leaving, but he hadn't. Nothing prevented him from tracking her down right now. On the other hand, he scared the crap out of her. But back on the first hand, he didn't scare her as much as whatever it was she saw in the boiler room. She couldn't help but ask herself if that was wise. Should she be afraid of Thomas?

Who else, she wondered. Who would know Alexander? *Briony.* Didn't Alexander say that was the name of her Guardian? Zoë couldn't help but smirk a little. Angel rules seemed bizarre and illogical, so she hoped they didn't consider themselves superior beings. But of course, she had to acknowledge they probably were, if for no other reason than the scary shape-changing mojo, and she suspected that was only the beginning.

"Briony?" she said tentatively. "Briony, can you hear me?" Zoë waited long moments in the silence. Nothing. *Crap.* Unsurprising, but still crap.

Sighing loudly, she dialed the phone.

"Thomas' office. How may I help?" Zoë recognized the voice as the same one that had answered the first time she called. She immediately dismissed the idea that this could be the lovely but tormented Camille.

"My name is Zoë Pendergraft. I need to speak with Thomas, if he's available."

"One moment." The warm voice was soothing and pleasant, but Zoë twitched with nervous energy after the woman put her on hold.

An impulse told Zoë to hang up. She pulled the phone away from her face, and was about to press the red 'off' button to disconnect. As her finger reached the button, a familiar voice said "Hello, Zoë."

His tone was warm and welcoming and for the moment, completely human. "Hello, Thomas, I'm sorry to bother you. I didn't know who else to call. I need to find Alexander, but he doesn't have a phone. It's...it's important. I saw something. I...Thomas, I didn't know what it was. I need help." She hadn't planned to say any of this, but her thoughts ran away with her, and she hated how pathetic she must sound. Poor little human needed the big angel to rescue her. Yuck.

The continuing stillness on the line shook her. "Thomas?" she said. "Can you hear me?" She was afraid for a moment he might refuse.

"He's on his way," Thomas said.

Zoë sighed with relief, and decided not to think too hard on what just happened. Telepathy? "Thank you, Thomas. And I'll be sure to ask him how to get in touch with him directly, so I don't have to bother you again."

"You did me a great service the other day, and put yourself in peril."

At any other time the expression would have made her grin. *In peril.* Who talked like that? "I'm sorry about what happened." She hadn't done anything wrong, but it seemed appropriate. "The way I acted, then leaving like that. I hope I didn't offend you." That much was true. She had no idea what an angel, free or otherwise, would do when affronted, but she didn't want to find out.

"I am not offended," Thomas said. "Are you?"

Now Zoë did grin. Like it would matter. "No, Thomas. I'm not. A little afraid of you, but not offended." How could she be? He hadn't done anything to her. In fact, he helped her release Jackson Burly. "I told the spirits you helped me. The ones who came to pay tribute for Jackson. I know they aren't always cooperative with angels, but I thought it was right they knew."

The stillness on the line returned. Not even the normal buzz of telephone electricity interfered. Was he communicating with someone or thinking, she wondered, but didn't dare interrupt either way.

"Spirits paid tribute to you?" he finally asked.

Now she felt awkward. Fortunately, she heard a whoosh of air outside, as a stiff breeze buffeted the windows. "I have to go, Thomas. Alexander is here. Thank you so much. I can't tell you how much I appreciate this." She said goodbye and hung up.

When she flung open the front door, happiness and relief washed over her. Alexander walked toward her from the front path. Zoë looked up and down the street, wondering if anyone could have seen him, but no one was outside, not even Mrs. Paez.

"I checked," he said with a smile. "Thomas said you needed me."

Zoë stepped up to him, and melted into his warm embrace. She breathed deeply of his comforting scent. "Alexander," she said, and then nothing more came, because without warning, Zoë started to cry.

He squeezed her gently, and kissed her hair. He didn't shush her or try to make her stop crying. He just held her.

Finally she said, "Let's go inside." She walked in the house, but turned around to find he hadn't followed her. It took her a moment to register why as she extended her senses. Gran had returned while Zoë slept, taking up her spot in the upstairs room where she always sat and stitched on a piece of needlework that would never be finished. "We can go. Someplace quiet, please."

He nodded. "Are you all right?" Alexander extended his hand to her, but still did not cross the threshold.

Zoë grabbed her things and turned off the lights in the front room. She wanted to tell him she was fine, but she didn't know how to answer the question. Soon she was in his arms again, standing on the front porch. The familiar warmth of him enveloped her. "May I take you?" he whispered.

"What if I said no?" she asked.

"Then I could not."

For some reason, that pleased her and made her feel less helpless. "Yes," she said.

He paused for a moment, as though listening, and then everything shifted. Just as before, it felt like he had spun her around, although he hadn't moved his feet.

New sounds and smells told her they'd arrived, but she didn't want to let go of him right away.

"Zoë, you are trembling. Are you afraid?"

"A little," she said, still not looking at his face.

"Of me?" The words rumbled in his chest. She didn't have to be a mind-reader to know he wanted her to say no.

But she couldn't make that assertion. "Should I be?"

"I will never harm you."

The air crackled, as though something significant had happened. This was no idle promise, Zoë thought. With everything in her, she believed him.

He gently released her, and she stepped back. She was surprised to see they stood in what looked like a hotel corridor. Before she had a chance to wonder about his intentions, he said, "This is where I live. It is safe here."

She marveled that somehow he had known what she needed more than anything: to feel secure and protected. Finally, she looked up at him and nodded. They walked together through the hallway. At the end she saw a blue shimmering wall.

"How many of these are there?" she asked and pointed at the portal.

"You can see it?" Alexander sounded perplexed. "You should not be able to."

"Alexander," she said with a smile. "I shouldn't be able to see a lot of things."

He held her hand as they walked through it. This barrier did not repel her as strongly as the one in the BART station, and she idly wondered whether it was because of its smaller size, or that she was gradually becoming used to them. The second they passed through the barrier, they were no longer in a hotel, but in an immense garden. It smelled fresh and green, and Zoë instantly relaxed, releasing thoughts and worries that stung her. The sky above was a perfect shade of cornflower blue, and a warm wind kissed her skin.

"Is this real?" she said in a hushed voice, taking in the riot of colors around her, the flowers and trees, the perfectly shaped shrubs. Butterflies flitted and bees went about their work, flying from one perfect bloom to another.

Alexander considered and then said, "Yes."

Zoë knew there was more to the answer than that but decided it didn't matter. She felt safe. "Is there a place we can sit?"

Alexander faced her, and brushed a curl out of her eyes. "You are weary," he said.

She nodded.

Without another word, he swept her up and carried her into the garden, walking along a path of amazing colors. Vines brushed her hair as they passed through an archway into what she could only describe as an outdoor bedroom. A huge gazebo dominated the center of a cluster of trees, and on it stood an immense bed. Its twining wooden headboard had green sprigs growing out of it, and white linens covered mounds of down pillows. Lanterns hung under the gazebo's sheltered overhang and creaked in the breeze. A couch and a couple of chairs stood to one side.

Zoë stared up at Alexander. "This is where you live?" she said. "It's like an enchanted fairy forest." She laughed, and his expression turned sharp for an instant, and then it melted away so quickly she couldn't have sworn it hadn't been her imagination. He carried her to the bed and laid her on top of it, taking a moment to slip her shoes off and drop them to the floor.

She considered objecting to the bed. After all, they'd only had one date, but the comfort and tenderness were precisely what she needed. He lay down beside her, and nestled her into the crook of his arm. "You are safe, Zoë. You have nothing to fear from me."

His heartbeat was steady and strong, and she knew he was telling the truth. She wasn't sure how. Her abilities didn't make her a human lie-detector, and it wasn't as though no one had ever lied to her before, but when he spoke, every mote of air around her vibrated, testifying to the truth of his words.

Within moments, she was asleep, this time without dreaming. The warm security took her into a place of perfect rest. Even the fragrant air restored her as she lay with Alexander, enjoying the rise and fall of his chest as he breathed with her.

When she woke, darkness had fallen and the lanterns around the gazebo glowed. Alexander still lay beside her, but she had rolled away from him in her sleep, and he curled up behind her with his arm protectively over hers. She stirred, and he pulled her into his body. It surprised her to feel evidence of his sexual excitement. So, she thought, angels can get horny. And based on her reaction, it was contagious. A pang of desire shot through her as Alexander propped himself up on one elbow, pulled her curly hair aside, and kissed her neck with soft, wet flicks of his tongue mixed with gentle nibbles. Her body shuddered involuntarily.

"Alexander," she whispered hoarsely. The name tasted delicious in her mouth. Before she could think to stop herself, she pushed her hips backward into him. "Alexander," she said again, this time with more force. If she wanted to stop, it had to be now.

"Yes," he said, but it was not a query. It came out as an answer to a question she hadn't asked.

She rolled over within his embrace and faced

him. Their noses nearly touched. Her mouth hungered for his. The scent of fresh cookies made her smile. "Alexander, why do you smell like baked goods?"

He paused for a moment and laughed. It was a wonderful sound. He put his mouth close to her ear. "Your brain does not know how to process the scent of otherness about me, so it translates into something more familiar. In your case, cupcakes."

A grin spread across her face. "More like snickerdoodles." She sniffed. "Or cinnamon rolls. It's hard to pin down." She touched his face, and he closed his eyes as she traced unexpected stubble on his jaw. Abruptly changing the subject, she said, "I'm not ordinarily impulsive."

He didn't respond with words. Instead he waited with what seemed like infinite patience.

"But here I am. In your bed. I barely know you. I know less about you than any man I've ever met. Because you aren't a man at all." She became acutely aware of what some of her romance novels would call "his manhood" pressing against her at that moment, and it took an abundance of will to ignore it.

"You are worried you will discover something about me that will cause you to regret any intimacy with me."

She wouldn't have put it that way, but he'd fairly well summed it up.

"I will wait, if you wish. How long does it take to be certain?"

Unfair question, and he probably knew it. But he had a valid point. She knew better than to think she could ever truly be certain about another person, whether *person* was precisely the right word for him or not. She corrected herself. Of course Alexander was a person. He just wasn't a human person.

Zoë pondered, and Alexander let her. He watched her with intensity in his green eyes. His gaze pulled at her, caressing, even taunting. The doubts would wait, she decided. Tentatively, she tilted her head toward his and whispered, "Kiss me, Alexander."

He complied without reservation. She couldn't help but wonder how many human women he'd kissed in the centuries he'd been in the mortal timeline, as he put it. He'd had a long time to practice, but then surely angels didn't go around seducing women on a regular basis. As the kiss deepened, the thoughts melted away.

His hand slid from her back down to her bottom, and he pulled her tightly into him. His body thrilled her, and she ached for him with surprising intensity. She returned his kisses, loving the taste of his mouth and the solid certainty of the way he held her.

She began to unbutton his white shirt. As she unfastened the last button, she pulled the cotton material over his shoulder. It flickered slightly, and disappeared. Zoë gasped, and Alexander grinned at her. "I forgot you could do that," she said.

Zoë moved toward the edge of the enormous bed, keeping her eyes locked on his. He crawled after her, their movements slow and sensual. Her feet touched the wooden slats of the gazebo. They felt cool and smooth to her bare toes.

Alexander positioned himself to sit on the side of the bed, with her standing between his knees. His hands rested comfortably on her hips. In one swift movement, she pulled the knit top over her head. His hands slid upward to her belly, then inched toward her breasts. His fingertips trailed over the lace on her pale yellow bra. She gasped as they glanced her nipples.

Zoë unbuttoned her trousers and let them slip down over her hips before stepping out of them. When Alexander's hands began to roam southward, she grinned at the delighted expression on his face. He touched her panties at the hips, tracing the web of flowers in the lace. "Humans," he said, "have many layers."

She leaned over and kissed him full on the mouth, her hunger and anticipation building. "Like gift-wrap," she said.

"What a precious gift you are, Zoë." Alexander slipped his fingers inside the lower elastic of her panties.

"That tickles," she said, giggling. She gave him a little push, indicating he should lie back. Then she pointed at his pants, and shook her head. "Those have to go."

A flush warmed her as his trousers melted away and she took in the beauty of his body. When she'd seen him nude before he hadn't been aroused. An unwanted thought crept into her mind. "Oh, Alexander, tell me you have a condom. Please, tell me we don't have to stop." She took her time looking over his body.

He smiled. "I am not susceptible to and cannot transmit human disease, and I will not impregnate you."

Zoë exhaled with relief. She began to unfasten her bra. When she managed the hook and let the bra fall, self-consciousness stopped her cold. He was so perfect, and gorgeous, and next to him she felt mortal and plain. Before the doubts could take hold, he stood and wrapped his arms around her, taking her into a strong embrace. He spun her slightly and lifted her onto the bed. His kisses were fierce and so full of desire she didn't question them.

He kissed his way to her neck. She arched her back with delight, pressing her stomach into his. He slipped his arm under her, biting at her neck and shoulder while she purred with delight.

Then he licked a trail down to her left breast. He teased the hardened nub, flicking and sucking until she moaned wildly. He turned his attention to her other breast, and squeezed it, kneading gently, and then he gripped them both, licking one and then the other.

Alexander's pulse had quickened, and the night around them stilled, as though the garden itself watched and listened. A breeze wafted over Zoë's bare chest as his hands went to her panties. He slowly peeled them down over her thighs and then tossed them aside.

When his mouth began to move down over her

tummy, Zoë tensed in heady anticipation. He gently spread her legs, touching her with strong hands. Another moan escaped her lips, followed by a sequence of many more.

She had no concept of how much time had passed, and Alexander was intent in the way he pleased her. When her body grew taut with impending release, Zoë panted hard, gripping the bed linens with her hands and thrusting her hips upward. Her body trembled and she screamed in a way she never had before. Alexander held her through the waves until the last of them passed, her body so sensitive and electrified she begged him to stop so she could breathe.

She kissed him hard, empowered and alive. With a smooth motion, she was astride him, and without further preamble guided him inside her. Pleasure pulsed within her as he filled her completely. She leaned backward, moving up and down on him, letting the rhythm take her to a second height of bliss.

Alexander grabbed her hips and began to thrust upward from beneath her. She swayed forward and braced herself on the bed, her face inches away from his. They looked at each other as their bodies rocked, and she'd never experienced anything as intimate as watching each other's eyes, tasting each other's breath as they flowed together.

"Zoë," Alexander said, his breathing ragged with excitement. He wrapped an arm around her and with enormous strength, moving to a kneeling position while still inside her. "Zoë," he said again.

"Little Zoë, do not be afraid."

He began to glow, as though light emanated from his pores. Zoë gasped, and the light travelled into her. She rode his hips, her feet touching the bed, her back supported by his strong arms.

"Don't stop," she cried out urgently. Zoë had difficulty telling where he ended and she began. "Come inside me."

He thrust with abandon, and took her with him as he submitted to pleasure. Light blazed around them, and Zoë had to close her eyes. Its warmth enveloped both of them and they lost themselves together. The intensity of sensations and emotions overwhelmed her completely, and tears ran down her face and sobs choked her. Alexander gripped her until the light faded. He laid her down beside him, and she snuggled close.

"Tell me, little Zoë, that I did not hurt you."

She took his face in her hands, and made him look into her eyes. "No," she said as firmly as she could in her current state. "No." She kissed him on the lips. "I...I haven't got words. I feel," she paused, searching, "beautiful."

He smiled and touched the tracks her tears had made down her cheeks. "You cried."

"Yes. Now, shush." She kissed him again, and then lay listening to his heart as it slowly returned to its natural rhythm.

CHAPTER 9

"THOMAS SAID YOU NEEDED to tell me something," Alexander said after a nice long while.

Zoë tore herself back to reality. If Alexander's enchanted garden could be called reality. "Yes," she said, shifting her position and propping herself up on some pillows. "Something bad happened today." She wasn't one for equivocation, but she couldn't bring herself to go directly to the scary part. Even as she skirted around it, she tensed.

"You are shaking," Alexander said, took her hand in his and looked up at her.

"I found a body at work." She looked away, focusing somewhere in the dark distance of the garden. "I saw something..."

"You saw him die?"

She shook her head. "I found him soon after. I could see the spark, floating above. And then this... horrible thing...a huge, tall thing came and took it."

Zoë gripped Alexander's hand. "Just came and took him. Put him in a jar, of all things, like a kid collecting a bug. But it was no kid. It had to be the most terrifying thing I've ever seen."

Alexander sat up and looked her squarely in the eye. "Zoë, are you changing?"

Of the responses she'd anticipated, this one came as a complete shock. "Changing how?"

"Do things look different to you, feel different even? Can you do things you previously could not? See new things you know are not of the human realm?" Alexander's voice was crisp and clear, not at all the tender bedroom tone he'd used a few minutes before.

Zoë pulled the blanket to cover herself. "I don't think so. A lot of the new stuff happens when I'm with you. And this thing I saw, well, I've never been around a ...fresh body before, so I can't say." She lowered her voice. "What was it?"

Alexander paused, as though deciding how to phrase it. "One of the Higher Angels, known as the Powers by some, although they have many names. It was taking the soul out of the timeline. They do that in special cases."

"The Grim Reaper," she whispered. "That's what it looked like, sort of. I never thought of it."

Alexander kissed her hand. "We have existed for longer than humans in this world. We are everywhere you are, and if you look at the legends and mythology of every culture, you will find us."

"It came at me. I thought it was going to take me. It's ridiculous, I know."

Alexander sat up. "It took notice of you?"

Zoë nodded. "I sort of yelled at it. And it moved straight at me. I was terrified." She refused to admit she'd passed out. That made her look too weak and girlie. "One of the maintenance guys was with me. He sorta rushed me out of there. I dunno what happened. There was a lot of confusion." After a pause, she said, "Could it have taken Henry? He's a spirit that lived there. My friend."

"He is gone?" Concern spread over Alexander's face. "It is possible. Tell me from the beginning, please."

Zoë told him about Henry and related everything she could remember from the time she went down to the boiler room until she called Thomas. She did smooth over the bits where she might have screamed or fainted or done anything that would sound hysterical, which was exactly what she had been. "I'm worried about Henry," she said.

"If the Powers took him, then he is beyond our reach and where he is supposed to be."

"Yeah, but is he where he *wants* to be? He seemed mighty happy in the Fiskers boiler room, no matter what you and I think about that. If he doesn't want to be where that Powers thing took him, then he shouldn't have to be there."

Alexander smiled. "Little Zoë. You are so courageous. Let me find out. If the Powers have taken a rogue spirit, then it will be known." He threw the blanket back and stood, his clothing forming around him.

Zoë had the feeling by "courageous," Alexander actually meant "incredibly naïve," but at least he hadn't said so. "Are we going somewhere?" She stared out at this strange enchanted garden, reluctant to leave it, and wondered why her life had taken such a bizarre turn.

"Not we. You can stay here. I will not be long." He took her hand and kissed her knuckles. "You are safe here. I have closed the doors so no other beings can enter unexpectedly."

Zoë didn't want to chew on the question of what types of beings *might* have been here, had he not done that. "Alexander, um, is there someplace I can tidy up?" Angels didn't need bathrooms, so it seemed unlikely he would have one here in this strange place.

He pulled her gently by the hand. "This way." The soft ground soothed her bare feet as they stepped down from the gazebo onto the cool grass. They wound their way through a garden path, through trees and wild vines until they came to a small clearing with a glassy pool. "You can bathe here. The water is warm and pleasant. If you require anything, call the name Liana, and a servant will come to you."

Servant? Zoë smiled to be polite and to cover her surprise. Every time they spoke, she added a dozen more items to her list of things she didn't understand about Alexander and his world. "Thank you," she said.

"Are you hungry?" Alexander pointed to an archway. "Beyond there you will find food."

Zoë nodded. "Okay." It occurred to her his understanding of "I will not be long" and hers could be totally different.

Alexander pulled her close, running his hand down her naked back. "You have nothing to worry about, little Zoë. I will return." He kissed her, brushing his lips against hers with feather-light pressure.

With that, Alexander turned back and made his way down the path. Zoë watched him go, and when she couldn't see him any longer, she felt for his presence, noting the very second he passed through the barrier to the outside world. She extended her senses as far as she could, and detected no one else, which meant only no spirits or angels were near enough to sense them. Humans passed under her radar, but she sincerely doubted she would encounter any of those in Alexander's garden.

She walked to the edge of the pool and knelt beside it. Her fingers grazed the glassy surface of the warm water, releasing a light, clean scent. She spun her legs toward the rim and dipped her toes in. A tingle went through her body as she edged her legs in one inch at a time, until she was standing in waist-deep water. The floor of the pool was smooth stone, and she found a nice ledge she could sit on. When she splashed handfuls of water on her face, it tasted sweet. Was it because of this "otherness" Alexander had told her about?

"I'm in another world," she said to herself. The

longer she stayed in the pool, the more it felt like a dream, and she became slightly dazed as she tried to take it in. After a nice, long soak, she reluctantly stepped out of the water, looking for something to dry herself with. But it wasn't as though she had carpets to worry about, so she walked through the trellis, naked and glistening with water, in search of something to eat.

The garden gave way to a large green lawn. More lanterns were scattered about, some hanging in trees, some on crooks atop poles, others forming a path to a small pavilion. When she approached the cluster of furniture, she found a table surrounded by four wooden chairs and one place setting with elegant silverware. A domed serving plate held a scrumptious dish of glazed figs, pomegranates, and a bright yellow fruit she'd never seen before. Zoë served herself and sat down to eat. She wondered mildly who had cooked it, or if Alexander could somehow conjure food out of thin air.

Once she'd finished eating, she stood and looked around the pavilion. She couldn't help but wish Alexander were with her. It seemed strange to wander around this place alone. She feared she might inadvertently go somewhere she shouldn't.

Part of her wanted to poke around the gardens, but she decided that would be as rude as going through a friend's closets while they were gone. She went to a low soft seat, and didn't have any trouble relaxing, as she curled her legs under her. She grabbed a folded blanket from the back of the chair and pulled it around her.

By the time Alexander returned, she'd fallen asleep. She felt his presence several minutes before she saw him. His question earlier returned to her. Was she changing? For some reason, she didn't like the sound of that. The idea of changing into something *else* didn't sit well, particularly if she didn't have any say as to what that might be.

The smile on her face faded as she saw Alexander's expression. "What's wrong?" she asked.

He sat beside her and kissed her hand. "I do not know where Henry is, and neither do the Powers, but they are aware of him, and are now looking for him."

"Why?" she said, sitting up.

"Henry was a person of interest since even before his death. They think he may have killed Kent McGee."

"No," Zoë insisted. "Never. Henry is a gentle soul. He would never harm someone else." She paused. "Wait. I thought Kent had a heart attack or something. Are you saying someone killed him? But there wasn't any blood."

"The Powers know when a life is taken wrongly." Alexander's tone was gentle.

"It doesn't matter what they think. Henry didn't kill him. Wait. There was someone on the stairs, someone who nearly knocked me down when I went into the maintenance area. He wasn't one of the usual people there. He didn't work at Fiskers."

"Zoë," Alexander began.

"Is it possible they're wrong? Truthfully. Is it possible?"

Alexander thought carefully. Finally he spoke. "The lower angels do not often question the judgment of those in authority."

"Then it is possible." Zoë felt triumphant. "We have to find Henry. We can sort this out, and they'll leave him alone, right?" When Alexander didn't answer she repeated, "Right?"

"I do not know."

"What will they do to him if they can't be convinced he didn't do this?"

Alexander looked away. "He will be detained."

Between the expression on his face and the tone of his voice, Zoë got a chill. "For how long?"

"Eternity," Alexander said.

Nausea overwhelmed her. "Are we talking hell?"

"There are many things you do not understand, Zoë."

"You're right. There are. The sooner you start talking, the sooner I'll understand."

"It depends what you mean by hell. It is a place of utter darkness. He would float for eternity without contact, feeling, or meaningful existence in the bleakness between reality and unreality."

She shivered, cold all over. "Do they do the same thing to live humans that kill each other? Who are they to judge? Maybe Henry had a good reason for anything he did." Zoë felt scared for Henry and furious at the same time. When Alexander didn't answer any of her questions, she said, "You do what you want, but I have to do something. I want to go home."

"Slow down, Zoë," Alexander said. "I will help you find your friend. If you will allow me to."

"And what if he's guilty? Will you turn him over to them?"

"We will hear what he has to say, and we will decide."

Zoë wanted to trust him, but found that difficult. If forced to choose, Alexander would likely side with his own kind. It's what she would do. But she nodded anyway, and said, "Okay." At least she wasn't completely alone.

"When we go back, would you take me to my car? It's still at Fiskers," she said as they made their way through the pathways to the bed.

Alexander agreed and waited as Zoë got dressed. When she reached to pick up her purse, she said, "Oh, I didn't even get a chance to ask Henry about this knife."

"Knife?" Alexander asked.

"It's not an ordinary hunting knife, I can tell you that much." She pulled it out of her purse and it slipped comfortably into her grip. With her left hand, she removed the sheath.

When Zoë glanced up, she saw that Alexander had backed away from her, and his skin had begun to glow. "Alexander, what's wrong?"

He didn't answer at first. A low rumble came from within, like the beginning of a growl. He backed away from the gazebo completely, but never took his eyes off her. "You are a Stalker." He spat the words, and his tone rung with betrayal.

"No," she said. "No. Alexander, I don't even know what that is."

Without warning, Alexander's skin took on a bluish tint, and he began to change.

Zoë watched in horror. She glanced around to see if there was anywhere she could run, but he was standing between her and the only exit she knew of. The blade sang in her hand as though urging her toward him.

The change in Alexander was not instant as it had been with Thomas. It seemed as though he fought it. The strain wracked his features. He crouched as ice-blue scales appeared on his face, arms and chest. A beak formed on his face and his legs twisted to a muscular cat form. He looked like a great, scaly blue griffin, but he stood on two legs and had human arms, enormous and incredibly powerful. Leathery blue wings unfurled behind him, and Zoë was both awed and terrified.

"Zoë," he growled, his voice echoing strangely in her head. "That is a Stalker's weapon, a chaos blade. And you brought it *here*." He roared the last word with anger.

Her heart pounded as adrenaline pumped into her body, giving her heady alertness and energy. "I didn't know, Alexander. Please. It was given to me by a spirit. After Thomas freed Jackson Burly. I only had it with me because I wanted Henry to tell me about it." Her hands shook. She fought to stay calm, but it was proving nearly impossible. She wanted to scream, but she thought fear would be the wrong reaction.

Traces of the familiar Alexander showed still in the strange, bird-like face. He tilted his head with a solid black eye trained on her, and she tried desperately not to look like prey.

"Alexander," she said evenly, "I'm going to put this down, okay?" She crouched slowly to put the knife on the ground. It vibrated as she got closer.

"No," he roared, and in her fear, she dropped the blade. When it touched the ground, the green grass immediately turned gray, and dissolved around the knife, leaving nothing but mist. Alexander winced as though wounded. "Zoë, take up the blade." His breathing was ragged, whether from fear or a frantic attempt at self-control she was not certain.

Zoë snatched the knife and put it in its sheath, and then stowed it in her purse. She trembled from head to toe as she watched Alexander warily.

Alexander relaxed and the gray patch of grass began to heal itself, slowly returning to a more natural color. Still watching her with a wary stare, his human form returned, and he rose from his defensive crouch.

"I don't understand what just happened," she said with a quavering voice.

"A chaos blade is one of the few things that can

kill my kind." He looked away, as though ashamed he was in any way vulnerable. "They are made of mordicite, and are forged in another realm. The only creatures I have ever seen possess them are Stalkers. Assassins." He paused, his mouth set in a grim line. "Angel killers."

"Demons?" Zoë asked quietly.

"No, this was created by the elder race. They are the ones who created us, the demons, the fae, and humanity."

"Alexander, you must believe me. I am not one of these Stalkers. I'm just a normal person." More or less, she thought, but a time like this called for absolute assertions. "I would never hurt you." He looked wary, so she added, "Just as I have to trust you wouldn't hurt me. It would be easy for you, wouldn't it, especially when you're like that?" The sight of him transformed had stirred so many emotions. He was magnificent and utterly terrifying.

He nodded. "That is true. Then, you will not run from me now, as you did from Thomas when you saw his exalted form?"

Zoë took a tentative step toward Alexander. "He surprised me, and I was afraid. I thought it was because he was Fallen he looked like that, that he changed."

Alexander shook his head. "Our normal appearance is similar to yours, and we rarely assume the other when we live and work among you. Our other form, however, is a part of our true nature, albeit a more primal incarnation. Demonkind can also alter their appearance, although their ability works differently. The fae and humans do not shift."

She'd never been so acutely aware that the man in front of her was not human. She couldn't bring herself to ask why he'd seduced her, if he was even capable of loving her. Her heart twinged when she thought about the incredible, lusty experience. Not that she expected commitment when things were this new. But it would change things to believe he *couldn't* ever love her.

"I have to find Henry," she said finally, doing her best to push her emotions aside. She knew with certainty Alexander would not be coming with her to search for him. They both had a lot to think about, and trust issues had wormed their way into the mix.

"May I come to you again?" It sounded formal, and somewhat tentative, as though this strange and powerful being actually feared her rejection.

She paused and considered before nodding. "I need to be able to get in touch with you without having to call Thomas. Can you get a phone?" She looked around. "Although I'm not sure where you'd plug in the charger."

For the first time in what seemed like ages, a grin spread across his face. "I think I can manage that. In the meantime, take this." He bent down and picked up a small stone that lay near the arch. He pressed it between his palms and it glowed for a moment. Alexander's skin paled slightly, as though the process hurt. He handed her the warm stone. "If you call to me while you are holding that, I will come. But do not let the blade touch it, or it will be unmade."

She nodded, certain that would be a very bad thing. She put the stone in her pocket, afraid even to put it in her purse with the chaos blade close by.

She walked toward the arch, coming within inches of him, and when she passed him, he turned with her. She wanted to kiss him, to throw herself into his arms one more time, but she held back. His eyes looked warm now, having lost the frost of his transformation.

"I'll call you," she said and passed through the arch. Once again, she stood in the hotel corridor, and she set off to find the elevator and the way out.

In this ordinary and real building, bleak lethargy overtook her. The colors seemed dull and the sounds indistinguishable and soft. Even in the shadows of the late evening, it pressed on her. The elevator opened into a bar. People meandered in an open area with glass walls overlooking a swimming pool. Low music filtered through the din of chattering voices and the clink of glasses. A few people stole glances at her, and Zoë unconsciously ran her hands over her hair, afraid she must stand out, as though surely they could see her recent experiences played out on her face, or in some kind of strange aura. She forced a smile and wound her way through the bar to the reception desk, where she picked up a hotel brochure.

"May I help you, madam?" asked a middle-aged man who wore a green jacket with the hotel logo embroidered on the breast pocket.

"I need the hotel's address," she said and looked at the leaflet in her hand. She tried not to look shocked when she saw she was in Redwood City. She had assumed, rather foolishly she now thought, that they were somewhere in San Francisco. "And a taxi please," she said.

It wasn't long before a taxi arrived to take her to the CalTrain station. From there she headed to San Mateo. Within forty-five minutes of leaving Alexander, Zoë was in the Fiskers parking lot, fumbling with the keys to her car.

The building looked strange in the darkness with only a few other cars around. The requirements of the Fiskers servers meant they were monitored twenty-four hours a day, but even with cars dotted around the parking lot, it seemed desolate. Zoë wanted to get away from there as soon as she could. She hugged her purse to her body and shivered, even though the night was warm.

After a long moment of considering, she steeled her nerve and dialed the tech department on her cellphone. "Brad? Hi, this is Zoë Pendergraft. Listen, I'm outside in the parking lot. I left, um, kind of unexpectedly today, and I need to get some stuff out of my desk for the weekend."

Of course, everyone would have heard about Kent McGee and how she'd been taken away in an ambulance. Brad, one of the database techs who regularly worked the night shift, came and let her in without even questioning whether or not he should.

"Thanks, Brad," she said when the thin young man opened the door.

He shoved his wiry glasses up onto the bridge of

his nose. "No problem, Zoë. So, you found Kent, huh?"

"Yeah," she said. "Look, it was awful. I don't much want to talk about it." She frowned and tried to look distraught, but not helpless, because the last thing she wanted was him trying to stay and comfort her.

"Oh yeah, of course not," he said. He dallied for a moment after walking her to her desk, but when she didn't offer any details, he said, "Okay, I guess I'll see you Monday. If you're all right to come back."

She smiled reassuringly. "Yeah, I'm fine. It was a shock is all. I'll see you Monday."

As soon as Zoë was alone, she left her desk and headed for the maintenance door. She steadied her nerves and pushed it open, turning on the lights as she went. No point, she decided, in floundering around in the dark.

An occasional thump in some distant pipe broke the deadly silence. Zoë jumped at each sound, even though she knew it was ridiculous. She couldn't feel a spirit or angel anywhere nearby, so she forced herself to proceed until she arrived at the boiler room and pushed the door open.

"Henry?" she called, knowing he wouldn't be there. Part habit, she told herself, and part wishful thinking.

She flipped the light switch and held her breath as she passed over the area where Kent McGee's body had fallen. She didn't know why she'd come. If there were any clues to how Kent had died, the police would have found them. The floor was as clean as always, and she could find no sign anything amiss had happened.

But the Powers, she reminded herself, said Kent had died wrongly, whatever that meant. It wasn't until she reached the back of the boiler room she saw anything unusual, and it was something the police would never have noticed. The pegboard where she hung gifts for Henry had been partially stripped. The door near it, which she had never seen opened before, had definitely been disturbed.

Zoë walked closer and tugged at the door handle, but it wouldn't budge. Could it have been her imagination? She did her best to remember what had hung on the pegboard. She saw a pocket knife, an old money clip, and a few other odds and ends. The only things missing were the keys. She had bought Henry at least a dozen. Now gone. All of them, including the one that had shimmered strangely when Henry touched it. Or had she imagined that? Even with all she'd been through before, she found it difficult to accept the sudden changes in her life.

Zoë hesitated. Should she tell the police? She couldn't think of a way to explain why she had such an odd collection of things and why she kept them in her company boiler room. "Gifts for Ghosts" didn't seem like something the average cop would understand.

She gathered up the rest of the items and put them in her purse. Although she wanted to tell herself Henry would be back here soon, she couldn't bear the idea of someone taking them. When he had lived here, Henry could have kept people away. A strong spirit like Henry could have made himself felt if he wanted to. But now, her strange little shrine had no protection.

With her treasures packed up, Zoë glanced around again before leaving, turning off the lights as she went. It chilled her that someone had come into the boiler room looking for those keys. It had to have happened that way, because otherwise, why take them and nothing else? The truth sank in. That meant whoever went down there knew about Zoë, her habit of leaving things, and where to find them. That also meant, as if the first part wasn't strange enough, Zoë had been partially the cause of Kent's death.

Whoever went down to search for Zoë's keys would never have been there to kill Kent if she hadn't left those things there. And Henry wouldn't have gone away. Now she was certain a third person had been in that room. So why did Henry run, and where did he go? Did he know the Higher Angels were searching for him?

She had to find him. She couldn't ask the police most of the questions that filled her mind. Saving a spirit from the Powers wouldn't exactly fall under their jurisdiction. She supposed it fell under hers.

On the drive home, Zoë considered alternative scenarios. Who knew she took gifts to Henry? It wasn't common knowledge. Of her human friends, only Simone knew about Henry, and it seemed bizarre to imagine she'd tell anyone else. How on earth would it come up? Other spirits knew, like

Gran especially, and Zoë might have mentioned Henry to one or two others, like Cecil, who lived at the library, and Drecker, a spirit she'd encountered at the DMV. She'd had time to kill, so she chatted with him, deciding if she was going to look like a total loon talking to someone nobody else could see, the DMV was the place to do it.

Even with going over every possibility she could imagine, few ideas sprang up. Spirits, in her limited experience, didn't want to hear about each other, or even necessarily, the person they were talking to. They wanted to talk about themselves, their days in life, and their family and descendants. Curiosity wasn't a usual indulgence. It made conversations one-sided, but Zoë didn't mind. She liked listening to their stories as much as they liked telling them. But their self-centered conversational style made it hard to think of any she might have told about Henry.

By the time she slipped her key in the lock of her front door, Zoë was exhausted. Even the naps at Alexander's place didn't make up for her horribly long day. Her heart clutched when she thought about him. Why had she let herself tumble into bed with a...a non-human entity? *Being*? Whatever...with someone she barely knew? He'd asked her when anyone could be certain they wouldn't regret intimacy, and she'd talked herself into thinking that meant "anything goes." *Stupid, stupid, stupid.* No matter what the answer to that question was, it surely took more than one date.

Zoë locked the house and stuck her head in the back room to say goodnight to Gran, who hummed to herself as she stitched. The old spirit looked up with a nod and a smile and then went right back to her needlework without a word. The clock on her bedside table told her it was well after midnight by the time she curled up under her duvet. She turned off her alarm. The library wouldn't open until ten on Saturday, so there was no reason to get up too early. She hoped Cecil would be there, because right now, she didn't have too many places to turn for help. It took a little time before Zoë could let herself relax, but exhaustion won out eventually, and she slept.

CHAPTER 10

ZOË WOKE CONFUSED. The sun filtered through a murky haze and diffused shadowless light between the upturned blinds. Her body had the satisfying sensation of recent and spine-tingling sex, but soon the harsher memories invaded: Alexander's bizarre transformation, the so-called chaos blade, and the unpleasant shock of Kent McGee's death, and Henry's disappearance.

After a few minutes of staring at imperfections on her bedroom ceiling, Zoë hauled herself out of bed. She threw on jeans and a polo shirt and shuffled into the kitchen. Sniffing the half-gallon of milk in the fridge, she discovered it had started to turn and opted for toast with strawberry jam.

Once she'd finished breakfast and tidied up, she grabbed her purse, hesitating only a moment when considering what it concealed. The spirit who'd dropped the knife at her feet must have done so for a reason. Alexander feared it, without even stopping to reason that "little Zoë" would never harm him. *Are you changing?* She asked herself, echoing his question. She had no real answer. "Everything changes," she said to the empty room and grabbed her keys, heading out to find Cecil, the San Francisco Library's strongest spirit.

After a tedious time finding a place to park, Zoë entered the main branch building to search for Cecil. She couldn't help but enjoy the beautiful surroundings and the splay of light as it filtered down from the nautilus-shaped skylight and the spacious floors below. A hundred million dollars well spent, she thought. Though the library rebuild had been controversial, she rather enjoyed the effect and the different types of people who meandered within. Although that included a few obviously homeless people huddled around the lobby, she liked that the library gave them shelter. No one hurried in a library, and that made her relax as she followed the pull of Cecil's presence up to the Filipino American Center on the third floor.

So far this morning, the small section had only one living occupant. He sat at a table with a stack of books. He smiled at Zoë when she entered, giving her a slightly puzzled look. She grinned back, knowing she looked anything but Filipina. Cecil sulked in the corner nearest the men's room. He gave her a sour nod.

Zoë walked to the shelf nearest him. "Hi, Cecil," she whispered.

"Hmph," he grumbled.

"Cecil, it's been years. You're still upset?" Zoë

spoke as quietly as she could, trying to appear as though she was reading something aloud from a book she had gotten off a nearby shelf.

"They could have fixed the old one," he said.

"Cecil. You know why they rebuilt the library. Quit being such a baby. It's really very nice."

"Nice? Nice! How about I tear down your house and build some big, gaping monstrosity of so-called modern design in its place. New people will come in and tread all over, moving your favorite books, which you can't even find anymore." His upper-class English accent made the rant impossible to take seriously. She didn't know why, but it did. Besides, he'd had ages to get used to the new place.

"I know, Cecil. It must be hard."

"And anyway, why don't you come visit me anymore? You used to come all the time."

"I'm sorry, Cecil. I tend to read eBooks a lot more these days."

"Eee books," he said, the disgust thick in his tone as though she'd told him she'd become a rock n' roll groupie. "Zoë, my dear, those aren't books at all."

She fought the grin that tugged at her mouth. Cecil didn't like being laughed at, but she couldn't help it. The shuffle of papers reminded her someone else was in the room, and she glanced over her shoulder to find the other occupant of the room trying very hard not to stare at her.

"I need a favor."

"Oh," Cecil said, throwing his arms up

dramatically. "You don't come for over a year, and now you want something. Isn't that grand?"

Zoë decided to ignore his attitude and just ask. "Remember me telling you about Henry? The, um, guy that lives," she lowered her voice even further, "in the boiler room at my work?"

"Ah, yes," Cecil said. "The railroad worker. You told me." His tone was heavy with disdain.

"Um, has anyone come around asking about him? Or me?"

Cecil's misty eyes narrowed. "Why would anyone do that?"

"Just, have they?"

"No. I haven't talked to a living human since the last time you were here. There's a disturbing lack of sensitives lately. I used to get seen quite frequently. Probably people of any taste won't come into this horrifying excuse for a library anymore."

Zoë put back her book and selected another, opening it to a random page. A thought occurred to her. "Cecil, why do you stay here, if you hate it so much?" She watched the spirit closely, afraid for a moment he would fade out. Spirits could be touchy.

"I can't leave," he said finally, sniffing as though he still had the snuff habit he'd acquired in life.

"Why not?"

"Zoë, don't be ridiculous. I can't."

She stared at him. "Do you even know why you can't leave?"

A troubled expression passed over Cecil's narrow face. "This is my home," he said, but uncertainty riddled his voice.

"Are you bound by an object?" she persisted.

"You impertinent girl."

"I'm sorry," she said. "Henry is missing, and I have no idea where to look." She turned around to see the man at the table now openly staring, so she gave him an apologetic shrug. Without a word, he gathered his books and papers and left, probably thinking a table in General Collections sounded good right about now. Zoë rolled her eyes. People could be so intolerant, she thought.

Cecil scratched his chin absently. "I see," he said, and then as though discussing something shameful, stepped closer and whispered in her ear. The chill of his nearness crept over her skin. "When the old library was destroyed, I found myself pulled back to England. I hadn't been there long, in my life, so the tie was not strong. But when the rebuild finished, I was here again. Disgusting," he added.

"I have heard," Zoë said, choosing her words carefully, "Of spirits being bound by objects as well as places."

"Necromancy," Cecil spat, flinging himself away from her. "I heard about your encounter."

Zoë wondered how spirits knew things when they hardly behaved as though they were interested in each other, or left the places they normally lived.

"Is it true you speak with angels?" he said.

She nodded and looked away. After a pause she said, "Cecil, can you tell me anything that would help me find Henry?"

He considered her carefully, as though weighing options. "Calling a spirit is unwise, Zoë. It is too close to the black arts, and you may do injury to yourself or to the spirit you wish to call." He held up a hand to stave off her budding protests. "However, if you have something which belonged to the person when they were living, you may be able to enhance your own abilities, assuming he's still even in this plane. Henry will likely be someplace of significance to him in his mortal existence, or near an object of consequence. Do you know his descendants?"

Zoë shook her head. "I don't think he had any. I can try to find out for sure though."

"That would be a place to start."

"Thank you, Cecil." She put the book back on the shelf.

"It was a pleasure to see you again, Zoë." Cecil gave her a stiff bow.

"Cecil," she said slowly, without making eye contact, "Do you know anything about chaos weapons or Stalkers?"

Cecil's embodiment vibrated with excitement. "You have seen such a thing?"

"Yes," she said.

"Do you have it with you?" Something in his eyes gleamed greedily.

"No," she lied. An uncomfortable shiver passed

through her body.

"Then no, I don't know anything," he said and flickered out of sight.

Zoë stared at the place Cecil had been for a few moments and then looked around to see if anyone had observed the last part of her conversation. The area was still empty, much to her relief. Pausing briefly, she collected herself and then returned downstairs, and went out the Larkin Street Entrance on the second floor.

On the drive home, Zoë considered her options. If she needed something that had belonged to Henry, or to go someplace that had been important to him, she had no idea where to start. The internet was as good a place as any. She'd helped Simone track down information about potential boyfriends before, so maybe it would hold the key to learning something about Henry's life and family.

Because she didn't own a computer, she made her way to an internet café close to home, and soon she settled in with a latte in front of a Wi-Fi enabled machine. She pulled a notepad from her purse and began to browse. The first bit of discouraging news was that "Henry Dawkins" was a more common name than she had thought possible. Artists, British Members of Parliament, surgeons and boatloads of regular folks, both living and dead, had shared that name. *Damn.*

Refining the search with the names of towns and cities he'd mentioned in his stories yielded nothing more. An hour of scouring dozens of websites left her with either too many possibilities or none at all.

She was getting nowhere, and she needed someone who knew more about this than she did.

She pulled out her cellphone and hit the speed-dial for Simone. "Hey," she said quietly when her friend picked up. "How was the big date?" Details poured out. Zoë laughed as Simone described the way Dustin danced and commiserated when she learned he hadn't even kissed Simone goodnight. Apparently it had been more of an 'awkward hug' parting, but Simone hadn't yet given up hope.

"Listen," Zoë said as she gathered up her things to go, aware of the annoyance of café patrons around her, "Remember telling me your Uncle Shel was obsessed with genealogy?"

"Hell, yes," Simone said. "He actually wanted me go to some old cemetery with him. I think he was hoping I'd pick up the baton for the family history. I said no thanks."

"Do you think he'd look something up for me? I need to find if someone has some living descendants."

"I'm sure he'd be thrilled. He loves a good family mystery. What's the name?"

"Henry Dawkins," Zoë said, throwing her purse into her car and sitting down behind the wheel.

A pause filled the line. "You're serious?" And then, "Sure, okay, no problem."

Zoë could tell Simone was covering for an inability to deal with things spiritual and unseen, bless her. If the positions had been reversed, she hoped she would be as open-minded as Simone at least tried to be. "Thanks, Simone. I don't know if he was born in San Francisco, but he died probably very near here, maybe even in San Mateo where Fiskers sits now. He worked for the Pacific Railroad Company at one time and also in a mining town at Lament, California."

"Lamont?"

"No, Lament. As in 'crying'." Zoë spelled it. "It was between Sacramento and Lake Tahoe."

"Lament. That sounds ominous. Why would anyone name a town something like that?"

Zoë sighed. "I have no idea." She said her goodbyes, thanking Simone again for helping her with her research.

Heading home, Zoë tried to formulate a plan. Shel's research should help with the possibility of descendants, so now she had to tackle the other prong: finding a place significant to Henry's life. She had no idea where exactly Henry had worked for the Railroad, except that he had been a stake-driver. The idea of finding a precise location seemed remote, at best, considering he'd worked his way over miles and miles of California. She figured there was likely a Railway museum in San Francisco somewhere, but there was no way they'd have anything of significance to one person.

Lament, California was over two hours away, but a drive sounded like fun, and she had the entire weekend with no commitments. It wasn't like she expected her new maybe-boyfriend to call and ask her out again. Did she want him to? If she was honest, yes, she most certainly did, and not because of the toe-curling sex. Well, not *only* because of the toe-curling sex.

When Zoë arrived home, she parked on Guerrero Street and waved at Mrs. Paez, who was outside fussing with some plants on her porch.

"How's that nice young man of yours?" Mrs. Paez was beaming at her like a wistful elderly aunt.

"He's doing great," Zoë said.

"Seeing him again then?"

Zoë grinned. "I hope so, Mrs. Paez." She waved again and made her way indoors before her neighbor could ask any more questions. She liked that she had a neighbor who cared. Up to a point.

She threw snacks, bottles of water, a road atlas and a few CDs into a rucksack. A road trip sounded like fun, she thought, but she sort of wished she wasn't going alone. It took a moment before she even let herself go upstairs and fetch the stone Alexander had given her. She could think of ten reasons to try to put this angel stuff behind her, as soon as Henry was back where he belonged and cleared of Kent's death, that is. And not an overwhelming quantity of reasons sprang to mind in favor of seeing more of him.

He was hot in bed, but she didn't want that to be the deciding factor. Maybe she'd never met anyone so celestially hot. *But you can't have everything*, she thought. As much as her brain filled up with cons, the one pro outweighed them all: she really liked him, and she couldn't help herself. He accepted what she was without question or disbelief, and maybe that wasn't the best reason to be with a guy, but it wasn't too shabby a place to start.

She turned the stone over in her hand and considered. "I can always take it with me, and decide once I get there." It wasn't as though Alexander would have any difficulty meeting her there. The dark stone felt smooth in her fingers, and she could almost detect his scent on its faintly striated surface.

A loud banging sounded at her front door. She stuffed the rock in her pocket and ran to answer it. She saw a male form through the stained glass of the front door. Her heart beat faster as she rushed to open it.

Alexander stood there, with a faint smile on his lips. "You called me," he said.

It was all Zoë could do not to respond, "I did?" She'd figured she would have to say his name or... what? Dammit, she told herself, life was too short to throw away a chance like this. She hesitated only a moment before throwing her arms around his neck and kissing him. He wrapped his arms around her waist, lifted her slightly off the floor and walked in, all the while engrossed in her lips.

"Are you sure no one saw you whoosh in?" she asked and then realized that might sound as though she was ashamed of him coming to see her. Fortunately, he didn't look offended.

He grinned. "I can be unseen if I want to."

"Really?" Of course, that made sense. "I wonder if

I can sense your presence when you are invisible. Let's try," she said and stood back.

"Okay."

After a moment, she said, "Well?"

"Well?" he repeated, cocking his head to the side. His skin had taken on a slightly bluish tint, and for a moment, she feared he was going to transform, but nothing happened.

"Do your thing."

"I am." A frown crinkled his forehead. "You can see me?"

She nodded. "You sure you're doing it right?"

Alexander looked up at the ceiling. "Yes."

Zoë shrugged, "At least now I know you can't sneak up on me." She tiptoed up to kiss him lightly on the lips, and when he still frowned said, "Anyway, I was going on a road trip today out to Lament. You'd said you wanted to come, but then, last night was kind of weird. I mean the ending. Not the sex part. The sex part wasn't weird. I wasn't sure if you still wanted to. Or what. But if you want to come, you can." *Shut up already. Jeez.*

"A road trip?"

"Yeah, oh…I guess you haven't done that before? We get in the car and drive a couple of hours out past Sacramento, and we probably eat a lot of junk food, or at least I will, you don't have to. And we sing along with the radio and play car games." *God. I'm too dumb for words*, she thought. *Car games? What am I? Eight years old?*

A huge smile spread over Alexander's face. "That sounds wonderful. I will even eat junk food."

Zoë happily relaxed. The tension that had sprung up between them the night before melted away, and today they were going to have fun together, like a normal couple. The phrase "normal couple" stuck in her head, but she dismissed the unease it brought. She'd dated guys of different races, religions, and a couple guys back in college from different countries, so different species shouldn't be that hard, she told herself.

All she had to do was stay open-minded and be patient with the differences when they came up, as they would. Like, oh, the fact that he had never taken a road trip before, and didn't have to eat, or go to the bathroom. The thought reminded her she needed to do just that, so she excused herself. *Can't start a road trip with a full bladder.*

She would have to deal with these issues, but not at once, and not right this minute. For now she wanted to have a pleasant day, and when she arrived in Lament, do something to help Henry. Nothing could let her lose sight of the real reason she was doing this: her dear friend, who faced a terrible and unfair judgment. The idea of it seemed so surreal that she wrapped her head around it with difficulty, but Henry, on the other hand, was real and important, and she missed him.

Emerging from the bathroom she said, "I'm ready when you are." She grabbed her purse, and Alexander carried her rucksack to the car. He agreed to help her navigate once they got past Sacramento and into the smaller back-roads of the California countryside. As she was putting the car in gear she said, "Alexander, we're okay then?"

He smiled. "We are okay." He leaned over and kissed her.

So many questions, and she didn't want to ask any of them. Not now, not when she was relaxed and having a good time, even if doubt tinged the edges of her day. Determined to enjoy the moment, she headed for the highway.

The first half of the trip was easy and fun, with little in the way of navigation required because Zoë knew how to get to Sacramento. Alexander asked normal questions, like any new boyfriend would about her life and opinions and places she'd always wanted to go. The conversation turned to her family, and she simply said her father had died a long time ago, and her mother had walked out when she was young. An uncomfortable silence followed that bit of news, so Zoë filled it by changing the subject, telling Alexander about Simone's potentially disastrous date with Dustin Bittner. She tried not to remind herself at least Simone and Dustin were the same *species*.

After the first hour, Zoë became acutely aware she'd done most of the talking. "So, um, if you're over two hundred years old, how come you have never been on a road trip before, and don't know how to make coffee?"

She stole a glance at him and saw him grin. "Not all of my years in the mortal timeline have been spent doing human things. Until recently, I have seen little of humanity up close." He paused. "Before I came here, I was advised to keep my distance, because humans, they told me, were not capable of taking in experiences outside your own narrow view."

Zoë would have taken offense, but for most people, that assessment was right on the money. "But you didn't keep your distance." She blushed and remembered exactly how little distance there had been between them last night. When he didn't answer, she said, "Alexander, how much trouble are you in? Are you going to get in deeper over me too? About...last night?"

"Do you regret our intimacy?"

"No," she said quickly. "No, Alexander. I like you. And, well, yeah, I like you. I just don't know what's going to happen next."

He touched her cheek with the back of his fingers. "Neither do I."

"Is it common, I mean, for angels and humans to...be together?" She would have rolled her eyes at her fumbling if she had thought he wouldn't see it.

"No."

Well, that's simple. "So." She hesitated. *How do you ask about the mating habits of your boyfriend's species?* "Angels can procreate then? I mean all I know is from Bible stories, and there isn't a lot of angelic sex in there."

"We are living creatures, like you, and mortal in a similar sense. We require energy, but not from food.

We rest, but not by sleeping. The books you may have read would give no more a complete picture than if I read Beowulf for a complete understanding of your people. We have been called *yazatas, jinn, malakh, deva,* even gods by some. I am not holy, and neither am I a member of a heavenly entourage. We use the word 'angel' because it is the word humans use to describe us, but its meaning is clouded in muddy human mythology. It would be better if you would forget the stories you have heard, and instead learn everything from the beginning."

"Okay," she said. *Like I have any choice.* She also noted he didn't answer the question about sex, but figured it would be rude to push. Too much like asking about old girlfriends. *That* was tacky. He could, as she could testify, have sex, and he had an excellent feel for how everything worked, so she could assume he'd done something like it before.

It was much too early to ask him how he felt about her, although she couldn't help but wonder what he saw when he looked at her. He'd tell her eventually. Probably. If he even understood human women liked to hear things like that. It probably had never occurred to him security in relationships would come up. Did angelic women get insecure? Her thoughts went to the sad angel in Thomas' office, and she knew for certain they could display an entire range of emotions and needs.

They passed through Sacramento and stopped on the other side of the city at a convenience store. She filled up the tank while Alexander went inside and bought drinks and candy bars. He proudly showed her a CD he'd picked up called *Broadway's Greatest*

Hits. "I asked inside about music for singing in the car, and she said this was perfect. We have not sung yet," he admonished, "And you said that was an integral part of a road trip."

Zoë laughed. "No, no we haven't." She slid her credit card through the "pay at the pump" scanner, cleaned her windshield, and checked the oil. Soon they were back on the road, and she and Alexander sang *Open a New Window*, and *Oh What a Beautiful Morning* while heading down Highway 16 toward Drytown, where they would make a turnoff. He had an amazing voice, and she marveled that he knew the words without missing a beat, where she got stuck somewhere around *I Got the Sun in the Morning*. Show tunes were not, in any way, Zoë's normal listening fare, but Gran loved films like *My Fair Lady* and *Fiddler on the Roof*. Watching old musicals with a spirit had filled more than one dark winter evening in her adult life, even though Gran seemed more pleased by the happy atmosphere and Zoë's company than anything coming out of the television. Not that Zoë would admit any of this to most people, but Alexander was not most people.

South of Sutter Hill, Zoë turned down the music so she could watch for the turnoff for Lament. Alexander helped her look out for signs, and she was glad it hadn't occurred to her to ask him to transport them to the ghost town. She laughed when she realized he not only could have, but certainly would have. But then they would have missed the fun of doing something so commonplace.

Maybe that was why he hadn't offered, she thought. Maybe he liked doing run-of-the-mill human things. Why he would, she couldn't understand. Not when his world seemed limitless. He could have spent the day at the Pyramids and then gone to Paris for dinner, and that didn't even cover the places like Thomas' bar and his private, magical garden. Who knew what other places there were that she couldn't imagine. Instead, he wanted to take a road trip, drink sodas, and sing show tunes. She couldn't help but smile. She *really* liked him, she decided. *Really, really.*

By the time they rolled into Lament, it was late afternoon. The state of the town surprised Zoë, who'd expected a ramshackle ruin. People did, in fact, live in and around this semi-ghost town. A few of the restored old shops were actually open, either as functioning stores, or as tourist attractions.

She found an all-day parking lot with a visitors' map of the town. A nearby sign bore the opening hours of the attractions, which included the Masonic Hall, a schoolhouse, a Methodist church, and a few hotels, one of which still operated. She wanted to be sure to visit the place with a tearoom downstairs and a historical exhibit upstairs. Ruins dotted the outskirts of town, including a jailhouse and two cemeteries.

The town history fascinated Alexander as much as it did Zoë, and they strolled through the streets, stopping to look at the wooden wagons and walk through the remains of what once had been a magnificent outdoor amphitheater. "It's almost like a movie set," she said, looking around as they stood near a row of old wooden facades on what must have been the main street.

"Can you sense Henry?" Alexander said quietly.

Zoë shook her head. "There are more people than I expected. I thought we'd be nowhere, not in the middle of Wild West Disneyland." That was an exaggeration. Only a couple dozen families milled around on this warm summer day, but her senses had to contend with fifty more people than she had expected.

"They are interfering?"

"More like distracting. Let's find a quiet place to sit."

Lament's town planners had virtually overlooked outdoor seating, and it seemed like most of the tourists would rather go inside the old music hall anyway. It had a sign outside saying they sold old-fashioned ice cream. Zoë and Alexander walked down a trail, which led to one of the town's cemeteries. "Anyone?" Alexander asked.

"No, this place is dead," she said. "You'd think if you wanted to find a spirit, a ghost town would fill the bill."

He grinned at her. "You would think. But then, humans have a funny way of naming things. Los Angeles does not have a higher ratio of angels than any other city."

Zoë sat on a stone bench and focused her thoughts around them, testing the physical distance of her senses. She couldn't detect any spirits nearby, but she'd never tried to figure out at what distance she could detect their presence. "You're glowing at me," she said finally.

"I am what?" He looked adorably confused.

"Your angel glow thing is blocking out everything on that side. I need some space." If she sounded crabby, it's because she was. She'd enjoyed the trip out here, but she'd expected…something. Not all this nothing. It occurred to her to apologize, but before she could, Alexander planted a kiss on her cheek.

"Okay," he said. "I want to see the jail house, and then I am going to check out the hotel. Come find me when you are finished." He stood and wound through the path and headed out of sight, stopping to give Zoë a wave before he got too far for her to see.

She waved back with disbelief. It was nice, she thought, to be taken at face value. Alexander never questioned anything she said, thought about subtext, or what she *really* meant. If she said she wanted space, he assumed she just wanted space. Wow.

CHAPTER 11

ALEXANDER'S PRESENCE MOVED away. She traced it beyond the cemetery, and although she had to concentrate, she felt him travel to the other side of town. That sweet, otherworldly scent filled her mind as though someone carried carnival funnel cakes just out of sight.

On the upside, the glare of his aura no longer interfered with her senses. Not that any spirits appeared upon his departure. The graves around her felt as dead as they had a few moments before. She walked up and down the rows, looking at the crumbling monuments. Little wrought iron fences surrounded the stone memorials, nearly all of them jutting at odd angles, probably due to earthquakes and shifts over the decades.

Part of her hoped she might even see, if not Henry's name, then another Dawkins, but no such luck. Judging from her lack of positive results, Henry had left the town before his death. She also knew he wasn't here when an earthquake had moved the gold vein, making this town no longer a viable mining spot. A crooked lane wound back to the dusty main street and through alleyways toward the actual mines.

Somewhere below the earth, the soul of a trapped miner glimmered. Even in death, he hadn't made it out. Pain choked her for a moment, knowing he was in some kind of hell, still stuck in a cave or maybe even solid earth. Why didn't he move? She wondered why the Powers that had come to retrieve Kent's soul had left this one behind. Alexander had said the Higher Angels came to retrieve people in special cases. What the hell did that mean, anyway?

They were angels, right? Supernatural? How could they overlook some souls, leaving them here on earth, when according to their rules human souls had to move on? But Alexander had told her in the car that angels weren't what she thought, or at least told her to forget the myths. More questions, and not nearly enough answers. She'd remember to ask him about it though. At least maybe this one soul would want to move on, rather than spend eternity beneath a ghost town.

The mines themselves were not accessible to visitors. Steel grating covered the flat, open tops for safety purposes. Old mine carts and tracks littered the ground around the entrances, rather artfully, probably thanks to the local tourism board. A few yards away a shell of a building bore a large sign reading "Assayers Office", and farther down she saw a saloon and an entertainment hall.

The second cemetery sat behind the Methodist church not too far away. Some of the names on the cracked, aging tombstones had faded with time, some too much to read. Others she could see clearly. A few had stone crosses with no visible markings, and two graves were piles of rocks and nothing else. It wasn't until she reached one that read "Rose Wilson" she paused. The name rang a bell, and she remembered Henry had mentioned her. She thought back. Yes, he most certainly had, but she recalled that when she'd asked, Henry had refused to say more.

Zoë reached down and ran her hand over the tombstone, wondering why it was in the back, separated from the others, lonely under a tall, twining oak. "Oh, Henry," she said. "Where are you?" She detected an ethereal shift or pull, but nothing more. A dead end, she told herself, then rolled her eyes at the pun before setting off to find Alexander.

It wasn't difficult, considering she could sense his presence, and he stayed in one place rather than milling around. She caught up with him in the town's sole open and functioning hotel. "Zoë," he called to her when she arrived inside. "I have reserved a room so we can stay the night."

"Have you?" Zoë said, blushing under the gaze of the narrow-faced young woman behind the desk. "How nice," she said and smiled up at him. Sure, he should have asked. She might have had plans. She might not be ready to stay overnight with him, and it was presumptuous. But in truth, she didn't have plans, and she liked the idea. Besides, why shouldn't they throw out all the "normal" relationship rules?

Ready or not.

The woman at reception beamed at Alexander and then glared at Zoë, as though pegging her as a common trollop, clearly not good enough for him. Zoë ignored it. Alexander took her by the hand and led her upstairs. On the way to their room, she told him she hadn't found anything helpful to do with Henry.

On the third floor, they made their way down a corridor, where Alexander unlocked a wooden door with a real brass key, not one of those swipe cards modern hotels used. Entering the room was like stepping back in time, until Zoë noticed the room did have modern conveniences like an en-suite bathroom and a telephone, and even a television and alarm clock. Everything else had the early California look, with delicate flowers on the bed linens and solid wooden furniture of simple, but sturdy fashion.

When he closed the door, she put her purse and rucksack on the foot of the bed. He slipped his arms around her waist from behind and kissed her neck. His breath tickled her ear when he whispered, "I cannot stop thinking about making love to you, Zoë."

She trailed her hands over his arms, and smiled. "I've been thinking about it too."

"Really?" He sounded surprised and pleased.

"Oh, yes," she said. "Really." She decided to show him exactly how much the memory delighted her.

It was nearly seven thirty before Zoë found all her clothes again. They decided to go to the hotel's restaurant so Zoë could eat. She envied that

Alexander didn't have to wash up or dress. Just *whoosh*, and he was spanking clean and wearing whatever he had a mind to. On the other hand, he did enjoy "unwrapping" her, and he watched her with a smile when she bent over to look for her socks, so dressing and undressing weren't all bad.

Once seated in the cozy dining room, Zoë ordered roast pork with fresh apricot sauce, local string beans and homemade bread. Alexander wanted steaming apple pie with old- fashioned vanilla ice cream. The waitress looked perplexed when Alexander asked her to bring the food together, rather than serving her meal first and his dessert later, but one look at his startling green eyes, and she nodded fiercely, making a note on her pad. "Right away, sir," she said, ignoring Zoë altogether.

During the meal, Zoë watched Alexander watch the other diners. "Why are you so interested in humans?" she asked.

"Humans are fascinating," he said, his eyes wandering around the restaurant. "See that man in the corner?"

Zoë turned to nonchalantly take a peek. "The one in the blue suit?"

Alexander nodded. "He is cheating on his wife. By that I mean he is having sex with someone else."

"I know what it means," she said, looking again, this time taking notice of the pudgy, nondescript woman with him. "How do you know?" She turned back to look at Alexander, who stared at the couple openly. "I thought you couldn't read minds."

He gestured with his fork. "He wears a ring. She does not. He listens to what she says. When he talks, she leans forward, and yet she keeps blushing. At the same time, he is looking around, as though worried someone will see them."

That pudgy little woman was the mistress? Surely not. "Maybe she can't wear the ring. For all you know she's gained weight and it doesn't fit anymore. Maybe they're in love, and maybe he's a good listener. And *maybe* he's worried someone is watching them because someone is." She gave Alexander a quick boot under the table. "Quit staring. It's rude."

Alexander grinned. "You are wonderful," he whispered and then turned his attention back to the couple, before letting his gaze travel. "Humans are full of conflict because they have both free will and a veil of ignorance. You do not remember where you came from or what you are, so you spend entire lifetimes either trying to figure it out, or cope by creating purpose. Somewhere in that muddle of confusion and suffering, humans are capable of growth and even greatness, hopes and aspirations."

"We also have fears."

"Yes," Alexander agreed, but he sounded more impressed than anything.

"But angels have free will too. Otherwise you wouldn't be here with me. You choose to be here, unless I'm some bizarre mission from..." Zoë failed to come up with an appropriate word, so she pointed at the ceiling. Alexander looked up and then chuckled.

"No, you are not an assignment. I choose to be with you."

"So you're not that different."

"My little Zoë. I am infinitely different. I know what I am. I have no doubts."

"And that changes everything?"

"More than you can know."

She considered, and thought it would be wonderful to *know*, to never experience uncertainty. "You told me earlier you don't know what's going to happen."

"The conflict humans suffer does not come because they do not know the future. It happens because they do not understand the present, but when they do find the truth, there is growth and change, and that is the key."

"To what?"

"To your innate superiority over other life forms in this world, my love."

Zoë's breath caught in her throat, and she coughed for a few seconds. Grabbing the cloth napkin next to her plate, she covered her mouth and closed her eyes. *My love?* Did he mean that? *Good grief. Pull yourself together, Zoë.*

"Sorry," she said. Clearing her throat she added, "Something must have gone down the wrong way." Alexander nodded, but with a smile that told her he read her better than she'd hoped. So much for keeping her thoughts to herself. This might prove to be yet another complication to a potentially fraught relationship. *Love?* She rolled the word around in her mind and considered if she could someday be, or already was, in love with Alexander. *Maybe*, she thought. She'd never been in love before. Her relationships had never lasted long enough for her to consider it.

When she lifted her gaze from the tablecloth and met his, he watched her with such intensity she flushed. "Do you want some air?" he said.

"No. No, I'm fine. Why don't we make it an early night?" Her voice was quiet, barely even a whisper, but he stood and held his hand out to take hers.

They returned to their room in silence, as though they'd known each other a long time. She tossed her purse on the dresser and watched Alexander in the mirror. He propped a pillow against the headboard and leaned into it with his hands behind his head.

Zoë slipped off her shirt slowly and slid her jeans down over her hips. She had worn basic black panties and bra, not expecting any of what had happened today when she'd dressed this morning. With a pang of regret, she wished she'd worn more feminine underwear, something that would make her boobs look perky and accentuate her hips.

"You are beautiful," Alexander said, meeting her eyes in the mirror.

"And transparent," she said with a chuckle. "Do you always know what I'm thinking?"

"No," he said, his face serious. "Your thoughts are for you alone, little Zoë."

"You make me feel so human. I'm...so imperfect compared to you."

He moved to the foot of the bed, and sat close enough to reach her. Running a finger along her waist and down her hip and thigh, he said, "Everything about you is real. My human appearance is a shell. The whole of you, the light in your smile and the thoughts that dance across your face, the way you tangle your fingers in your curls and the freckles on your nose made by the sun's kisses— these things make you perfect."

He stood and turned her around, tilting her chin with his hand so she looked into his eyes. "Your beauty will deepen with age, with the natural change and growth that comes in life. Those things are beyond me. If you could see yourself the way I do, you would be in awe and would know why I cannot help but love you."

The kiss that followed left Zoë breathless. Any thoughts clouding her mind had vanished, and she felt completely grounded in the present moment, unable to worry about anything. "I need to take a shower," she said finally. She disentangled herself from his embrace and walked slowly and deliberately to the bathroom door, feeling him watch every step. At the door, she lowered her eyes. "Join me?"

His warm and fulfilling presence moved closer. She turned on the water without looking around, but she could feel him as surely as when he touched her. His hands went to her bra clasp, and he carefully unhooked it and let it fall to the white tiles at their feet. He tugged at her panties and pulled them down to her ankles. She laid a hand on his naked shoulder to step out of them. The disappearing clothes thing would take some time to get used to. She might even miss the pleasure of undressing him from time to time.

He stepped into the shower first, and the droplets bounced off his skin, spraying her with mist as she took his hand and joined him in the tub. Soft, wet kisses followed, kisses that trailed from their lips and explored the flesh down their bodies, flowing with rivulets of warm water. They soaped each other's skin, exploring the darkest, most intimate crevices and folds. Tender probing became intense desire and need, and their movements grew more urgent.

When they were thoroughly washed Zoë said, "Take me to bed." She ran her hands over the hair on Alexander's chest, down the solid line of curls leading to his groin, and then slipped her fingers around his solid erection. He turned off the faucet, swept her up and carried her, dripping water all the way to the bed.

Swimming in desire, she wrapped her legs around his hips as he laid her down and cried out as he thrust into her over and over again. His release came soon after hers, and again she was bathed in warm light as he groaned with ardent pleasure.

She smiled when she looked into his eyes as the glow faded. He kissed her again, still breathless, but now contented. Tiredness overtook her as he lay down beside her and pulled her into him. "I love you too." She barely mouthed the words, not sure she was ready to say them, but also not doubting the truth of it. A low murmur rumbled in his chest, like a growl laden with contentment, telling her he had, in fact, heard her.

When Zoë woke, she extended a lazy arm, and quickly realized Alexander was not in bed. Peeling her eyelids open, she sensed the presence of an angel even before her vision adjusted. As the blur of sleep cleared, Zoë recognized it was not Alexander standing over her. This angel, in monstrous "exalted" form, swathed in cobalt light, thought it was invisible to her.

Her heart pounded and fear thudded through her veins, electrifying her body. With as smooth a motion as she could make in her excited state, Zoë made a grab for her purse, grasping the smooth chaos blade and quickly unsheathing it. She stood atop the bed, which allowed her to look eye to eye with the immense being. The knife was tiny compared to the being in front of her, and she felt even more vulnerable because of her stark nudity. "Who are you, and where is Alexander?"

The creature looked something like Thomas had when he transformed back at his office, sharing the square dragon-like head and six arms. But this angel was definitely female. Sculpted breasts stood out on her chest, seeming incongruent with her reptilian sparkling red scales. Tendrils of red came from her head and cascaded in a floating mass around her face. The exalted angel stepped back from the bed, but slowly, as though taking her measure. The female's voice reverberated as she spoke. "I can see

why you are a person of interest, Zoë Pendergraft."
Her eyes flicked to the blade in Zoë's hand. "I was
aware, of course, of your quirks, but did not take
them seriously. How wrong I was."

My quirks, Zoë thought. *What a thoroughly
insulting way to put it.* "Who are you?" she repeated.

With a *whoosh* of air, a second angel appeared.
Thomas. Zoë was relieved he was not trying to cloak
himself, and that he had appeared in human form.
Oddly, he wore a tuxedo, although his bow tie hung
loose around his neck, and his black hair looked
disheveled. She had to remind herself angels always
looked exactly like they wanted to look, but she
couldn't help but wonder what he'd been up to
before popping in.

Whether it made sense or not, relief washed over
her. *Better the angel you know*, she thought.
"Thomas?" Zoë said, still pointing the blade toward
the female, but feeling more ridiculous and awkward
at her nudity, especially when she noticed Thomas
taking in the view appreciatively.

"This is Briony," he said. "Obviously you can see
her. How interesting."

The blue tinge around Briony disappeared, but
she did not change to her human form.

"My Guardian," Zoë said, not quite able to keep
the contempt out of her voice. She didn't know why
she said it with so much bitterness, probably
because Alexander had told her Briony would not
have interfered if Zoë had been in trouble, making
her next to useless as a guardian angel, in Zoë's

opinion. "And what do you mean 'person of interest'? To whom? And where is Alexander?" She wished she didn't sound hysterical, but her frustration was coming to a boil and she wasn't convinced yet that Thomas was going to help. Even recalling how nervous the blade had made Alexander when he'd first seen it, she didn't think she could take two of them.

"Some things are not for you to know, human," Briony said, all six of her muscular arms flexing. Guarding Zoë seemed the furthest thing from her mind. The reptilian angel stepped forward, and Zoë crouched.

"Thomas?" Zoë said again, this time not caring now how nervous she sounded.

Thomas barked at Briony in a language Zoë could not understand. The Guardian backed off a step.

"Zoë," he said, "Briony is a warrior angel. I'm afraid she believes you are challenging her. You should put the knife away." He sounded casual, as though talking about the price of peas, but judging by his tone with Briony, he wasn't feeling casual. Why was Briony even listening to him, of all people, a so-called Free Angel?

"If someone doesn't tell me what the hell this is about, I might challenge both of you."

Briony sucked in her breath with a hiss of pleasure.

"And anyway," Zoë shouted at Briony, "I thought you were supposed guard me, not attack me."

The laugh that came from Briony's chest crackled. She squatted as though about to leap, but Thomas stepped between them.

He spoke to Briony again in the same harsh language he had before, his tone carrying command. Although she could not decipher his words, Zoë understood their sting.

Briony tore her gaze from Zoë and looked down at Thomas, her exalted form towering over his human shape. Even with the difference in size, Zoë was not certain which was stronger. But she wouldn't find out today. Briony glanced up at Zoë and then crossed her arms, and with a gust of wind, she disappeared.

As soon as she had disappeared, Zoë half sat, half collapsed onto the bed. She put the chaos blade back in its sheath, and threw it down on the mattress. Thomas turned and looked at her. "So you trust me?" he said.

Zoë vaguely waved her hand in response. She didn't know, but her nerves were shot for the moment, and she needed some answers. When Thomas' gaze slipped over her naked flesh, she pulled the rumpled sheet up to her chest. "Don't any of you people knock?" she said.

Thomas grinned. "Not usually." Then he turned serious. "Alexander asked me to tell you he had to leave. His trial is starting."

"Now?" Zoë said. "It's the middle of the night." The time of day wouldn't make any difference to angels, but it somehow seemed indecent to conduct trials after midnight.

"He is not permitted to leave until the process has come to a close, but he didn't want you to worry when you found him gone." Thomas smirked, as though the idea of being accountable to a human amused him. He looked around the room, taking in the old-fashioned décor, and the compact arrangement. "Frankly," he said, "I don't understand the appeal."

Indignation surged through her. "The appeal of what? Me? Or do you mean sex in general."

He laughed warmly. "Oh no," he looked at her in a way that made her wonder if he could see through the thin sheet covering her naked body. "You are very charming indeed." Somehow, she didn't think he meant her personality. "Alexander is fascinated with humanity." Thomas shrugged, as though that needed no further explanation.

"When do I need to come?" Zoë asked.

"Come?" Thomas said.

"To testify. I thought they wanted to question me at Alexander's trial."

"I am going to see what I can do to keep that from happening," Thomas said. "Alexander's relationship with you is not something that would reflect well. If I am successful, you will not need to come at all."

She felt embarrassed, began to argue, but then decided Thomas probably did know what was best, at least as far as what would go over well in court.

"Okay," she said. "When will we know?"

"It's impossible to say. If you are needed, I'll send for you when it's time."

"Hours? Days? Weeks?" She hated the uncertainty.

Thomas smiled. "I have to get back. The hearing begins soon."

Zoë held up a hand. "Thomas, wait. What about Briony? I'm... a little scared of her. *Is* she on my side?"

He tilted his head and considered. "I don't know, Zoë. Whose side are you on?"

"I guess I'm on my side," she said, then quickly added, "and Alexander's side."

He nodded thoughtfully. "Then we shall have to see," he said. "A word of advice though, Zoë." His eyes flicked to the sheathed blade. "I would be very wary of drawing that weapon, if I were you. You don't understand it."

All she could do was nod. He had that much right anyway. "Okay." When Thomas gave a little bow she said, "Thank you for coming to tell me, Thomas."

He nodded, and rather inexplicably, blew her a kiss. With a gentle push of air, he disappeared.

CHAPTER 12

AS SOON AS ZOË COULD MOVE again, she darted up to check the locks on the hotel room door, although she knew it didn't make any sense. She went back to the bed and picked up the blade, measuring its weight with her hand. It was her only defense against these seemingly invulnerable beings, and she was very glad she had it. She had no idea what it would do to them, but at least it meant they couldn't threaten her blithely.

When she looked at it closely, it shimmered in her hand. She considered Thomas' warning and decided she needed to learn more, but knew she had about a hundred other things more pressing right now.

It didn't take long for Zoë to know she wouldn't get any more sleep that night, so decided to head home. Alexander's trial could take ages, so she didn't see a point in waiting around.

A pang filled her chest at his absence, especially

so soon after having decided she loved him. With a shake of her head, she chastised herself for acting like such a *girl* and got dressed. Within minutes, she'd tossed her things into her rucksack, although out of habit she looked twice in every nook of the room before she grabbed the key and headed down to the lobby.

When she slid the key onto the reception desk and told the young, groggy clerk she was checking out, she was annoyed to find herself stuck with the bill. How had he managed to get by without giving them a credit card? She assumed he must have used some angel mojo, and she figured she needed to explain money to him. He never seemed to have any, and as far as she could tell, he didn't understand the entire concept of paying for things. She wondered briefly how he'd paid for the things he'd gotten at the convenience store. Surely he hadn't stolen them. It wouldn't surprise her if the cashier miraculously hadn't thought to ask for money.

Zoë settled the bill and as she put her wallet away, the clerk said, "Thank you, Mrs. Scott."

She blinked and then nodded. When he ducked out of sight to answer the phone, she grabbed the registration book and scanned the names. Sure enough, in bold looped handwriting was the name Alexander Scott about six lines from the bottom.

"I'm an idiot," she said quietly. How could she be in love with someone and not even know his last name? Or worse yet, that he even had one.

Zoë glanced at the clock on the wall. Two AM. When she stepped into the night air and made her way down the steps outside the hotel, she opened her senses to her immediate surroundings. She instantly recognized the sparks of spirits around her, and began to make slow, wary movements into the night.

The spirits she'd known had never shown aggression or even the inclination to harm a human, but Alexander made it plain that they could. The Powers wouldn't have accused Henry of something impossible.

Her wariness also had to do with the fact that she had never known spirits to appear and disappear *en masse*. Sure, they popped in and out, going she had no idea where, but for the entire town of spirits to appear and then come back when the sun went down? That implied some sort of outside force or organization she hadn't seen before in the dead.

Not that she knew much, she chided herself. She'd taken her abilities for granted, and never tried to learn the rules spirits lived by. She had spent her life running into them on a near-daily basis, and she'd wave or say hi, or answer a question or occasionally ask one, but never had she questioned their behavior, where they went, or their experiences after death. Zoë hadn't felt even a tickle of curiosity, and besides, they didn't like to talk about death, as a rule. Life was the way it was, and she had accepted that fact.

But lately everything had changed, and she needed to know, if for no other reason than to get her life in context. If she *was* changing, as Alexander had cryptically implied, she wanted to know what that meant. She understood when he'd said her problem wasn't not knowing the future, but not understanding the present.

As she walked through town, she passed spirits of varying ages, although most were young men. They watched her as though they could sense something different about her. Spirits knew she could see them, but instead of approaching her, they hung back, or even slipped into the shadows as she walked through the streets of Lament.

She lost her bearings, and found herself in a strange, deserted alleyway, but no living human beings prowled the streets of the ghost town. The moon shone in the clear sky, making her task easier. Those spirits floating through gleamed in the light.

For nearly an hour Zoë searched for Henry, hoping he might have cropped up with the others. She went from the jailhouse to the cemetery and back around the General Store to the amphitheater. The cross atop the Methodist Church loomed ahead, and she felt drawn to the graveyard behind it. A spirit wailed, as though in pain.

Zoë approached, but the keening spirit did not fade away like the others. In fact, it barely noticed her. The female figure wore a faded but sturdy brown dress. She leaned against the side of an old storage house. Its black door loomed, seeming larger than the building itself.

When the spirit yowled again, Zoë fought tears. The cry went beyond the natural senses and unsettled Zoë to her core. Now that she could see the woman's face, Zoë saw her great physical pain. The spirit clutched her rounded abdomen and grimaced with overwhelming childbirth pains.

"Henry?" the woman called. Her ethereal features melted with relief. "I knew you'd come back for me. I've been telling this baby he can't come yet. Not until you get home." Her face clenched with remembered pain.

Zoë stepped closer. "You're Henry's wife? Henry Dawkins?"

The spirit squinted at Zoë as though she had bad eyesight. "Who are you?" she asked.

"I...I'm a friend of Henry's."

"He's coming soon," the spirit said.

"I hope so," Zoë told her. "Ma'am, what's your name?"

"Rose," she said after another painful wail. "Rose Wilson." The look in her haunted eyes defied Zoë to make comment. She couldn't help but wonder if the child had survived.

"Rose, how long has it been since you saw Henry? See, I'm looking for him too."

"Six months. He was gonna meet me here. He promised." Her tone was so sad and forlorn Zoë couldn't stop the tear that slid down her cheek. She never liked talking to spirits who didn't realize they were dead, but that kind never sought her out. Fortunately, it hadn't happened as frequently as it could have.

Zoë stood in shocked silence as Rose relived the moment of her death. She clutched her belly, desperate to keep the baby from coming, but unable to stop the process. Then Zoë noticed Rose held something in her hand. When the last of her painful throes stopped, Rose lay back. Her features went slack in a terrible pantomime of her death, and a key slipped out of her hand.

The key's shank was long enough to fit into Rose's hand perfectly. Fashioned of what looked like iron, it had little ornament on it, and a simple, hollow round top. Zoë stared. She went to pick it up, a strange and foolish notion, she realized. The key winked out of existence seconds after it lost contact with Rose's translucent skin.

Moments after, Rose herself disappeared. Zoë stepped back and then jumped as she heard a wail behind her. She turned to see Rose again appearing as she had in life, but at the beginning of her labor. Picking her way through the graves, Zoë left as quickly as she could. She couldn't bear to watch Rose die again, alone and afraid. It didn't matter that it had happened more than a hundred and fifty years before. Zoë had seen it happen right there, right then, and that was also reality, no matter what any so-called normal person might say. She couldn't do anything to change the tableau played out in the Methodist graveyard.

Her car sat alone in the Lament parking lot. Most of the hotel patrons probably parked nearer, and the day visitors had long gone. Zoë felt strangely desolate, as though she was the only person still living in the entire world. "Lament" indeed, she thought.

Soon she returned to the road and headed toward San Francisco. She drove faster than she normally would, or than traffic would typically allow. Although once closer to Sacramento, Zoë shared the road with many more cars, the late night drivers never could equal their daytime counterparts in sheer quantity.

Zoë wondered where they were going at four in the morning. The truckers she got. But what about the others? Drunks or party-goers? Travelers? Nurses or waitresses who worked night shifts?

With deliberate effort, Zoë looked the other way when she saw a ghostly family in an equally insubstantial overturned car along the side of the highway. Four of them, it appeared from her passing glance, trapped together. Why had they not gone to the other side?

By the time she arrived home, the impending sunrise had begun to lighten the sky. She drove straight into her garage and stumbled up the stairs. Her mind heavy and clouded with doubt, she pushed her worries aside, hoping to fall asleep and get some peace. Just for a few hours.

When Zoë woke a few hours later, she realized she'd slept in her clothes. She couldn't wait to strip them off and get into the shower. Once she was clean and had downed a cup of coffee, she made a note to get some groceries and stop by the internet café to check her email.

Before heading out, she threw her sheets into the washing machine off the kitchen, ran a quick vacuum over the living room floor, and tidied up her main floor. She didn't worry about the state of her bedroom, because no one but her ever went up there, but at least the public areas of the house should be presentable. Her thoughts went to Alexander, and whether or not he would ever come into her bedroom, or if he planned to avoid her house completely any time Gran was around. Which, she had to admit, was much of the time.

She exhaled loudly. Most people had relationship issues, but with her boyfriend and her Gran both being practically immortal, she couldn't wait around for things to sort themselves out. "Talk to Gran" went on her mental to-do list.

By the time Zoë parked in front of the internet café and made her way inside, dread came from several corners. The outcome of Alexander's trial tugged at her, mostly because she didn't understand what was happening. Finding Henry seemed more and more impossible since she had no idea where to look. She didn't know what to make of this chaos weapon either. Then she had to consider that Alexander and the other angels seemed to know more about her than she did, and she didn't like the way they expressed that, either.

Part of her wanted to go home and forget, to hide under the duvet until Monday morning came around, and then she'd go to work and be normal. *Normal.* Yeah, but Henry wouldn't be there, and that wouldn't be normal, and he wasn't coming back, she thought, not unless she did something. Not to mention if the angels caught up with him before she did, she'd never see him again and he'd suffer forever. No, she couldn't turn her back.

Zoë shrugged when another patron of the café, who had apparently been watching her have this internal conversation, gave her a quizzical look. *Yes*, she thought, *I'm crazy. Deal with it. It's not like being crazy makes me stand out much around here.*

Gmail told her she had several new messages, and ignoring the usual nonsensical spam, she eagerly clicked on the one marked "Shel Wallace".

She read his letter three times, trying to soak it in. He had indeed found Henry James Dawkins, but said it appeared Henry had never had a wife or children, as far as he could find. Of course after seeing Rose, Zoë knew different. Poor Henry. Did he even know about the baby?

Shel had attached a copy of the US Census form for 1880. Zoë read the thin, scratching handwriting of Henry's entry. Without thinking, she touched the screen. It made him seem more dead, seeing the hard-copy evidence of his mortal existence. But she also experienced a twinge of guilt, as though she was spying by going through his personal life, even though that life had ended some time ago.

Under "Place of Abode", the census document showed Elm Street, Lament, California, and it listed four residents of the house, all men with the surname Dawkins, and all with a check mark under color: black. It took her a moment to sort out what it said under "Relationship to Head of Household", but it appeared the older man was Henry's uncle, and the other two younger men his cousins. Further on, the form showed Henry's trade as miner, and no check marks had been placed in the columns for

"Married within the year", "Attended School within in the year", "Persons over the age of 20 who cannot read and write", or "Whether deaf and dumb, blind, insane, idiotic, pauper, or convict". Zoë couldn't help but smile at that last one. Not exactly something she'd expect to see on a modern census form. And rather subjective, wasn't it?

Henry's birthplace was listed as Beaufort, North Carolina. She couldn't help but wonder why he'd wanted to travel so far from home. Down the page she saw another entry that made her blink a couple of times before she could process it. Rose Wilson had lived on the same street. A fine hand had checked the column marked color: mulatto. Zoë stared for a moment while she collected her thoughts and then hit the reply button. She thanked Shel profusely for the information about Henry, and asked him if he could find out anything about Rose Wilson, born in Bloomfield, New Jersey. She wrote that she believed Rose may have died in childbirth, and she needed to know if the child survived, and whether there were living descendants.

As Zoë finished up at the café and returned to her car, she marveled at how much information the internet held for those who knew how to look. She never could have found Henry on her own. *Thank God for Uncle Shel and for the World Wide Web*, she thought.

With one item checked off her mental to-do list, Zoë settled herself in her car and hit Simone's number on the speed dial. "Simone?" she said when her friend answered.

"Hey," Simone said. "What's new?"

Zoë told her about the trip to Lament, leaving out anything about spirits or other angels, hoping to paint a normal picture of a romantic getaway. She talked mostly about the town and their drive up, also omitting the small detail that Alexander hadn't returned with her. As much as she trusted Simone, her life had taken some strange turns, and she believed there was a limit to how much weirdness she could thrust onto one friendship.

In turn, Simone told her about Dustin Bittner. Seems he at least had the good sense to call after their lukewarm date Friday night, and somehow they managed to have another encounter Saturday night, this one having a much different ending than the first.

"I decided to take my clothes off, and see what happened," Simone explained. What *had* happened continued throughout the night, and Simone had just woken up about half an hour before. She sounded happy, so Zoë let her talk. The story finally ended with a confession that Dustin had left before Simone got up, but he left her a sweet note saying he had to get home to pack for a business trip, and hadn't wanted to disturb her. "He has that Chicago thing," Simone said.

Zoë agreed, when asked, it was terrible timing, but at least Simone had known ahead of time about the upcoming trip, so she hadn't been surprised or harbored suspicions he wanted the hell out of there. He still might have, Zoë thought, but no need to point that out. Cynical Simone would have already bludgeoned herself with the worst-case scenario. If she wanted to present Zoë with the best possible interpretation, Zoë would let her.

"By the way," she said, when it seemed Simone had delivered her news in its entirety. "I heard from your Uncle Shel. He really came through with that genealogy stuff. I wanted to say thanks for putting me in touch with him. I can't believe he got back to me so fast."

Simone laughed. "I talked to him yesterday. He always loves to have a new project. Since he retired, he's gotten obsessed in the worst way. Spends more time thinking about family below the ground than above it."

"I hope he doesn't mind, I sent a follow-up request. I found some more information, so I figured it was worth a shot."

"I'm sure he won't. You'd have to know Uncle Shel. He'll bore you to death with the stories if you let him."

Zoë didn't want to say it, but she doubted very much she'd be bored. She loved hearing Henry's stories, and those her Gran and others shared with her. In fact, she might even be able to return the favor someday and help Shel find information on relatives he couldn't track down using more conventional methods. She mentioned the idea to Simone.

"I'm not sure," Simone said. "Maybe. If you made it sound like you'd just run across something."

"So, he wouldn't want to know that I *know*." Zoë

had learned to hide her gift. Simone's suggestion surprised her, considering how open-minded she usually seemed.

"He's not really a believer in that sort of thing."

"Okay," Zoë said, putting aside her hurt since he was, after all, doing her an enormous favor. "I'll send a thank you note instead. I know how strange this seems to some people. I appreciate you helping me find Henry."

"You know, this is weird." Simone sounded thoughtful.

"Why?" Zoë fought her instinctive defensiveness, holding it in check. For the moment.

"Remember me telling you about that guy coming around the other day saying he had a letter for you from your Uncle Henry?"

"No. You didn't tell me that." Zoë felt a chill. She didn't have an "Uncle" Henry.

"He said he couldn't make out the last name on the slip. I found that strange too, because wouldn't you expect it to be typed? But whatever."

"When was this?"

"I can't remember now. Maybe Tuesday afternoon, late."

Zoë thought back. Tuesday was the day she met Alexander. She'd left work early. Wednesday, she'd talked to Dustin about Simone, so Simone had been distracted. Thursday, she'd missed work because of the meeting with Thomas, and Friday she hadn't seen Simone until she'd found Kent's body. But still.

A message on her desk wouldn't have been too much to ask, would it? "You didn't mention it. You say this guy left a letter for me?"

"He'd said you had to sign for it yourself, so he would come back first thing the next day," Simone said. "That's why I didn't bother mentioning it, I guess. He didn't show?"

"No," Zoë said.

"Anyway, talking about Henry and Uncle Shel made me think of 'Uncle Henry'. Weird coincidence, huh?"

"Yeah," Zoë said uneasily. Without a doubt this wasn't a coincidence. Someone had been looking for her: someone who knew about Henry. Then it hit her. Simone wasn't the only one who knew about Henry. Whoever had been looking for her thought Henry was her uncle. That person didn't know Henry was dead. "Simone, I have to go," she said, and quickly said goodbye.

She sat in her car for long minutes, trying to sort out her thoughts. Finally, she took off the parking brake and headed toward the Marina.

CHAPTER 13

MARCO'S ANTIQUES WAS OPEN on Sundays during the summer, thank God. Zoë didn't think she could wait until after work Monday to confirm her suspicions. The store sat back from the street, bounded by clean, clear sidewalks and shrubs and flowers so perfectly manicured they looked fake. Mosaic stone tiles spread into a flat-faced sun beneath Zoë's feet. She trampled on its eye as she approached the antique store.

A bell tinkled as the door closed behind her. Zoë loved the smell of antique shops. They invariably smelled of wood and sometimes dust, but everything had history, and that made her comfortable. Today, grim reality kept her from finding it soothing.

Marco's was quiet, both in the natural sense and the supernatural foot-traffic as well. She looked at the glass knick-knack cabinets on the East wall where she had discovered some of her treasures. She'd bought Henry keys because she thought he loved them. Now she considered perhaps he just loved Rose, and those keys reminded him of happy times. That key in Rose's hand at the moment she died...Zoë knew it held significance, but she had no idea what it had opened.

The key was the key, she thought, but didn't smile at her bad joke. Not only had the key meant something to Henry and Rose back in 1880, someone determined to steal *her* keys had started the series of events that led to Henry's disappearance.

Zoë braced herself. The direct approach, she decided, would work best and required the least effort. She walked up to the cluttered counter and said to the smartly dressed woman behind it, "I need to see Marco."

The thin-faced woman looked down her nose at her, eyeing her through thick, trendy glasses. "Marco," she said in an upper-class New York accent, "is unavailable."

Zoë leaned forward, tired and out of patience. "Oh, he'll see me. Tell him it's Zoë Pendergraft. And if that doesn't get his ass out here, tell him a man died because of him."

The woman raised an eyebrow, and Zoë could have sworn a malicious smile flitted across her face. "Certainly," she said in a clipped tone and briskly walked toward the back room.

Within moments Marco emerged, flailing his arms. His rust silk shirt and varicolored tie clashed with the pale trousers and waistcoat, but somehow he pulled it off with flair. The gold pocket watch struck Zoë as a bit much though. "Darling!" he said in exaggerated tones. "Miranda says someone died? How ghastly! What on earth happened?"

He shuttled her along to a side room where he sometimes took customers for private showings, and there indicated a hundred-year-old chair. "Sit, darling. Tell Marco all about it." He looked pleased at the excitement at least on the surface, but she knew he hid a deeper worry. Good, she thought, but held herself in check. She had to be careful if she wanted him to tell her the truth.

"I got a little visit Tuesday," Zoë said, watching Marco closely. "From a friend of yours. Someone interested in keys."

"Now, Zoë," he said, but she cut him off with a wave of her hand.

"He came back Friday, when he hadn't gotten what he wanted. He stole my entire key collection, although how he found it is beyond me. That I could live with. Just things, after all. But someone interrupted his escapade and that person is now dead." Marco lost his smile instantly.

"Zoë, I didn't have anything to do with that," Marco said, but his voice had gone up in pitch.

"See, you know how I know that isn't true? He asked about my 'Uncle Henry.'"

"So?"

"Henry wasn't my uncle. And you were the only one in the entire world to whom I'd ever called

Henry that. You made some snide comment about me buying gifts for an older man, and I covered by saying he was family." She fought not to blush at how stupid she'd been. "He was just some nice old guy at my work. When someone stole the keys, Marco, most of which I'd bought in your shop, did you really think I wouldn't put it together?" Okay, so it had taken her longer than it should have. But she'd been distracted.

"Look, someone needed to find this key. It had ended up in the display by accident." All traces of the flamboyant accent had completely disappeared. "He was desperate to have it back. I gave him your name. That's all."

"Desperate? Why, Marco? Why would someone be so distressed over something like that?"

"I wish I knew," Marco whined, "It doesn't make any sense to me either. He said the key opened something valuable, but I know my antiques, and that key was nothing special."

"Obviously you don't know as much as you thought you did." Zoë snorted. "You sent this guy to my work?"

"I had to tell him. Honestly, Zoë I didn't have any choice. I might have told him where to find you, but that was all. He said he wanted to talk to you. Ask to buy it back." Marco licked his lips.

"Uh huh," she said with disdain. "You didn't have to do that, Marco. I would have helped you out."

"I never meant for anything to happen." Marco's voice was thin, and sweat had broken out on his forehead. He mopped it with a linen handkerchief.

"When you didn't respond, he assumed you planned to hold out." After a brief pause he said, "Have you talked to the police?"

"Not yet." She knew the police wouldn't do anything. They seemed to believe Kent had died of natural causes, and she didn't think they'd thank her for bringing this new bit of information to light. The keys had been trifles, and none very expensive. Not knowing where Henry had gone bothered her, but scaring away a spirit was hardly a crime. Zoë shook her head. "I want the guy's name."

"Zoë, I can't have the police involved."

"Marco, honey." she smiled without humor. "I might look like a ditzy secretary to you, but believe me, there are things about me that would surprise you. If I have to send someone here to get the name from you, it isn't going to be the police, and I promise you, you will tell them what they want to know." Okay, she was stretching the truth. Thomas and Alexander weren't her personal thugs and she had no idea if they'd do what she asked, but Marco had already proven threats worked on him.

Marco met her eyes for a long, hard moment. When Zoë didn't back down, he flinched. "Peter Delancy."

Zoë sighed, not unsympathetic to Marco's fear. "Henry is gone," she said, more to herself than Marco.

"Darling, you didn't tell me your friend was the one that died!" Marco tutted and made large consoling gestures. "But all this was a horrible accident. You know me, darling. I'd never have told this...associate...where to find you if I thought he meant any harm."

Zoë started to set him straight about Henry not being the one who died, but decided not to bother since she didn't believe Marco thought this Peter Delancy person harmless. She could tell he was scared, and Marco, even with his flamboyant personality, didn't seem the type to spook easily. She didn't like that she enjoyed seeing Marco upset, but she did. Besides, Henry *was* dead, so it was only half a lie.

She pondered going to the police. She hoped she wouldn't see this guy again, but if he got what he wanted, surely he wouldn't return. But then, if he thought Zoë saw him, he wouldn't want to leave witnesses. Explaining to the police why she kept a collection of keys in her company boiler room would take enough creativity as it was. She'd think of something, if it came to that.

As she arrived at the shop's entrance, Marco made a display of giving her a goodbye kiss. "I'm sorry about this, Zoë, about your friend. I thought he was just going to ask to buy the key back." He lowered his voice.

After a few air kisses from Marco and some more empty reassurances that he'd take care of everything, Zoë returned to her car, trying to decide what to do next. The part she hated most in mystery novels was where someone had a key piece of information but didn't tell anyone. That was always the precise moment they got conked on the head and thrown into a ditch. Obviously she had to tell someone—and quickly.

She gripped the steering wheel. It was her fault. If she hadn't bought Henry those keys, none of this would have happened. And it was Simone's fault. If she had left a message for Zoë about this fake delivery person, she would have sold the key back to the guy, or given it to him for that matter.

She sighed. To know for sure what had happened to Kent, she'd have to ask Henry. That seemed the much smarter option than finding this "associate" of Marco's on her own. This was another sure-fire way to end up in trouble deeper than she could get out of. She was a lot of things, but not stupid. After getting the non-emergency number for the police in San Mateo, she called and asked to talk to the person investigating the death of Kent McGee at Fiskers.

"Homicide. Esteves."

"Uh, hi. You're investigating Kent McGee's death at Fiskers Technology Group?"

"Who are you, please?"

"Zoë Pendergraft. I found him."

"Yes, ma'am. Did you have any more information about the incident?"

"Yeah. I saw someone coming up from the boiler room when I went down the stairs. I, uh, recognized him, and he didn't belong at Fiskers. His name is Peter Delancy. I've seen him before at this antique store I go to all the time. Marco's on Union Street. I wasn't sure what his name was, but I just asked the owner."

"And you have reason to believe Mr. McGee's death wasn't natural?"

"I don't know anything of the kind. I just know Peter Delancy was somewhere he wasn't supposed to be, so I thought I should tell someone." Zoë stared out the window, not sure if she was being really smart or really stupid. "It just seems to me if this person did do something to Kent, if I recognized him, he'd probably recognize me too, right?"

"Can you come by the station so we can talk this over?"

"Sure. Tomorrow on my lunch hour, if that's okay." He asked her a couple more questions she'd already answered twice, and in the end agreed to let her come in tomorrow to sign her statement. Zoë felt she'd done her thing by telling them Peter Delancy's name, even though she'd only done it to avoid the classic mystery-movie deathtrap, figuring now that she'd told someone official, nothing bad would happen. It wasn't logical, and if she was honest, she just wanted some time to think how she'd keep herself from sounding like a nut job. If they questioned her more closely about why she had gone to the boiler room in the first place, she'd have to do some quick thinking.

She hung up the phone and pondered. The important question, other than the cause of Kent's death, was if this information would get Henry off the hook with the Powers? She needed to call Thomas and see what she could do about that. Looking at her short list of recently called numbers, she found his and redialed.

The usual warm female voice answered the phone. "Good afternoon. Thomas' office."

"This is Zoë Pendergraft calling for Thomas, please."

"I'm sorry," the woman said in a sympathetic and soothing tone. "Thomas is at the High Court. Can someone else help you? One of his associates?"

Thomas has associates? "No, I'm afraid not. Any idea how long he'll be?" Zoë said, hoping she could also get some word on how Alexander's hearing was going, in addition to asking for help with Henry.

"No, I'm sorry. When he checks in, I'll tell him you phoned." The line was abruptly disconnected.

Zoë noticed she hadn't asked for a return number, but then nothing ever seemed to stop angels from finding her. She stared at the phone for a second, frustrated and annoyed by the dead ends, and uncomfortable about the whole situation. She thought through the possibilities and couldn't come up with one single thing she could do to hurry things along, either with finding Henry or with Alexander's hearing.

She started to call Simone and see if she wanted to have a girl's night in, but decided just as she was about to hit the button to connect that an evening alone wouldn't be horrible. Once she got home though, cleaned everything she could stand to clean, washed her hair and painted her toenails, she couldn't deal with the silence anymore. Even Gran wasn't about, and darkness had completely fallen.

Zoë caved and hoped Simone would pick up, secretly glad that the apparent new boyfriend had this "Chicago thing". "Simone," she said, "I need some company. Want to bring over some Chinese?"

"Damn, I hear you. I'll be there at seven. Go get us a movie, and not a chick-flick either. No crying. Let's watch things blow up."

Zoë agreed, feeling happier knowing Simone would arrive soon. So she sucked at living alone sometimes. So what? Alone was overrated. Right now, she needed a friend.

CHAPTER 14

BY THE TIME MONDAY MORNING rolled around, Zoë felt prepared for her meeting with Detective Esteves at lunchtime. She had worried for nothing, though. When she went to make her statement, Esteves wrote down everything she'd said on the phone, asked for a description of the person she saw, and then repeated the same questions she'd been asked at the scene. As far as she could tell, they still thought Kent had died of natural causes, but they were tight-lipped about the whole thing. She tried to worm a bit more out of them, but all she got was their thanks for "coming forward". *What a waste of time.*

After lunch, Zoë realized she was worried about Alexander. The police business had distracted her, but with that taken care of, she now had time to notice that she hadn't heard a word about his hearing in the past twenty-four hours. Monday slid into Tuesday, and by then she was close to frantic.

How could the hearing take this long? And why the hell hadn't Thomas returned her call? She thought about calling again, but believed without a doubt the message had gotten through, and he just wasn't willing or able to speak to her. Angels, she reasoned, wouldn't forget to give a message, and she doubted things slipped their minds.

Finally, around four in the afternoon, her cellphone beeped once and then vibrated, indicating she had an unread text message. *I'm coming to get you.* Relieved it was from Thomas, Zoë grinned, even though beneath it all she did not feel particularly cheerful. She knew Thomas wouldn't understand why the message sounded like a threat straight out of a B horror movie any more than Alexander would. For an angel who prided himself on his thorough understanding of humans, and despite Thomas' admitted disapproval of her relationship with Alexander, he could be clueless sometimes. Even though it meant nothing, she enjoyed the fleeting sense of superiority.

The feeling passed as soon as she saw him pop into the room right next to her desk. His skin and clothing were tinged with blue, telling her most people wouldn't be able to see him. She smiled when she saw him, but her smile faded when she saw his expression. "Thomas, what's wrong?" she whispered once she made certain no one else could overhear them.

"The High Court is in recess right now," he said, fading to normal visibility. He plopped himself down next to her desk.

"It's not going well?"

"They want to hear your testimony first-hand," he said.

"Okay." Zoë waited. She knew Thomas had hoped to avoid this, and she worried what this would mean. "What if I refuse to testify?"

Thomas looked up, his eyes sharp and probing. "No," he said.

"What if I do? They can't force me. It's not like a human court where I'll get held in contempt, is it? How can they arrest me? I didn't even know they existed until a week ago. Look, if it's going to hurt Alexander's case, I'll refuse."

"Zoë, when the celestial High Court summons someone, they go."

"Or what? I'm only asking, you know. I'm not saying I refuse. I just want to know what my options are."

Thomas stood, took her arm and pulled her close to him. "You have no options, Zoë. If you do not go, they will come get you. If you do not want to speak, they will compel you. This is not a formality. You have no choice."

Her stubborn streak flared. "I always have a choice." She jerked her arm away from him even though she didn't feel as confident as she hoped she'd sounded. "Don't worry. If you tell me going is the best thing for Alexander, I'll go. But if it's not, I'll refuse. I'll get my own lawyer if I have to."

"Is everything okay here?" Marilyn's voice came

from her office doorway. Before either of them had a chance to answer, Marilyn looked at Thomas. "Who the hell are you?" Turning to Zoë she said, "Are you all right?"

"I'm fine," Zoë said, although she didn't feel fine. Thomas had wound himself into a tizzy and the tension tainted her mood. She had to relax and smooth things over if she was going to help in court. "I have to leave, Marilyn," she said. "I cleared it with Personnel. I'm testifying in court today."

Thomas relaxed at that pronouncement, but Marilyn's eyes narrowed. "Today? Zoë, it's after four."

Zoë shrugged and bent down to get her bag. "I know. Crazy, huh?" When she'd gathered her things under Marilyn's watchful, but slightly confused supervision, she turned to Thomas. "Shall we?"

He nodded to Zoë and then gave Marilyn a small bow, to which she responded with an incline of her head. The entire scene would have seemed comical to Zoë if she wasn't growing more terrified by the minute. After they made their way to the Fiskers entrance, Zoë said, "Thomas, why are you upset? What aren't you telling me?"

"I wouldn't even know where to start," he said, and without any warning, he again touched her on the arm, but more gently this time. "May I?" She looked up at him, not certain at first what he meant.

"Sure, but..." she started, and suddenly they shifted together. It was much like when Alexander had whooshed her places, as she called it, but this journey jarred her senses. A hard chill went through

Zoë's body and made her bones ache, as though a thousand human spirits invaded her at once or like she'd been dunked in a river flowing straight from a frozen mountaintop. The process left her in agony. She couldn't move or breathe. She would have struggled, but her body no longer responded to her brain's commands. Her eyes saw nothing but black for horrifying moments, and then suddenly light surrounded her from every direction, and she collapsed into Thomas' arms.

Zoë gasped for breath and shook all over. "Dammit," she whispered, just before losing consciousness.

When Zoë opened her eyes again, her first thought was how annoying it was that she'd passed out twice in a week. Kick-ass independent women, a group she always wanted to belong to, did not faint, for goodness' sake. If this kept up, she'd have to...as this thought flitted into her head, it faded away when she realized she was nowhere. Not just nowhere *in particular*, but literally nowhere.

She sat with her head in Thomas' lap, a far more intimate pose than she had ever wanted to adopt with him. Moving into an upright position, she looked around. The two of them sat on a gray stone bench placed on a flat gray surface. It went on forever. As far as Zoë could see in any direction— nothing. No walls, no horizon, no ceiling, not even a sky. Gray above, gray below, and it never stopped. She turned to Thomas. "I feel sick," she said, and thrust her head down between her knees.

"Sorry about that," he said. "Your entrance was

blocked. Well, not just yours, but all humans. Took a moment to sort out with the authorities."

Zoë wanted to ask why. It wasn't not like humans could get here without an escort anyway, or could they? Her good sense told her to stick to the more pressing matters. "So, uh, what now?"

Thomas had gotten even more tense than he had been at Fiskers. "When the court reconvenes, they'll come get us."

"Can I see Alexander?" She looked around, hoping in vain that he'd pop up.

"No, witnesses are held in isolation. Since you're not one of us, I assumed this experience would be disconcerting for you. I asked to stay with you while you wait."

Zoë sighed and straightened up, even though her head still throbbed. "Thank you." Disconcerted wouldn't have begun to cover how she would have felt if she'd woken up here alone. "Thomas, why are you upset? Can you tell me how things are going so far?"

"As to my discomfort, no Free Angel would find comfort here, especially me."

"But you're a lawyer, Thomas. Don't you come here all the time?"

Thomas chuckled. "I'm Alexander's advocate. I'm not a human lawyer. I don't come to the celestial realm any more often than I have to. As to the hearing, there isn't much to tell. They've questioned Alexander, Celion and few others."

"Celion. Alexander's mentor, right?"

"Yes. The court found him guilty of negligence this morning."

"Wait, they've already ruled?" That didn't sound like good news. She hoped it didn't mean things looked bleak for Alexander.

"Against Celion, yes. His case was heard separately. Alexander, however, will face the same committee."

"Okay." Zoë breathed in and out a few times. She had never liked public speaking. The few times she'd had to give oral reports or presentations in school, she usually managed to fall "sick" that day. Trying to talk to a classroom full of kids while seeing spirits no one else could did not exactly make her feel comfortable. Not that spirits showed up every time, of course. But she was always on the lookout for them ever since she'd had that dead janitor shuffle in to hear her talk on George Washington Carver in the seventh grade. Of course, she sincerely doubted she would see any human spirits in the celestial realm. Looking around at her dismal surroundings, she shivered. Endless nothing would drive her mad, and she had to fight to keep herself from pondering what it would feel like to get stuck here.

"What are they going to ask me?" Zoë straightened her blouse and then tried to fix her hair with her fingers. She wished desperately she had a mirror with her, but this so-called waiting room didn't exactly seem to have a ladies' room where she could freshen up.

"The same type of questions I asked you before. Most likely about your relationship with Alexander, the day you met, and possibly things that have happened since then."

"Most likely?"

"Technically, they can ask you anything they want."

"Anything?"

"You are their witness, not mine. I will be allowed to make statements at certain times during the hearing process, and I will ask you questions, but I cannot interfere with their questioning." Thomas shrugged. "Although we angels are very organized when it comes to laws, we don't have the same limitations as humans. The committee has the power to do what they must in order to find the truth as to whether or not Alexander interfered with mortality to the detriment of the timeline progression plan."

"Did he?" Zoë said quietly.

Thomas put his hand over hers and squeezed. For a moment, he seemed more like himself, more relaxed. "If you don't understand something, it's okay to say so. The proceedings are formal and structured, but allowances will be made for you."

They fell into a silence, sitting together and waiting. At first it seemed unbearable to Zoë, but after a while the urgency faded, and with it went her nervousness and fear. Finally she asked, "What's taking so long?"

"I don't know," he said. "Angels do not tend to

hurry." But then, with a twitch of his head, as though he'd heard something in this vast expanse of nowhere, Thomas stood. "They're reconvening. It's time."

Zoë nodded. "Okay." She exhaled again and stood beside Thomas, facing him since there were no doorways or other indication of which direction they would go. She reached up to straighten his dark tie. As she touched it, it disappeared, and his suit melted into a dark blue robe that flowed from a high collar down to the floor. A subtle insignia appeared at either side of the neck: some sort of shield or device.

His coal black hair grew long and then stopped as it touched his shoulders. The stubble on his face vanished before her eyes, but at the same time deep lines creased his cheeks, making him look older than she'd ever seen him. Suddenly he looked more than old, he looked ancient. His deep gray eyes, however, shone with the same familiar glint. Even with long hair and wrinkles, she would have known him anywhere. And despite the change, he was still compelling to look at.

Before she could ask, he answered the question budding in her mind. "Out of respect, I observe certain traditions." He pushed back the long sleeve of his robe and offered to take her hand. "May I?"

"It's not going to hurt like last time, is it?" she said warily.

"I doubt it."

Although she found that less than comforting, Zoë nodded, and the gray world jerked around them as they shifted.

Deep reds replaced the gray, and Zoë had to fight not to leave her mouth hanging open. The courtroom didn't have the Judge Judy layout she'd expected. Instead it brought to mind the British House of Lords with rows of deep red benches on either side of a long, narrow room. Its inhabitants, on the other hand, were like nothing she had ever seen.

Though every angel within the chamber was in human form, their long hair and formal robes in varying dark shades made her feel like she'd stepped back in time. "What do the colors mean?" she whispered to Thomas.

"Different factions," he said in a low tone.

Angels murmuring among themselves filled nearly every one of the some two or three hundred seats in the hall. It had occurred to her earlier they might be in exalted forms, with bird heads and serpent bodies and a hundred other variations she could imagine, and she found herself somewhat disappointed that they each had two arms, two legs, no wings, and their skins were plain old beige to mahogany in color.

"Which group is the committee?"

"All of them."

Zoë snapped around and stared at Thomas. "I'm going to be questioned by all of them?"

"Possibly. Probably not."

"I hope they plan to give me a bathroom break and a sandwich," she muttered.

The angels occupied themselves with the pleasantly mundane task of finding their seats, so Zoë took the opportunity to look around. Behind and above them, in the rear of the chamber, a visitors' gallery perched like box seats at a baseball game, except the railing was carved wood and its inhabitants dressed in ornate, formal clothing. Unlike the committee, those sitting above wore jewelry, sashes or ribbons. One man and a woman in particular caught her eye. Splendidly dressed, they stared directly at Zoë. The woman wore a golden sheath dress of heavy damask with dark green jewels at her neck. A delicate golden crown rested in her pale blond hair, but her eyes were sharp and calculating. The man next to her wore a long robe of the same gold color and a similar, but heavier crown.

"Who are they?"

Thomas followed her gaze and then urged her to look forward as the crowd began to settle.

He leaned over and put his lips close to her ear. "Alexander's parents, Trill and Zedane."

She met the woman's eyes once more. Zoë couldn't help it. The woman wore a crown, for goodness' sake, and she remembered very distinctly Alexander had told her his parents were named Duncan and Emily or something like that. "But..."

Before she could ask anything more, Thomas gave her a warning look. The chamber fell silent. She and Thomas faced forward, and Zoë felt the weight of the gazes in the chamber on her. Her hands shook, and she wished she had long sleeves like Thomas' to hide them in. Instead, she crossed her arms in front of her waist and hugged herself.

At the head of the room and positioned above the benches sat an immense throne covered in soft red velvet with a lily carved into the wood casing around it. When an ancient angel entered in a long white robe and a beard nearly the same hue, she expected him to take the throne, but he did not. Instead, he crooked a knobby finger at Zoë and Thomas, and motioned them forward.

He eyed Zoë from beneath bushy brows. "So you are the girl, are you?"

She stiffened. *The girl*, indeed. "I'm Zoë Kathryn Pendergraft."

The old angel grinned. "So you are. Good for you."

When he stepped to the side, she saw Alexander had come in behind him. He looked tired and his face lacked the usual sweet humor she loved so much. He also wore a golden robe exactly the shade as the man in the balcony above. When their eyes met, she took a couple of steps forward, wanting nothing more than to fling herself into his arms. The startled and pained look on his face stopped her in her tracks. It had been, she suddenly realized, exactly the wrong thing to do with every eye in the chamber on them.

Dammit, she said to herself. She hadn't even opened her mouth yet and she'd already made things worse.

"I am sorry," he said softly.

For what, Zoë wondered.

The older man watched the exchange and then

motioned her to a solitary chair at the center of the chamber. If someone had actually sat in that enormous throne, she would have had to crane her neck upward to make eye contact. Thomas went to a podium to her right, and the bearded angel to her left.

Zoë didn't want to look at Alexander. He looked lonely, and his defeated expression pained her. For a moment she forgot her fear of the questioning to come and berated herself for having indulged her selfish worries. As uncomfortable as recent events had made her, his situation was a hundred times worse. After all, he knew these people, and he stood to lose his position. Seeing the formality of the chamber made this seem less like the employment tribunal she'd first pictured. Instead, it had the feel of a senate judicial hearing, including the overwhelming trappings, except that she didn't have so much as a table to hide behind or a glass of water to sip.

"Zoë Kathryn Pendergraft," the white-haired angel began from behind his podium, "We are here to determine whether the celestial being you know as Alexander did interfere with mortality to the detriment of the timeline progression plan. The committee had discussed the matter of your humanity and whether or not this would preclude you from acting as a suitable witness."

He talked about being human as though it were some kind of handicap, and this got Zoë's ire up. She bit back the remarks that she longed to let tumble out of her mouth.

"Some suggest you should be questioned as any of us would. Others believe humans incapable of telling the truth for a long enough period to satisfy our purpose. With that in mind, a third group has suggested we compel you to tell the truth." He stopped and looked at her closely. "Do you wish to comment on this?"

She did. She wanted very much to comment on the cheek of thinking they would have to force her by some means she didn't even want to consider. The presumption of dishonesty came under the twisted opinions of people who probably didn't even know any humans personally. It took all her self-control simply to say, "I don't like the idea of you compelling me to do anything. How about I swear to tell the truth, the whole truth and nothing but the truth, so help me God?" Even people in fake TV courtrooms got sworn in, didn't they? But seeing as how angels didn't lie, it did make sense they might not cope well with someone who at least knew how.

A murmur went up in the chamber, and Zoë glanced at Alexander, who looked something between amused and horrified. If they had this much trouble with just getting started, this might take a while.

The old angel cleared his throat and gestured for silence. "We are prepared to allow you to exercise your free will," he said after the commotion had died down. "This is our way, but remember, false statements will hurt your already limited credibility."

"If my credibility is so limited, then why am I here?" The words fell out before she could pull them back.

"You are here to answer questions and submit to the will of the High Court."

Well, then. She had no answer for that, so she nodded.

"When you met Alexander, he posed as a message delivery worker. Is that correct?"

"Uh, yeah. He came to my work and said he was the postman. Wait, no. He didn't say that. He came in dressed like a postman and carrying the company mail. So, you know, I guess I assumed it."

"Did he seduce you, or did you seduce him?" came from a woman on the left.

Zoë looked up to find the speaker. The narrow-faced woman wore a dark green robe and stood at her seat. "Well," Zoë said, feeling a rush of heat on her face, "I suppose I suggested giving him my phone number or something like that, and he asked why. My friend Simone explained."

Another brief bout of whispering went around. Zoë could tell not everyone knew precisely what a phone number was, so she clarified. "I suggested we see one another again. Alexander agreed, and he came to my home that night after work."

"And you commenced an intimate relationship involving sexual intercourse."

Not a question, she noticed, but Thomas didn't make a move to object, so she said, "Well, not that night, but yes, we, erm, yes." Despite trying to avoid looking at Alexander, Zoë met his eyes, and his tender expression relieved her. He didn't appear embarrassed by their relationship. Not that she was. Her mortification came from having to tell hundreds of strangers about it. Of course, it couldn't be easy for Alexander, with his parents sitting behind her. But then, it surprised her that in a couple of centuries he hadn't gotten over that concern. As that thought flitted through her mind, Zoë realized she cared very much what his parents thought.

A committee member a few seats down stood and asked, "We are aware you have super-human abilities. Please describe them in detail. Do they include detecting Alexander's divine nature, even though he presented himself in human form?"

Super-human? Right. That made her sound like a crime-fighter. *Up, up and away.* She cleared her throat. "I can see the spirits of humans who have died. And, yes, I knew when I first saw Alexander he definitely wasn't human."

"Anything else?"

"Oh, I can see you guys even when you go invisible, and I can see those blue wall thingies."

The old angel opposite Thomas leaned forward on his podium. "What blue wall *thingies*?"

"You know, the barrier things. Like at the train station?"

"She means she can see a Pale, my lord," Thomas interjected. "Apparently they look blue to her."

Zoë was surprised to learn what she had called a force-field and what the angels called a Pale didn't look blue to them too, but it didn't matter. "Right," she said. "Sorry, I didn't know what you call them."

The old angel flicked his wrist and pointed at her, and suddenly she was surrounded by four blue translucent walls. The aversion to them crept over her skin, and she wanted desperately to get away, except they surrounded her. "Hey," she said, jumping to her feet and pushing her way through the barrier. Zoë glared at the questioner. "That was pretty rude," she said.

"Oh," he replied absently. "I had thought to verify you could see them. I forgot you would feel it as well." With another gesture the walls disappeared, and Zoë took her seat again, but slowly, fearing the walls might come back at any moment.

Zoë wanted to point out that they had agreed to trust her, but decided not to press her luck. When she'd imagined giving testimony, this wasn't at all what she'd had in mind.

The angel who had asked about her abilities continued as soon as she had settled herself. "What other super-human abilities do you have?"

"I don't really know," she said.

The old angel asked her, "What do you mean?"

"I mean that I don't know." Zoë shrugged. "I'm only twenty-five years old. I've seen spirits as long as I can remember. I didn't know until last week I could detect angels, and I'd never seen a Pale before. So, either I just haven't run into any, or my abilities are growing. Last week, if forced to label myself, I would have used the word medium. In the past seven days,

I've been called a few other things."

"Like what?" the old angel asked her.

"My friend Henry Dawkins, he's dead, called me a seer. Alexander seemed to think I was a Stalker." She quickly added, "But of course I'm not."

If the interruptions before had been a mild chattering, the word Stalker made the place explode. Angels stood right and left, and a whirring of activity swirled around her.

Cries of "Take her!" and "No!" and a hundred variations of fear and outrage clattered in her ears. Their voices grew thunderous, and Zoë stood, helpless in the center of the commotion. She bolted from her seat and ran to Thomas' side and stood with her back to Alexander, between him and Thomas.

Alexander rippled as he shifted. She couldn't see it, but she felt him grow taller and then saw the edges of his blue wings in her peripheral vision, and even Thomas backed away. A predatory bird-like screech came from deep within Alexander's chest and the entire chamber fell into a hush. His arms clutched her protectively.

The first time she'd seen Alexander shift, she had been afraid of him. Now she felt nothing but grateful. Her heart thudded, and no one moved for an eternity. All eyes in the chamber fixed on the pair of them.

Finally Alexander spoke. "Zoë is no assassin."

A voice came from behind them, but because of

the grip Alexander had on her, she couldn't see its source. "How do you know?"

Zoë trembled, but she answered, "Because I don't kill people. That's why. Even angel people." She felt stupid saying it. Even with the chaos blade she couldn't imagine being able to hurt one of them, especially when she felt power rolling off Alexander like musky cologne.

"You possess a chaos weapon?" the old man asked her.

"It's not like I asked for it. A spirit dropped it at my feet."

"And you picked it up?"

"What the hell was I supposed to do? Leave a hunting knife lying under my sofa? I didn't even know what it was when I found it."

The old angel looked up at Alexander, still in his exalted form, towering over Zoë. "And even knowing what she might become, you would side with her over your own people? Your own family?"

Alexander growled. "She is innocent."

"And if it turns out she is a Stalker? How far will you go to protect her?"

"She has done nothing wrong. It is not her nature," Alexander said.

The old angel tugged his white beard for a moment, and then looked up and behind Zoë and Alexander, to the visitors' gallery. He nodded in the direction of Alexander's parents and motioned for the rest of the committee to sit. To Alexander he said, "She will not be harmed, unless she commits an act that requires intervention. We will give her the opportunity to exercise free will."

Alexander stayed standing, and did not return to his human form, but his grip did loosen.

When the rest of the chamber had finally taken their seats, the old angel said, "I think we have heard enough from Zoë Kathryn Pendergraft, unless anyone has any questions for her?" He squinted around the hall, but no one spoke. "Thomas?"

Thomas looked up at Alexander, then down at Zoë and he sighed. "No, I require no further testimony from Zoë. If the committee will allow me, I will return her to her home, and then we can proceed."

"Agreed," the old angel said, his expression probing. "It has been interesting meeting you."

"Likewise," she replied, but only because politeness dictated she say something. "Interesting" wasn't the word she would have chosen.

Alexander released Zoë, and she turned to face him, staring into that strangely beautiful beaked face with large black eyes. "You can't take me home?" she asked, not caring who heard or what they thought.

"No," he said. "I am sorry, little Zoë." He leaned over and nuzzled her. "Goodbye," he said and bowed to her before stepping back to allow Thomas to take her arm.

She wanted to hold on to him, to beg, cry or just scream, but instead she stepped close to Thomas, and nodded when he asked if he could transport her home.

CHAPTER 15

"THE WORD 'DISASTER' comes to mind," Zoë said.

Thomas still wore the long robe, not having bothered to change since he'd transported directly into her living room. He didn't answer her assessment, but his expression was grim.

Looking at him made Zoë's stomach twist. "What now?"

"Now I return to the hearing, and they call their next witness."

"Who?"

"Briony, I believe."

"My Guardian? Why are they interested in me? I thought this was about Alexander. Am I on trial too?"

Thomas shook his head. "Isn't it obvious? I told you his relationship with you wouldn't reflect well, and them knowing you're a Stalker makes it worse. It makes Alexander look as though he was either duped or irresponsible."

"I am not a Stalker," Zoë said glumly. "How many times do I have to say that? How can someone who has never killed another living soul be considered an assassin? Thomas, don't you understand? I see death every day. Every freaking day. Henry. My Gran. A stranger here or there, sometimes one at a time, and sometimes by the hundred. If anyone knows death doesn't get rid of people, it's me. Why would I kill someone who could make me more miserable in the afterlife than before?"

Thomas looked at her curiously. "Zoë, have you ever seen an angel's spirit?"

She could tell it wasn't a question. "Angels don't have souls?"

"Of course we have souls, but we don't leave them behind when we die. Zoë, think about it. All Stalkers are seers. You can't kill what you cannot see." He scratched his chin, obviously missing his usual stubble. "You do raise an interesting point though. Your ability to see human spirits is unusual. I don't know that it has anything to do with the other, or if the two abilities are unrelated."

"Unrelated? How can that be? That doesn't even make sense."

"I don't know, Zoë, but I will try to help you if I can. If it's all the same to you, I'd rather you stayed on our side."

Zoë gave a weak smile. "It's not all the same, but I'd rather be on your side too, Thomas." She plopped down onto her sofa, tossing her bag to the floor.

"What a crappy day."

"Goodbye, Zoë. I will see you when the committee has ruled."

"Thanks, Thomas," she said, and before she could even raise a weary arm to wave in his general direction, he'd pulled his arms in close to his body and popped out of the house.

After a few long moments of staring at the ceiling, Zoë forced herself to get up and make a sandwich. She flipped on the television and watched as a variety of barely-talented singers humiliated themselves and then listened as a panel of celebrity judges picked over their fame-seeking carcasses. Usually she enjoyed the spectacle, but tonight she had far too much empathy for those hapless folks in the spotlight. She pressed the power button before the announcement of the final results, and headed upstairs.

That stupid knife. And it happened because she'd saved Jackson Burly. She wasn't sorry she'd done it. No matter the unintended consequences that had piled on since then, she would save him again if she had the chance. Zoë couldn't think of anything more wretched than spending who knew how long having someone as repulsive as Ren Jones leech her soul. She didn't have the experience to guess what would have become of Jackson, had she not interfered. Zoë tried to spend her life worrying about the now, and not the here-ever-after. She'd seen enough spirits to know fretting about the afterlife was a pretty big waste of time, just like living about the past.

Without a plan in mind, Zoë retrieved the knife

from her dressing table. She felt its cool weight in her hand. Someone had given it to her for a purpose, and she wasn't convinced she'd ever fully understand it. She pulled the knife from its sheath and examined the strange metal that seemed to glow from within. *You'd think a bequest like this would come with a manual*, she thought, *if not an actual sit-down chat explaining the wheres and hows and whys of it all.*

Absently twirling the knife in her hand, Zoë considered the options. She could try to call the person who'd dropped it at her feet, the same way she hoped to call Henry. The knife could act as a focal point, assuming it had meant anything to the mysterious spirit. On the other hand, Thomas had warned her about handling the knife too much.

With that in mind, Zoë looked at her hands in time to see her fingers spinning the blade as though doing a strange dance with it. She hadn't even noticed what she was doing. She made an odd strangled peep and stared. Even if she'd wanted to, she wouldn't attempt a maneuver like that with a sharp instrument. That was a sure way to lose perfectly good fingers. In her shock and confusion, Zoë froze, and she expected the knife to clatter to the floor. Instead, it hung at the end of her fingertips, as though held in place by sheer attraction.

"Oh crap," Zoë said to no one. She slipped her hand down and closed her fingers around the handle. This, no doubt, would qualify as one of those aforementioned super-human abilities, even though she had no idea what it meant. Having said abilities was not, upon reflection, desirable. Evolution should take millennia, not days. She didn't know what the end result would look like.

Just as Zoë moved to put the knife on the dressing table, she heard loud grating sound, like stone scraping against stone. Since she hadn't turned on the overhead light, her bedroom was dim, and shadows clung in the corners.

One of those shadows expanded, straightened, flattened, and became a solid black archway. Through the archway she could see more darkness. Zoë backed away.

She wildly cast out with her senses in hopes Gran might be nearby, but felt nothing. Neither could she sense Alexander, Thomas, or any other within range of her abilities. She listened hard, but no sounds came from the archway. Her vision couldn't penetrate the darkness, and she didn't dare touch it.

Indecision kept her rooted in place, staring at it. If she went through into nothingness, she would jump in blind. She had no experience to tell her what this might be, and not even an insubstantial instinct. This particular unknown terrified her.

On the other hand, if she didn't go, she would always wonder what might be on the other side.

But back on the first hand, she had a lot to lose. Her life for one. Smart women, she thought, don't jump into other-worldly archways that come from nowhere. That would be like going into the basement with a dodgy flashlight when there was a serial killer on the loose, or being the character in the monster movie who says, "Let's split up," when investigating a scary noise.

Back on the other hand, she didn't know how to make it go away, and she didn't relish the idea of sleeping with a big gaping hole in reality next to her bed. Thoughts jumbled back and forth, pushing her in every direction. Finally, a thought hit her. The archway appeared when she'd picked up the knife.

Cautiously, she put the blade in its sheath and laid it on the bed. As soon as it left her hand, the archway vanished. Zoë walked to the far side of her room and waved her hand where it had been. Nothing appeared out of the ordinary. Eager to make a second test, she stepped back and picked up the knife again.

With it in her hand, she focused, but nothing happened. She turned the knife over without any luck. She unsheathed it, flicked the blade around, letting it flow in her fingers, and again nothing changed.

Zoë blew out a loud sigh. At least now she wouldn't have to decide anything. She wondered briefly if Alexander's trial had started up, or if Thomas was waiting. As her thoughts turned to the strange vast plain of nothingness where they had first arrived and imagined Thomas sitting there, the portal creaked into existence again.

"Okay, that's weird," she said and moved toward it. When she got close enough to step through, she peered into the darkness. An odd sensation came over her, and the light shifted, bringing a new view into focus. "That's *really* weird," she said. Inside the archway she saw a gray floor extending as far as she could see, and a plain stone bench. It had to be the same one she and Thomas had sat on when waiting for the committee to call her.

But remembering the difficult time she'd had transporting into the celestial realm, she didn't want to risk getting caught in that cold, airless place. This time she wouldn't have Thomas to save her. At least now she knew why those precautions existed. It *would* be possible for a human to travel to their realm. She couldn't help but stare for a moment, wondering if she would make it, and if she did, whether she could find her way out again. She looked around the room for a moment, and found an elastic hair band. Tossing it toward the archway, she instinctively stood back, but it didn't explode or bounce off. Instead, the hair band landed a few feet shy of the bench and skittered on the smooth floor. That didn't mean she could survive the trip, but still, it gave her something to think about. It also made her wonder if someone on the other side could have seen her, or even walked into her bedroom. Not a nice thought, actually.

None of the possibilities filled her with confidence. On top of that, she didn't think getting caught spying on angels with the aid of a chaos blade would help anyone believe she wasn't a Stalker.

With deliberate effort, Zoë turned her mind away from Thomas and the trial, and tried to make the archway disappear. No matter what she did, it stayed. She did the only thing she could think of and put the knife down. Just as before, it vanished, and Zoë exhaled a loud breath she hadn't realized she'd been holding in.

She took the knife, wrapped it in a t-shirt and stuck it in her sock drawer. *Behold the magical shielding power of cotton*, she said to herself, rolling her eyes.

This thing definitely should have come with an instruction manual. Grappling her way in the dark didn't seem promising, and sooner or later she would do something colossally stupid she couldn't undo.

Unable to figure out what to do next, Zoë did the only thing that made sense: she brushed her teeth and put her pajamas on.

* * * *

In the light of day, Zoë could pretend none of yesterday's strange events had actually happened. It worked for a full fifteen minutes while she lounged in bed and ignored the nagging alarm clock.

In the end, she moved because she had to. Activity was the only antidote to the awful thoughts that played over and over in her head and asked questions like, "What if you *are* a Stalker?" She'd decided she loved Alexander, and she believed he loved her too, but asking him to hang out with an angel assassin? What did Stalkers do anyway? Was there some kind of criteria or club? Or did these Stalkers just go around, well, stalking. Zoë didn't even like to kill moths, but beyond that, it seemed a horribly hazardous line of work. She simply didn't have the physical strength or the temperament for it. She'd seen *La Femme Nikita*. She didn't have romantic ideas about a future as an international woman of spiritual intrigue.

So Wednesday morning Zoë put on her business clothes, scrunched her untamable hair with styling cream, put on some lipstick and went to work. The best thing Fiskers had going for it right now was pure normality. The drive to San Mateo calmed her, and she spent the morning attacking meaningless paperwork with grim ferocity as though her sanity hung on the quarterly throughput finalization management something-or-other.

Around midday, she got an email that sent her mind moving in a completely different direction: a lead on Henry's descendants from Simone's Uncle Shel. He'd found her a name. Robert Benson. According to Shel's email, Robert Benson was something of a history buff himself and the one who'd posted much of the family tree on a popular genealogy website.

Rose's baby, Louise Wilson, had lived. Henry's name hadn't appeared on the birth certificate. Strange, Zoë thought, but possibly Rose hadn't told anyone. She'd sure told Zoë willingly enough, but death did change people, and spirits would tell secrets they'd held close in life after they died.

It took Zoë a couple hours to work up the courage to call Robert Benson, another to figure out what to say, and less than that to find a phone number for him. She thanked her lucky stars Robert Benson was listed.

When she got his voice mail, she left a number and a message saying she worked for the Lament Historical Foundation. The angels were right, she mused. Humans were a bunch of liars, with her on top of the big, fat liar list. Zoë sketched out a brief but plausible request for information, family records, or any other data of interest to the ghost town. She found herself getting into the role. She'd enjoyed her trip to Lament, and thought that if she wasn't wrapped up with inter-species strangeness, she would have had fun working for the Lament Historical Foundation.

Zoë needed to find out if Robert Benson had anything that might have once belonged to Henry. A long shot, but her only hope. She needed an object Henry had touched while living. Of course she'd considered telling Robert Benson the truth, but she couldn't risk him dismissing her call as a crank before she even got her foot in the door. She'd learned somewhere around second grade that sharing her *extra insights* invariably led to confusion, doubt, and trips to the shrink.

Robert Benson returned her call as she was leaving work for the night. He readily agreed for her to come to his home in St. Francis Wood that evening, confirming his obsession with his family history. He seemed more than willing to talk about his early California ancestors. Before leaving the office, Zoë printed out Rose's family tree, planning to memorize what she could before she met with Benson at eight o'clock.

The nervous flutter in her stomach stayed with her until 7:58 PM, when she parked her car on Santa Anna Avenue. The inside of the house was lit up, and she stood outside for a moment, looking in. This was such a long way from the gold mines of Lament,

California. What would Henry and Rose say now, to see their sixth generation grandson living in a place like this? The immaculate lawn spread up from the street to a row of perfect hedges surrounding the bay windows. Even in the moonlight, complimented only by the lighted path, she could see the muted and understated colors of the house. Robert Benson had good taste, and he obviously lived in comfort.

Zoë followed the herringbone path to a series of circular bricked steps at the looming double doors. Her hands trembled as she reached for the doorbell. Footfalls sounded on hardwood flooring, approaching fast. She took a deep breath and pasted a smile on her face as the door opened, and light flooded the green front lawn.

Robert Benson's dark face split into a friendly smile. "Miss Pendergraft," he said, extending his huge hand. His rich baritone voice and friendly manner helped her relax. She searched his face for a moment as he stepped back to allow her into the house, hoping, she supposed, to see something of Henry in him. His head was shaved, and the short, sculpted beard around his mouth had nearly as many white hairs as black.

"Can I offer you some coffee? Tea, perhaps?" he asked, showing her through a beveled inner door. She had seen the bookshelves from the street, but still marveled at his library, now that she stood inside it. From floor to ceiling, books lined three of the room's four walls. And these weren't books picked for their covers either, because the stacks of papers and cozy atmosphere told her he often used this room. She couldn't make out the books' titles without staring, but they certainly weren't the cheap paperbacks she had littered around her place. No, Robert Benson's books were thick, expensive and scholarly.

"Thanks, but no. I just had some and it'll keep me up all night," she said, her nerves indeed jangling, but for another reason completely. She hated lying to Robert Benson, but how could she tell him the truth? He'd never believe it. "I appreciate you seeing me, Mr. Benson."

"Doctor," he corrected. "But please. Call me Robert."

Zoë sat on the deep burgundy camel-backed couch he indicated with a gesture. "Thank you, Robert," she said, running her fingers over the velvety surface. "You have a lovely home."

"Why don't you tell me what you'd like to know?" He sat opposite her, resting his hands on his chair's curved wooden arms. He scrutinized her face as she spoke, narrowing his eyes, which were so dark the brown was nearly indistinguishable from the pupil.

"Have you ever visited Lament?" she asked, forcing herself to smile. "It's a wonderful little town, and the Lament Historical Foundation has worked so hard to preserve the look and feel of it for today's visitors."

He nodded, sitting back and smiling, but without taking his eyes off her for a moment. "Yes, I know."

"Your great-grandmother, some six generations back, Rose Wilson, I'm hoping you could tell me more about her. I thought you might even have some photographs or letters? Something. Anything to build a picture of who Rose was." Zoë reached into her purse and pulled out one of the brochures she'd collected in Lament, handing him one describing an upcoming historical exhibit. "We want to present the residents of Lament as individuals with histories, families, records and as much as we can find about them. Lament needs to be more than a collection of buildings."

"Why do you specifically want information about Rose?" he asked quietly.

"I'm researching many of the town's residents." Zoë feared her smile looked as fake as it felt. She was going for pleasant and perky. She wore it like a clown wig.

Robert went to his desk and got a small stack of papers topped with a photograph and handed them to Zoë. She instantly recognized Rose, standing in front of the Methodist church next to a rotund man and his dour wife and four children of varying sizes. Three other men stood with them, wearing equally serious expressions. Zoë's throat closed up as she remembered Rose's awful death and the way the woman relived it over and over even to this day. She looked through the papers: all had to do with the Methodist Church. Rose had worked there, apparently, paid a meager sum to clean and prepare the church each week for services.

"Thank you," she whispered. "Do you have copies? I can make some and get these back to you right away."

Zoë suddenly noticed the far wall. She hadn't

been able to see the shadowboxes from the street. Ten boxes arranged in a row, all the same size and lined with velvet in colors varying from deep red to midnight blue hung in a row. Each one contained an antique key. She looked from the keys to Robert and back again. She realized her mouth hung open, but she couldn't help herself. "Oh my God," she said.

Robert's eyes sharpened and he watched her closely. "You like keys?" He stood and went to the collection, and ran his hand over the cases.

The parallel between this and Henry's key collection left Zoë close to speechless. "They're amazing," she began, but her mouth clamped shut when she saw that as he passed his hand over each key, it shimmered, just as the last key she'd given Henry had done when he'd touched it. Her thoughts went instantly to the chaos blade. It wasn't exactly the same, but something about them was distinctly similar. Zoë's stomach knotted up.

Robert pointed to one in the center, the plainest of the ten keys. Zoë recognized it instantly. "This is the only thing I have of Rose's," he told her. "It goes to a building behind the church that held supplies, extra hymn books and old chairs. Rose kept the key."

"She died with it in her hand," Zoë said, her voice barely audible.

"She died in childbirth," Robert said, a curious expression on his face. "A single woman. A mixed-race outcast who refused to name the baby's father. But the old Reverend Sprayberry stood by her to the end, not letting them run her out of town. There was speculation, of course, that he was her lover. That rumor didn't go away when he and Mrs. Sprayberry took the child in after her death."

"He wasn't the father," Zoë said quickly, wanting irrationally to defend Henry, but she regretted the words as they leapt out of her mouth.

"What makes you say that?" Robert moved away from the shadowboxes. As soon as his presence grew more distant, they stopped shimmering and mostly looked like ordinary pieces of metal, but now that Zoë had made the connection with the chaos blade, she thought she detected an internal gleam.

"Miss Pendergraft," Robert said, "May I call you Zoë?"

She nodded, dragging her eyes away from the keys and back to Robert. The expression on his face stopped her cold.

"No one in Lament has ever heard of you."

The blood drained from her cheeks and she fought the urge to bolt, instead gripping the couch seat with her fingers.

"Obviously, you didn't know I'm on the board for the Lament Historical Foundation. Your call surprised me, to say the least. After we set our appointment, I made some calls, and not a single person I contacted knows you. I honestly didn't think you would show up.

"At first I thought my ex-wife sent you to check up on me, but in that case she would never have told you to pose as someone from Lament. It also occurred to me you might be some kind of con artist.

But then why ask for pictures of a woman dead for a hundred years? You don't seem to want money."

Zoë shook her head, biting down on her lip.

"I would think you are a reporter, but honestly I'm not interesting. In the end, I couldn't resist the mystery. I'll ask you again, what is your interest in Rose Wilson? I can tell by your face you have some connection. Her picture sure did shake you up. I get the feeling you're not telling me something."

If she hadn't felt so panicked, she would have laughed at the understatement. Zoë had no idea what to say. "I'm... a friend of the family." She glanced toward the door, wondering what he would do if she made a run for it. But how in the world was she going to get that key? If anything would call Henry to her, it would be that. Now that she saw it, she knew it and the others had special properties, even if she didn't know exactly what that meant. Surely it did more than open a dilapidated old store room in a dusty semi-ghost town.

"Uh huh," he said, and Zoë couldn't blame him for his skepticism. She was a useless liar. *A friend of the family?* She wondered with an inward groan what had possessed her to say that. "An explanation would seem to be in order," Robert added after the awkward silence stretched beyond an acceptable limit.

"Maybe a glass of water would be nice, Dr. Benson. If it's not too much trouble?" She didn't have to try very hard to get her voice to croak.

Like Zoë, Robert Benson wore his emotions on

his face. She could tell he was caught in a dilemma and had figured out that she'd lied her way into his house, but he couldn't think of any reason to deny her refreshment. On one hand, he must see she was a fraud. On the other, the scientist in him must want to verify that she had some connection to the family. Zoë hoped the curious family historian would win the struggle over the reasonable, middle-aged, law-abiding citizen.

At last, his gentlemanly instincts overrode his suspicion. "Of course," he said. "Sparkling?"

"Just tap water, thanks." Zoë smiled, hoping she didn't look scared. She'd never committed a crime before, at least none more serious than speeding. Stealing was out of her realm, but she had no choice. She had to find Henry. She couldn't do anything to help Alexander, and in fact, she had probably doomed him with her big mouth and her stupid super-humanness, but she could help Henry. She steeled herself to do whatever it would take.

As soon as Robert left the room, Zoë jumped off the couch and darted for the row of shadow boxes. The one containing Rose's key came off the wall with a minimum of fuss. Without pausing for reflection to ask if she was doing the right thing, she tucked it under her arm and raced for the front door. She'd gotten as far as to have one foot on the porch when she heard the rich voice behind her. "I'd like to have that back," he said.

Zoë froze. "I promise. I'll send it back when I'm done with it." Her knees shook.

Robert stepped toward her. "I must insist, Miss

Pendergraft. It's of great sentimental value."

Zoë's mind whirled in one direction and the next. She didn't have many options that appealed to her. She could make a break for it. She doubted he would chase her, but what if he called the police? Covering her tracks wasn't something she had anticipated needing to do. Zoë braced herself to do something completely outside the realm of her normal life: tell another human being the unvarnished truth about herself. "I think we both know it's a lot more than that."

"You wouldn't be the first person to try to take them from me," he said.

Peter Delancy. Dear God. He had been after that last key she'd given Henry because it had some magical property just like Rose's key. "If I wanted to steal from you, I wouldn't have given you my real name, and I wouldn't take just the one, even though I can see they're special. I can see a lot of things most people can't. Please, Dr. Benson. I need this key. I promise you I'll bring it back."

"There's no rational reason for me to believe you. You've lied to me, and now you're trying to take something that's precious to me."

Tension bundled in Zoë's shoulders and she clutched the shadow box so tightly she worried she might shatter the glass cover. "Henry Dawkins," she said as she turned to face Robert on the darkened path.

Robert raised an eyebrow, and said nothing.

"He was your great-grandfather, not the

Reverend Sprayberry. Rose probably died because she didn't want the baby born until he got back. They said he ran off and left her, but in truth he died before she did. Like you, Henry knew there was something special about this key."

"How do you know this?" he said, his tone slightly excited, but still tinged with skepticism. Zoë could almost see him mentally poring over his records.

"Henry was...is...my friend. And Rose told me he was the father of her child." Zoë slowly took a few steps backward, down the brick steps.

"She told you." Robert stared. His bold features contorted with obvious conflict.

"Yes. She told me. Like I said, I see things, Dr. Benson. Do you even know what is special about this key? Does it do something supernatural?"

"No. Maybe. I can feel it. When I touch it, it vibrates. The eldest child in our family has always kept this key. We passed it down from one to the other, like a family secret. It wasn't until I found a second one that I realized it wasn't singular in its properties. I've searched all over the world and it has taken my entire life to find nine more."

"Henry had the same ability. I thought he loved keys, but now, obviously, it's much more than that." If Peter Delancy knew of its properties, and she felt certain he did, she hoped he would leave her alone now that he had Henry's collection. On the other hand, if he discovered Robert Benson's, he'd likely stop at nothing to have it.

"Zoë?" Robert said.

"Sorry. When I came here, I wasn't certain what I was looking for. Now I am." She tapped the shadow box in her hands. "I swear to you I will bring this back. I don't want the key. I'm just trying to find Henry. His spirit, I mean. He's disappeared, and he's one of my closest friends. I need to find him, and this is the only way I know."

Robert nodded, but he didn't look any less bewildered. "This has been the strangest night of my life," he said.

"I wish I could say the same," she replied, and she smiled, genuinely this time. Stepping back toward her car, she watched for signs that he would object. When he didn't voice any protest, she turned and walked the rest of the way to the curb.

She stopped as she unlocked the driver's side door, and called out to Robert, "Thank you." Zoë got in the car and drove away. She didn't look back, but when she looked in her rear-view mirror, the light that spilled onto the street told her Robert Benson still stood in the doorway, staring after her.

Her knuckles whitened because she gripped the steering wheel so hard. "Damn," she said softly. He believed her. Maybe.

Soon Zoë pulled into her garage and shut the door behind her. She grabbed the shadow box and her purse and headed upstairs, Robert Benson forgotten, and her mind going over what she needed to do. Cecil had warned her against summoning spirits. She wasn't even entirely sure how to do it, but knew she must try, and damn the consequences.

CHAPTER 16

ZOË STEPPED INTO HER LIVING ROOM and swore when she saw Thomas sitting on her couch, frowning at the wall. She made a sound that came out something like "gaahk."

He gave her a brief half-smile, and then his brow returned to a furrow. Abruptly he said, "It's over. Alexander is gone."

"Gone," she repeated, putting her bag and keys on the kitchen bar, with the precious shadowbox. "In what sense." No preamble, no softening it up, just bad news: wham. *Great bedside manner, Thomas,* she thought.

"He's been summoned by the queen."

Zoë stared at him, at his expensive suit and his gorgeous face and studied his expression for a hint of humor. "The queen of what?"

Unflappable Thomas raised his eyebrows. "You don't know?"

Zoë fumed. "Would I have asked if I did? Spit it out before I strangle you."

"Alexander went home," Thomas said. Zoë didn't interrupt with another outburst, because she could see how he weighed his words. "He didn't tell you who his parents are?"

Her mind went to the two golden angels Thomas had said were Alexander's parents. Oddly, with everything that had happened in the past two days, seeing Alexander's parents not only wearing crowns but having different names than she'd thought had barely registered on the importance meter.

"Yeah about that. He told me who his parents are: Duncan of Edinburgh and Emily of some place I can't remember."

"Aemilia of North Uist or *Uibhist a Tuath*." He pronounced the Gaelic naturally. "It's an island in the Outer Hebrides of Scotland."

"Yeah, and then you tell me those people at the hearing are his parents, and now he's gone to see a queen, so I assume you mean her, and not the human British queen. But if his parents are Duncan and Aemilia, who are Trill and someone else?"

"Zedane. Let me explain. We angels name ourselves. Since we come into this world as you see us, there's no reason for us to name each other, unlike humans who enter the timeline in a less... capable state. We choose a name we like and sometimes even change them periodically. One angel can have many names and even many titles. I'm called Thomas, sometimes Thomas of San Francisco,

Thomas Black, and a few other things. I've been called Yamuna, Hoff, Bomani..." He waved his hand to brush the idea aside. "Alexander didn't lie. His parents are Duncan and Aemilia. They are also Trill and Zedane. The celestial king and queen of Europe...roughly. Our borders aren't precisely the same as yours."

"King and queen. Of...Europe." Zoë watched Thomas. He obviously wanted, for some reason she couldn't puzzle out, for her to believe Alexander hadn't deceived her by giving her the names Duncan and Aemilia.

"Including part of Russia, the Middle East and India. Not Saudi Arabia, of course, and not China. Mostly. I could show you on a map, I suppose, but it's not important."

"Alexander is some kind of prince."

"Yes."

"So, why did he hire you and not some big-shot royal lawyer? For that matter, why did they charge him to begin with? Why didn't his parents protect him?" More than anything she wanted to know why he hid the truth from her. Didn't he trust her? Would she have talked to him at all if he'd said 'Hi, I'm Alexander, celestial prince of Europe and the Middle East but not China'? Probably not.

"What makes you certain I'm not a big-shot royal lawyer?"

"You're a Free Angel, Thomas. I might be new to this, but I'm not stupid." She had barely resisted using the term "Fallen".

"No," Thomas said. "I can see that. Zoë, he asked me to help him because he knew he would lose."

Zoë blinked and waited for him to explain.

"Alexander left his parents' court to learn about humanity, or as we sometimes call you, the Fourth. He began work as a Guardian, starting with one charge, Ronald Underwood."

"My postman."

"Yes. How much has Alexander told you about Guardians?"

"I don't know anything, really." Zoë exhaled. Another huge understatement.

"They are not fairy godmothers, as human mythology would have you believe, waiting around to protect you from stubbing your toe. It is not the humans they're guarding."

The truth dawned on Zoë. "Briony isn't here to protect me. She's protecting you *from* me."

"Not us specifically. The entire mortal realm. The timeline we live in. Yes."

Zoë sank down into the chair opposite Thomas, trying not to wonder what specifically Briony guarded against. "And Ronald is like me?"

"He's a person of interest."

"And my postman and I are a threat to the entire mortal realm?"

"Not yet. Potentially. Possibly. Guardians watch and wait. Most of the time nothing happens. You are simply an unknown quantity."

Zoë swallowed, trying to take in what this meant. Her heart ached. "So the trial is over. When will Alexander come back?"

"I don't know."

"He lost his case, then. So he's no longer a Guardian."

"Zoë, it's difficult for you to understand, but the crime he committed was in fact a serious one. He's been cast out. He had a choice, but he found that option the more palatable of the two."

His tone alarmed her. "Cast out? Of what?"

"The celestial circle. Alexander is a Free Angel now. That is why he asked me to act as his advocate. He knew he would lose, and he didn't want his parents tainted with his choices any more than they had been, nor any of their kind."

"Oh no," Zoë said. She couldn't fathom what this meant. She wanted desperately to talk to Alexander, to comfort him and listen to him. "Not that...I mean no offense."

Thomas smiled for the first time in a long while. "None taken."

She wanted to ask, *What about me?* As selfish as it would sound, she didn't much care. She stopped herself saying it only because she couldn't bear for Thomas to see her fragile emotions. Instead she asked, "He might not come back at all?" Her throat felt thick.

They had gone on three dates, not that any of them were normal dates, but then they weren't normal people, either of them. After three dates, she could hardly expect anything. Back at the trial, he'd defended her, but knowing him, his personality and character, he would have defended any innocent person. She quickly wiped away the tear that slid down her cheek. *Dammit*, she thought. *Don't cry, you stupid cow.* "He's been cast out of the celestial circle, but he's still gone back to his parents? I guess I thought if he lost his case, nothing would change. That he'd still be here with us, just like before. I don't understand."

Thomas sat and watched as she struggled with her emotions. "Zoë, he's gone." He offered none of the usual comforts: no shoulder to lean on, pat on the back, reassuring words or even a glass of water.

"Damn," she said. Nobody was going to comfort her, so she would have to do it herself. She stood and went to the adjoining kitchen and poured herself a drink. Even knowing he didn't need to eat or drink, she couldn't help but play the hostess and be polite. "Want some? I have some juice, or I can put on some coffee."

He surprised her by accepting the offer, and she poured some orange juice into a tall, clear glass. He followed her into the kitchen and leaned against the counter, sipping his drink. Zoë got a sponge and wiped down the counters, wanting to be active, to do anything but think. How could she put any of this into perspective? She had no frame of reference for her new reality.

After she'd scrubbed the counter and sink, despite them not having been dirty in the first place, she said, "Thomas, I know you don't know me, but I wanted to ask your help."

"Zoë, I have done everything I can for Alexander." He paused. "Or is this about the chaos blade? Has someone contacted you?"

Okay. Who would do that? She didn't want to ask. However, she did consider telling him about the black arch she'd summoned with her chaos blade. He'd said after the hearing that he wanted to help her. She decided to focus on one thing at a time.

"No, this isn't about that. This is about my friend Henry Dawkins." She put down her soapy sponge and wiped her hands before turning to him and, as methodically as she could, explaining Henry's situation. She also told Thomas Marco's story and about her meeting with Robert Benson. "I can't let Henry be 'detained' for something he didn't do. He never touched Kent McGee, and had nothing to do with his death. If anyone is to blame, it's this Peter Delancy person."

"Do you have proof of Henry's innocence?"

"Other than the word of Marco that Delancy was at Fiskers and probably in the boiler room when Kent died? No. Maybe I can get proof. From Henry. I'm going to summon him using that." She pointed to the shadow box she'd laid on the bar separating the kitchen and living room.

Thomas put his hand on the shadow box and then drew it back suddenly. It did not shine like it had for Robert, but she could still detect something strange about it. His face remained unreadable.

"What do you need from me?" Thomas said.

"Be Henry's advocate. To whatever group might want to harm him. I don't have a lot of money, and I don't even know if angels have any use for money. Alexander sure never paid for anything." Guilt flooded her for her petty and bitter thought. She shoved that particular set of problems aside. "I will try to contact Henry. Perhaps he can tell us something that will clear him. And then you go and present his case and get him taken off whatever kind of list he's on. Make them leave him alone so he can exist in peace."

Thomas stared into the distance as he considered. "I'm not sure it's ever been done before, an angel representing a non-living human spirit." His thoughtful voice told Zoë the idea of a challenge appealed to him. "As for payment," he said slowly, "The key is interesting."

"The key belongs to Robert. I promised I'd take it back when I finished with it. I'm sorry. It isn't mine to give." Not that she would have given it to him anyway.

"I don't require money; however, you have talents that could be of use to me from time to time. You helped quite a bit when we first met and you spoke with my former clients."

Former clients, Zoë noticed. Did Thomas tell them to find another representative after he discovered what they'd done to the spirit of Jackson Burly? She considered, but let it go, not wanting to be distracted from the matter at hand. "I would gladly exchange my time and services to you, in return for your help."

"Good. That's settled. I'd like to watch you summon Henry."

"You won't be able to see him, will you? And he might not come if you're here. When Alexander and I went to Lament, the spirits stayed away. The moment he left, they came out of the woodwork, so to speak. I didn't put it together at first, but I think that's why. It's also possibly the reason my Gran has stayed away."

"If I'm going to help, I want to know everything. I'll see your reactions, even if I can't see Henry. And then you can tell me what he says."

Zoë hesitated before nodding her agreement. Tossing the dishtowel on the counter, she led Thomas back to the living room where they sat and made themselves comfortable. She picked up the shadow box and turned it glass-side down. With a fingernail, she slit the brown paper on the back. Half way down, it tore straight across the back, so she ripped it the rest of the way and said under her breath, "Sorry, Robert."

The shadow box had a set of small clasps that held the wooden backing in place. She rotated them easily and turned the glass-side up again, and the two wooden moldings that made up the deep frame slid off. It took a few moments of fiddling to loosen the hidden wires, which held the key to the backing.

Zoë set the frame assembly aside and took the key. It was heavier than she had expected, and the metal felt cool. A tiny thrum went through her hand.

She remembered the way Rose had clasped it tight at the moment of her death. "Oh Henry," Zoë said. "Where are you?"

She wondered if it would work like it had with Alexander and the stone she'd used to summon him. Did she just have to think about Henry and he'd show up? Probably not, or spirits would pop up everywhere on the planet as relatives fondled their inheritances. She'd read stories about people using incense and drawing circles and chanting rituals, but that sounded like hocus-pocus to her. The memory of the cursed fetish Josh Grieve and Ren Jones had used to tie Jackson Burly made her shudder. No matter what, she couldn't do anything like that.

She closed her eyes and rubbed the metal key, noticing a few spots where it flaked, a couple of bumps in the otherwise smooth and worn surface. Rose came to mind immediately, but Zoë pushed her image aside. The last thing she wanted was for the ever-pregnant spirit to arrive and re-enact her death.

As Zoë struggled, she saw flashes, but couldn't hold them. She opened her eyes and tensed under the weight of Thomas' stare. "Relax," she said to herself, and hoped Thomas would take the hint. Of course he didn't, so she closed her eyes and ignored him with all her might.

She thought of Henry, let his features fill her mind. His face was so nice. She'd never imagined him as a romantic figure, but she could understand why Rose would have loved him. His dark chocolate-colored skin had wrinkles and furrows, but he had a great face, full of care and personality. Zoë liked the idea of Henry and Rose happy and full of the joy of falling in love, the pitty-pat the heart would do when the image of someone made the world spin out of control.

Alexander intruded into her consciousness, but Zoë couldn't stand to consider that right now. She let him float away in her thoughts, concentrating on her friend.

The key warmed in her hand. What purpose did it serve? Henry perhaps knew it had some special properties, but the key had belonged to Rose and not Henry. Could Rose have known it too? Or maybe to Rose it was just a key. If so, Zoë could understand Rose enjoying the responsibility. Having a key to the church storehouse probably meant respect to her. Unless... The idea snuck into her head and made her smile. Of course. Neither of them lived alone. They were unmarried. With Rose under the watchful eyes of the Reverend Sprayberry, where would they meet for their moments of illicit passion? The storage room to which only Rose and maybe the Reverend himself had a key. Of course.

Zoë could imagine them sneaking behind that old Methodist Church in the dead of night to hold each other. "Henry, you sly dog," she said, hoping she was right. She loved the idea of her friend having those happy moments. The images in her mind became more vivid, and the face she'd imagined now began to move, as though speaking. "Henry," she said. "I need to talk to you." When she'd summoned Alexander with the stone, she'd done something similar, but also different. She reached out in her mind, conscious of threads of energy extending from the key into another dimension. It flashed. Zoë wondered if its properties would enhance her abilities even more than a normal object would.

When she opened her eyes, Zoë saw those threads. Like spun gold filaments, they twined and reached into a place she could see, but not reach. Henry stepped forward. He spoke, but she couldn't hear him. He looked tired and worn, and it broke her heart. Did she do this to him?

"Henry, please." Then, realizing what she had to do, she said, "Henry. Come here." She could have used flowery language about calling him forth from the shadows, but that sounded too melodramatic for her taste, and probably for Henry's too. As soon as the command left her mouth, he shifted from that other hazy realm into her living room and stood in front of her.

"Henry," she said. "I'm so sorry," She wanted more than anything to fling her arms around his neck. Instead she touched his arm, ignoring the chill his presence sent down to her bones.

"Miss Zoë," he said, his weary face smiling.

"Are you okay?" she asked.

He glanced to the side, as though listening to something behind him that she couldn't see. "It's dark there, Miss Zoë." His haunted expression disturbed her deeply.

"Why did you run away? I've been trying to find you. I want to help. I want to bring you home, and I need to know what happened. If you tell us, we can protect you."

Then Henry's eyes widened as he noticed Thomas. He took a small, backward step.

"He wants to help you too. He's promised me he'll do everything he can, speak for you to the Higher Angels and tell them you didn't hurt Kent McGee. I know you didn't, but you need to tell us what happened."

Henry retreated, putting a few paces of distance between himself and Thomas. "I swear to you that we can trust him." Her ferocity and certainty shocked her. Could she trust him? She didn't have any choice.

"You have Rose's key," Henry said, looking at the small object in Zoë's hand. Then Zoë noticed a small metal ring on Henry's belt. On it hung the key she'd given him just over a week before. It would take a very strong spirit indeed to perpetually carry around a physical object, but then, this was no ordinary object. "You brought me back," he added after a moment. He sounded relieved and tired.

"Of course I did. You're my friend. I'd do anything to help you."

Thomas spoke quietly. "I can't see you like Zoë can. But just start from the beginning. Zoë will tell me what you say."

Henry nodded, not taking his eyes off her, as though looking at Thomas was too uncomfortable to bear. His eyes looked even more glassy as he cast his memory back. "I hoped to see you that day, Miss Zoë."

She nodded.

"Someone came in. No one ever does except for a few I recognize. But this was someone new, so I stayed back and watched from the shadows. He was a white man, dark hair and he smelled like old tobacco."

Zoë tilted her head. She hadn't realized spirits could smell. "I saw him," she said. "He ran out of the stairwell as I went down." To Thomas she said, "Peter Delancy. Henry saw him and watched him."

When she turned back to Henry, the old ghost continued. "He searched around for something. He muttered some words I won't repeat in front of a lady. I could tell he was angry. Impatient. Then he found my treasures. He seemed confused and in a hurry, but he gathered them up quick as could be." Henry paused and licked his translucent lips as though they were dry. "I thought I'd jump out at him, see if I couldn't rattle him. I don't know if it would have worked. I've never tried before, but then Kent McGee came in."

Zoë caught Thomas up and then asked Henry, "What happened next?"

"Why, Mr. McGee yelled at him. Said to get his hands off your things, Miss Zoë."

"Wait, he said that?"

"Yes. He said first, 'Who are you?', and then when he saw what the man was doing, he yelled, 'Those are Zoë's. You get out before I call the cops.' Something like that. That scared the man. I could tell. Kent was none too young, and I think he got a bad feeling from him."

"I had no idea anyone knew about our treasures," she said quietly.

"A few of them knew. They like you, Miss Zoë. None of them can see me, but a few seem to know I'm around. Hadn't you heard?"

She smiled slowly. "No. I thought I was the only one."

"Nah, I'm a legend at Fiskers." Henry smiled as though the idea pleased him, and then his face darkened as his thoughts went back to his story. "They had words, them two. That man saying nasty things, threatening Mr. McGee."

Zoë sat upright. "Did he hit Kent?"

"Didn't have to. Poor Mr. McGee got all dark in the face, and started to jerk like someone had snapped his spine up. He clutched his chest, and his heart gave out."

Zoë closed her eyes and told Thomas what Henry had said.

"That man was cold. Even with Mr. McGee lying there on the ground, he looked around to make sure he had gotten all my keys."

"But he didn't get all of them, did he?" She pointed to the key on Henry's belt.

"No, Miss Zoë." The old spirit's hand went to the key, and a play of eerie light caught her eye. "This one is special, so I keep it close." His voice wavered with uncertainty.

Zoë nodded and sighed. "Henry, why didn't you come and get me?" He wasn't part of the living world anymore, so she had no right to expect him to act like it, but it bothered her nonetheless. Spirits had their own rules, their own view of right and wrong.

"I thought of that, Miss Zoë, but then I heard the alarm."

"Alarm?" she said. "What alarm?"

"I don't rightly know. Like a beacon calling down thunder." Henry looked distraught, as though he blamed himself.

Zoë hated that she'd assumed he wouldn't have tried to help Kent. She pushed aside her guilt, figuring she'd have plenty of time to sort that out, and asked Thomas about the alarm. "Does that make any sense to you?"

"Actually, yes. Henry is, like you, a person of interest to the celestial circle."

Zoë remembered Alexander telling her that before, but she had been so preoccupied she hadn't asked him to clarify. "But Henry isn't psychic or a medium. Are you, Henry?"

"Angels got nothing to worry about from me. There's nothing special about me."

Thomas went on. "I first heard about the Portal Keepers years ago, but never paid much attention. They're rare, and always of fairy blood. I knew he was a person of interest, of course, and I suspected his talent when you told me about his obsession with keys."

"Portal Keepers?" Zoë said. "You didn't say anything before."

At the exact same moment Henry said, "Fairy blood?"

Thomas nodded to Zoë, having not heard Henry's question. "They protect the portals that lead to a shadow realm, the place Henry has been hiding. Mortals can walk through the fringes of a specific astral realm, but accessing these places isn't easy. The most common way is a portal. Only a Keeper can open it, and he must have a mordicite key. There is such a door in Fiskers. That's likely why Henry has lived there. The door would have called to him."

"Mordicite?" Like the chaos blade. Alexander had told her mordicite wasn't from the mortal realm.

"The keys are not pure mordicite, but each of them has it blended into its core during the forging. If it was pure, I could not touch it. Even with it encased in ordinary human metal, I can feel it when I get close. This is a true portal key. I'm certain."

Zoë suddenly remembered the forbidding door in the back of the Fiskers boiler room. The one no one ever opened. The one that had looked different and disturbed after Henry's departure. She turned to Henry. "Did you use that key in the Fiskers door?" She pointed to the key on Henry's belt.

Henry fondled the key and frowned. It glowed as though it was caught halfway between the spirit world and the physical, living world. "I must have. Yes," he said. "Yes, and it reminded me of another time..."

"Wait, are we assuming Delancy would have known this? Then wouldn't he also know immediately the other keys weren't magical?"

"If Delancy is a Portal Keeper, an angel or a demon, yes, he would know right away, and possibly the fae, but I'm not certain. There are other abilities out there, some more like yours, Zoë. It could be the keys only look different to him in the presence of a Portal Keeper, or perhaps he senses astral or celestial objects, or any number of abilities. He would have known his key wasn't there, but taken the others back to test them. So if he's not a Portal Keeper himself, it's possible he's working with one."

"He wasn't an angel, of that I'm certain. When I saw him at Fiskers, he just seemed like a regular human. I don't know if demons or the fae would look different to me." She raised an eyebrow at Thomas.

"I don't know. My guess is you would sense something about a demon, since they share much of their nature with my people. The fae are more like humans, at least in that sense."

One of these days, Zoë thought, she would sit some angel down and get him to explain the universe to her. Until then, she had to press on. "What about this alarm?"

"The Guardians are watchers." Thomas said. "Two people of interest in the same room with an unexpected and violent death, with another." Thomas nodded toward Zoë. "On the way? Yes, a Guardian would sound the alarm."

"I don't understand," Zoë said. "If they were

watching, wouldn't they know Henry didn't do anything wrong?"

"Fully-trained Guardians are given abilities something like yours, Zoë. They can see the spirits of humans who, for whatever reason, have remained in the mortal realm. They also can sense violence. Henry's Guardian would have felt it and summoned the Powers. Guardians do not stay close to human spirits, since they cannot remain hidden from them, which is why neither of you have ever seen him. But they keep tabs on a person of interest as long as they are a part of the mortal timeline. Unlike you, we do not have to look at someone to track them and know their condition."

"Do you understand this, Henry?" Zoë asked.

"Some, Miss Zoë. Fairy blood?"

"Henry wants to know about the fairy blood," she said to Thomas.

"In Henry's case it came from Xoac. Around 1250 AD Xoac was a bit of a problem. He impregnated many human women. Not all of his descendants will have magic, of course, and some magic is very specific, like Henry's. There's never more than one Portal Keeper in a line, and the ability passes on death, not at birth."

Zoë didn't know what to say to someone who'd learned that more than thirty generations back they had a fairy in the family, so she said nothing.

Henry sat down, as though his spirit body felt weary. "I don't remember it all, Miss Zoë. When I heard that alarm, I wasn't about to stick around and meet these Higher Angels. I don't know where I was. I barely remember opening the door." He paused and thought. "Best I can describe it is some kind of in-between place. A bit like where I go when I'm not...awake. But different. Scarier. I'm grateful to have gotten away from there. It was so dark."

It brought to mind the place she had seen through the archway in her bedroom. A shudder traveled through her from head to toe.

Henry went on, "But I know for certain I'd been there before."

"When?" she asked. "Did you have a portal key before I gave you this one?" As soon she'd said it, she knew. "Rose's key." She turned to Thomas. "Does this mean Lament has a portal?"

"I would say certainly yes."

Henry looked down at her hand. "Miss Zoë, how did you get that?"

"From your sixth great-grandson. He's a doctor. I don't know what kind. His name is Robert Benson. Lives in a big house on Santa Anna Avenue. He has a whole collection of portal keys, Thomas. Ten of them. I take it this means he's a person of interest too?"

Thomas nodded. "Considering the nature of the Portal Keeper magic, I'd say certainly he has a Guardian, yes. I don't know who, but I could find out." He tilted his head to the side and his eyes went blank, then he looked at Zoë. "Cesara."

"Pardon me?" Zoë said.

"Robert Benson's Guardian."

Zoë stared. She sort of liked how blasé Thomas acted about the whole telepathy thing, and wondered who he had asked. She also wondered if Alexander could do it too, and if so, why he never used it to talk to her, like, say, to inform her that he never wanted to see her again.

Forcing that nugget of awful thought out of her head would take some persistent work, she realized. Willing herself to deal with the present issue, she looked at Henry. "I met Rose too."

"Rose," he said softly. "She didn't cross over?"

Zoë shook her head, unable to speak. "She's...a little confused. She's waiting for you." Turning to Thomas she asked, "Can you sort this out? About Kent's death? Clear Henry's name with the celestial circle so they'll stop looking for him?"

"I think I can," Thomas said. "But I want to be certain of my suspicions. I remembered that Henry is registered as a person of interest, but I don't actually have access to the official records of his gift. If I'm going to plead his case, I want to know everything. Shall we go?"

"Go?"

"To Lament. I want to see if Rose's key opens a portal there."

Zoë blinked. "Can't you just ask his Guardian?"

"I'm certain Henry's Guardian lost track of him when he left the mortal realm, and we don't want to alert them to his presence until we know what we're dealing with."

"Why Lament? Why not the one at Fiskers? That's where this all happened."

"They'll be watching that one. I don't think anyone else knows about the one in Lament. Henry just needs to put the key near the lock. This way we can check our theory before I take the next steps."

"Henry? What do you think?"

Henry had frozen. "That's how I died."

"What?" Zoë said.

"I remember now. It was a Tuesday. I had planned to meet Rose, like we always did. She'd given me the key because she had to run an errand for the Reverend. I'd noticed it before, of course, how that key called to me, but I'd never held it. Rose kept it close. She was a careful woman. The door opened to me, and...I remember what seemed like ages of darkness and I wandered and searched, losing a little bit of myself all the time. I kept searching for a way back to Rose, even after I, well, passed. Then after a long, long time, I found myself at Fiskers, even though it wasn't called Fiskers back then. Funny. I'd forgotten so much. Time wasn't like anything there."

Zoë nodded as his voice trailed off. "Thomas, we can't ask him to do this. It's too dangerous."

"I won't let anything happen to Henry. I promise."

"Henry?" Zoë said. "If you don't want to, we'll just go with what we have. We don't have to go through with this."

"No," Henry said. "I'll go. I should have gone back long ago. Back to Rose. I don't know why I didn't."

Zoë felt sad for him. She knew spirits didn't seem to have control over where they landed. She'd never seen one able to just flit around as they pleased, although they didn't, as far as she could tell, understand their limitations. Even the spirits who had paid tribute to her must have expended a great amount of will, and she wasn't sure why they'd been able to do what they had.

"Okay," she said to Thomas. "Let's go."

CHAPTER 17

THOMAS TRANSPORTED ZOË to Lament with an unceremonious yank through space. As much as she wanted and needed his help, Zoë believed Thomas was dangerous and somewhat reckless, although that didn't seem exactly fair either. Still, she didn't like the idea of taking Henry back to Lament. Knowing how and where he'd died made her suddenly very glad she hadn't leapt into that dark arch in her bedroom.

The two of them stood close together in the darkness in front of the old Methodist church. Zoë listened hard, wondering if Rose would approach, but the town felt as eerily still as the first time she'd walked its streets. A few moments later, Henry coalesced out of the darkness. They'd hoped he could use Rose's key as an anchor, and it didn't appear he'd had any problem. In fact, with each passing moment, Henry seemed stronger and more solid.

Henry immediately headed toward the cemetery and the storage building beyond. A small groan escaped him as he recalled the last moments of his life. "Here. I had the key in my hand, like this." Henry held up the key Zoë had given him at Fiskers. The metal gleamed in a most unnatural way. He started to move toward the door.

"Henry." Zoë felt uneasy. She didn't like the way the door called and enthralled him. "Henry, wait."

She was too late. She'd assumed he'd need Rose's key for this door, but now realized any portal key would open any portal lock. The mordicite was the key, not the physical shape. "Thomas, he's opening it," she cried.

Thomas moved with preternatural speed, straight for the portal. Henry yanked open the door just as the angel arrived.

Darkness roiled out of the door, and roaring filled Zoë's ears like wind through ancient underground caves. She ducked to the ground. Then silence descended on them, and she peered up. "What the hell was that?" she cried. That part certainly hadn't happened in her dark archway.

Henry stared into the emptiness beyond. "I remember the darkness that night, and I remember hearing that sound. I convinced myself my imagination played tricks on me. I walked in, not knowing anything was wrong at first. But as soon as I stepped over, everything went cold and black. I just remember wandering."

Although he'd died before she was born, Zoë

couldn't help but grieve at his sadness and the way this door had ripped his mortality from him. He'd had a happy life with Rose, and they were going to have a baby.

As though on cue, keening sounded behind them. Henry whipped around, his eyes narrowing. "Rose?" he called to her. "Rose!"

Rose appeared behind them, just as Zoë had seen her before, her hair pulled up in a tight black bun, her features stretched with pain as she clutched her middle. She leaned against a tombstone, weeping. "He's coming back for me. I know it. He didn't run off."

Fighting an invisible force that pulled him toward the portal, Henry struggled toward her. "Rose, I'm here. I'm here."

"Henry?" She frowned. "Is that you? It's time, Henry. The baby is coming. We've been waiting for you."

Zoë's throat clutched. That "baby" of Rose's had died nearly a hundred years ago. "Thomas, what can we do? Rose is here, but she doesn't understand what's going on. She's in pain. Can we help her?" She'd long suspected Thomas wasn't that bothered with humanity, but her earlier assumptions were shattered when she saw the concern on his face.

Henry caught Rose in his arms. "Shhh. I'm here. I'm here for you now. I came back. Just like always."

Rose cried out with pain. "The baby isn't moving right, Henry. I don't know what to do. What do we do?"

Henry looked up at Zoë. "Please. We've got to help her."

"Thomas?" Zoë repeated.

Thomas nodded. "I know a place of refuge. I can't leave you alone though. I will lead them away as soon as I get you protection."

"Protection? I manage just fine," she said with stubborn indignation.

"Zoë," Thomas said, "If you saw Peter Delancy, he saw you. He knows where you work, and it wouldn't be difficult to find out where you live. Henry kept the portal key, which means Delancy didn't get what he wanted the day Kent died."

"I gave his name to the police already," Zoë said, as though that actually changed anything. *Stupid*, she thought.

"If he's a Portal Keeper, the police won't intimidate him. The key will draw him, and he'll need more than anything to get it."

"Can't you do something about him?" Zoë asked when the reality of her situation sunk in. The idea of running from someone who could be a demon or a fairy or just a "person of interest" didn't sound good.

"Yes, and I will. I will tell the celestial circle he was responsible for Kent McGee's death. They will not allow him to carry on, once they know that. But this will take time, time during which you will need protection."

Zoë shuddered. She didn't know what the celestial circle would do to Delancy, but she couldn't say she felt sorry for him.

Thomas' face went blank, which told Zoë he was communicating telepathically. A loud pop sounded as a second angel appeared. When she saw Alexander, Zoë said, "No. Absolutely freaking no."

"Zoë," Alexander said softly. "Thomas said you are in trouble."

"Yeah, well, so are you. You sent your *lawyer* to break up with me? Are you kidding me?"

Henry cradled Rose on the ground. "Miss Zoë, please. I don't want anything to happen to you. Please let them keep you safe. For me."

Okay, now she felt like a selfish jerk. She nodded. "For you, Henry. Anything." She paused as she watched her friend comfort the woman he'd loved all those years before. "I thought you liked keys. I never knew about the mordicite or the portals. I feel silly now. Maybe if I hadn't been so dumb and bought those things, none of this would have happened."

"Don't you talk like that about my treasures, Miss Zoë. You thought about me, and that made me feel nice when I saw those things. You are like family to me. I don't know if you understand what a blessing that is."

Thomas nodded to Alexander. "You are a Free Guardian now. Treat Zoë as your charge."

Alexander stiffened. "Of course."

To Zoë, Thomas said, "I'll lead Henry through the portal. That's the best way. Henry? Hold Rose and stay close. I can't see you, but I'll take it slow. Take my arm. I can at least feel the cold and know you're with me."

Henry stood with Rose cradled beside him, as she wept with remembered pain. When he touched Thomas' arm, the angel's expression didn't change. What if they got separated beyond that door, she wondered. She was afraid for them all.

Thomas led them to the portal door and the blackness within it. "Don't worry, Zoë. I'll have them to safety before you know it. And we will do our best to protect you."

"And Robert Benson," she said. "He is a Portal Keeper too, and he has nine more of these keys. If someone came after me and Henry for one key, imagine what they'd do for ten."

"She is right," Alexander said. "If for nothing more than the mordicite alone."

"And even with this Cesara angel person as his Guardian—we all know how useless they are when it comes to actually protecting anyone." *Stupid angel rules*, she thought.

"I'll go to him after I finish here," Thomas said, "Later tonight. But he'll need something more permanent. Alexander, you will act as his Free Guardian. You will protect him the way you tried to protect Ronald. Keep him and the keys from falling into dangerous hands."

Alexander opened his mouth to protest, but Thomas interrupted.

"I command it," Thomas said.

Zoë blinked. *He did what?*

Alexander hesitated only a moment before he bowed his head slightly in Thomas' direction.

Zoë watched the exchange with interest, but decided the time was not right to ask why Thomas could command anyone.

Thomas went toward the portal, with Henry and Rose close behind. She hoped he could get them where they needed to go. The fact that he couldn't see them didn't instill much confidence in her. Knowing Henry had died in there reminded her that she couldn't do much to help. Besides, she had to have a little faith.

As soon as the trio passed through the portal, the ancient door slammed shut. Long grass in front of the storage room shifted slightly, but then suddenly everything went still, and the door looked for all the world like it hadn't opened in a hundred years.

"Zoë," Alexander said. "May I take you?"

"Will Robert Benson be safe?"

"Yes, Zoë. Thomas and I will do all we can."

"You may take me *home*," she said. With that he put his arms around her.

CHAPTER 18

THEY POPPED DIRECTLY onto Zoë's front porch. She didn't say a word as she unlocked the door and went in. Alexander didn't follow. Zoë sighed. She'd have to do something about this.

"Alexander, can you wait here please? I need to talk to Gran, and then you and I can talk." Her anger hadn't faded, but she didn't have much fight left in her.

The clock on the wall read eleven fifteen. Her back ached and she was drained and sore. Her legs dragged as she climbed the stairs to the upper floor to Gran's room. For the first time it struck her as odd that she had an entire room of her three bedroom house devoted to someone no longer breathing. Most women her age would plan to use it as a nursery someday. That thought made her laugh. "Get over it, Zoë," she said aloud.

She tapped on the door before walking in. Spirits didn't need privacy, since they could simply vanish if they didn't want to be seen, but she couldn't stop herself from treating them like living people. "Gran?" she said. The room was empty, as she had expected. She didn't have an object of Gran's to use as a focus, to draw her into the world as she had with Henry, but would she need it if Gran was only "resting" and not caught in some dark place like Henry?

"Gran," she repeated, closing her eyes. Something in her blood sang. She suddenly understood she wouldn't need an object. As a blood relative, she could use her DNA as the calling object. "Gran, please come here."

"I'm here," Gran said testily.

When Zoë opened her eyes, she saw the plump figure staring at her over her spectacles. "Hi. Thanks for coming." Before the old spirit could say anything about not having a choice, Zoë ploughed on. "Gran, why haven't you crossed over? Is it because of me?"

Gran smoothed out non-existent creases in her lilac pantsuit. "I wondered, sometimes, why you never asked me before."

Zoë lowered herself into a worn, overstuffed chair. "Are you like a Guardian? Making sure I don't mess up the world with my...quirks?"

A derisive snort exploded from Gran's mouth. "Quirks, my backside. And no. Well, sort of." She held up a hand to stop Zoë speaking. "I'm not like one of those *exalted* who go around telling people what is and isn't supposed to be. Anyone with any sense knows that's a crock."

Zoë smiled. Coming from Gran, this was

practically swearing a blue streak.

"You need looking after. Let's just say I know some things." She picked up her needlework, as though to end the conversation.

"You've been gone a lot." When Gran didn't respond, Zoë sighed. "Alexander won't come in if you're here."

"Good," Gran said haughtily.

"No, Gran. Not good. I know you want to watch over me, but I have to live my life." The words pained Zoë. It seemed rude to remind Gran that the old lady was no longer alive. "You can't protect me."

Gran look startled. "I see. That's what you think?" She took off her glasses and eyed Zoë. "You want me to leave?"

"No. That's not what I'm saying. I want you to stay. But only if you want to. Only if you like it here. Gran, do you want to cross over? You never know. You might like the other side. Maybe it's all streets of gold and milk and honey," she said, her voice soft. She got the feeling most stories about the afterlife and heaven didn't have anything to do with what was actually out there. "I'd miss you, of course. But I know you have your own soul to look after."

"I like looking after yours," Gran said.

"Do you ever wonder though? What's out there waiting if you go?"

Gran's gaze went steadily back to her needle and thread. "If it's all the same to you, child, I'll decide when it's time to go."

"I'm going to have some odd company from time to time, and I don't want you going off in a huff. And no scaring off the angels." Zoë grinned. She enjoyed seeing Gran savor that idea.

"All right," Gran said, pursing her lips. Zoë knew that stubborn expression.

Zoë stood and stretched. "I'm glad you're staying, Gran. I'd have missed you." She stopped at the door. "If it ever does seem like it's time to go though, I will understand. You can't baby me forever."

The expected retort never came. Gran concentrated over her stitches and started to hum to herself. Zoë almost recognized the tune, but couldn't place it. With a smile, she closed the door gently behind her.

Zoë headed to her bedroom. She picked up a few odds and ends lying around and stuffed them in the bottom drawer with her socks and the chaos blade.

Thomas' warning still bothered her. Did he know something she didn't know? She had to laugh. Thomas probably knew a hundred lifetimes worth of things she didn't, but his motives still were unclear. On the other hand, what about the purpose of the spirit who'd given her the blade in the first place?

She wondered if it would open a portal like the keys had. Maybe, if the metal was all the lock required. But then, who knew what went into forging a magical object? She didn't particularly like the word "magical," because that made it sound like a bunch of wand-waving and enchantments and stuff she didn't believe in. Of course, she hadn't believed in real-life angels until she met Alexander, so who knew what life would bring her.

She looked to the trove of items the spirits had brought her when they came to her after she'd set Jackson Burly free. Although they were strange odds and ends, Zoë now realized those spirits had done the equivalent of giving her their card. Each one, other than those too weak to create a bodily form, had given her an item she could use to call them. They'd basically said *We owe you one*. The understanding touched her deeply.

She dug Alexander's stone from her pocket. She'd nearly forgotten she'd tucked it in there. It embarrassed her slightly that she'd taken to carrying it with her ever since she'd testified at Alexander's hearing. But as Zoë began to toss it in with the other trinkets, she hesitated. Who the hell was he to walk out with no word? To have his *lawyer* come by to break up with her? To only come back because Thomas said so?

For a moment, her anger built again and mixed with confusion, sadness, and sheer overwhelming weight. She gripped the stone in her hand, trying to decide what to do. Her cork burst. "Alexander!" she yelled.

The telltale pop sounded out in the hallway. She stood in the center of her room with her arms crossed, waiting for him to enter. "Well?" she said to the door.

Her heart caught in her throat when she saw him. His brow furrowed as though he had a headache. Zoë steeled herself.

"You sent Thomas? Thomas?"

"Thomas likes you," Alexander said quietly.

Zoë couldn't decide between the fifty responses that popped in her head, so she threw the stone at him with all her will and anger behind it. He caught it easily, but still looked injured.

"What is wrong with you?" she asked.

"They cast me out."

"So what?" Zoë flung at him.

He blinked. "So what? Maybe you cannot understand what it means," he said, his tone heating up.

"You lost your position. You got excommunicated. So what? Life goes on. You knew what would happen when you did what you did. It was still the right thing, and to hell with the Powers for thinking they can decide who should live or die. And to hell with you for being too much of a coward to tell me yourself. If you don't want to see me again, just say it. Or don't. But don't send someone else to say it."

"I cannot," he said, his tone now softer.

"You can't love me, or you can't say you don't love me? Look, I know this is my fault. I messed up at your hearing. The whole Stalker thing came out of nowhere, and I never should have said anything."

He raked his hand through his hair. A gush of air escaped his lips as he exhaled. A clash of emotions played across his face. "I am sorry, Zoë," he said finally. "None of this is your fault. Any who did not know about the chaos blade would have as soon as

Briony testified. And even with it, I do not care. Zoë, I know you. You are not a killer."

Her anger dissipated in an instant, but the hurt remained. "Just tell me why" she said, annoyed that she cared after only three dates and that she didn't have more pride. "I thought it was special. I know the case went badly, but the way you stood up for me, I thought...I thought you cared." She dashed away a tear, but not before he saw it.

With a blur of impossibly fast motion, Alexander came to her and wrapped his arms around her. She melted into his embrace. He whispered as he kissed her hair, "I am sorry, Zoë. I am one of the Fallen. I knew from the start it probably would happen, and nothing you did or said could have changed that. This is my fault. But I did not want to face it once I met you. You allowed me to forget what the future would hold for me."

Zoë stiffened and pushed back from him. "Wait. You're telling me you left me because you're a Free Angel?"

He hung his head and opened his mouth as though he wanted to speak, but couldn't say anything. Instead he nodded.

She couldn't help it. She laughed. Alexander looked up, startled. "Alexander," she said. "Why on earth would I care about that?"

"But—"

"No. Look. Answer me this—are you evil now? Following some prince of darkness? Doing nefarious deeds on a whim? Morphed into a demon when I wasn't looking?" She tried not to laugh, but it was a struggle.

A grin tugged at his mouth. "No, but little Zoë, my love, you cannot know what it means. This changes everything for me. My position, my work...all of it is gone. My family even. My parents, they are coping, but a Free Angel can never be a king."

"You idiot," Zoë said, pulling him close, their faces now scant inches from each other. "You think I care about your position, your work, or your family? I didn't even know about your family until I saw them at the hearing and Thomas told me. Who in their right mind would want to be a king anyway? Sounds like a lot of work."

"I do not know what is going to happen to me."

"Alexander, I don't know what's going to happen to me either. So what? So we find out together. That's what a relationship is. If it's not working, fix it. If life is hard, we lean on each other. You don't run off to keep from inflicting yourself on someone else. If it gets too much for me, I'll say so, but *you* don't get to decide that for me."

He looked at her one last time, as though suspecting she might change her mind. "I might be an outcast forever," he said.

"I might be one of those Stalker things. You had it right," she said. "I am changing. I'm not sure how, but I feel it. I've started seeing more. Things are happening. We find out together, face it together."

Instead of answering or asking the questions she knew he must have, Alexander kissed her hard on the lips. "I do not want to be without you," he said.

"So don't. Besides, you have to stay and protect me now."

"Do not be afraid, Zoë. Thomas will have Henry to a place of safety. I will watch out for you and for Robert Benson, along with others. Things will return to normal."

Zoë couldn't help but laugh, now awash with relief, and truly believing that, at least for now, that might be true. "Alexander, you don't know what normal means."

He grinned. "I suppose I do not." He kissed her again, this time with need and urgency. Their bodies twined together and instantly the heat enveloped them. Zoë let the last of her anger and fear melt into lusty, aching desire. Tenderness could come later.

CHAPTER 19

THE MOONLIGHT SPARKLED, reflecting on the sheen of sweat on Zoë's skin. Alexander ran his hand from her throat down her chest, growling appreciatively as she rocked her hips in an urgent rhythm. She leaned down to kiss him full on the mouth and then playfully nipped at his lips.

It felt right, and the reality that she'd very nearly lost him intensified the feeling. This was the first time they'd made love in her bed, and she liked having him there and a part of her life. Sure, she enjoyed his place, and she couldn't even imagine what it would mean to have anything she could think of. At the same time, this house was *her* place, and as much an expression of her personality as his home was of him.

She realized suddenly how few of the men she'd dated she'd allowed in her bedroom. Usually she opted to go to them. Had she closed her life off and protected her domain? Probably, she decided.

Growing up, she'd hidden the *real* Zoë, spirit-friends and all. One of the things she loved about Alexander was that she didn't have to pretend.

They moved together, and Alexander held her hips tightly as his excitement grew. Zoë loved the rapture on his face and the honesty of his enjoyment. Exotic and seemingly forbidden thoughts raced through her mind, causing her to blush and shudder with delight at the same time. In his other form, he was bigger, in every sense of the word, not to mention ferocious in a way that frightened and excited her. Pleasure built deep within and she tilted her head back, hands resting lightly on his, and drank in the warmth as the familiar and telling glow began to build in Alexander's body.

She loved everything about him, from his dual nature to his ridiculous pride, to the adorable way he seemed befuddled by human machinery. As his body tensed with impending release, hers responded, and she leaned forward again to hold him close to her as their bodies were wracked with an exhilarating rush. She peaked just before he did, and, as though answering her call, he cried out with her, unleashing pleasure in throbbing waves. They lay intertwined in a long, delicious silence. Contentment made Zoë's eyelids heavy, and sleep beckoned her as she rested her head on Alexander's shoulder.

She looked up, opening her mouth to say, "I love you." She hadn't said it but the one time back in Lament, and it seemed ages ago, even though it had been only days. They'd come through the trial, Henry would soon be safe, and Zoë thought now was the time to make it clear: she meant what she'd said. She did love him. She'd always believed that when one meant them, those words couldn't be said too often.

Just as she began to speak, Alexander stiffened. "Zoë," he said. "Something is wrong." He eased himself away from her and stood, his clothing forming over his magnificent body.

"What is it? Is it Henry? What happened?" she asked, sitting up suddenly. All thoughts of sleep vanished. She swung her feet around the side of the bed and began to look for her clothes.

Alexander's skin took on a blue tinge, and for a moment Zoë thought he was going to transform, but he must have just turned invisible. "I will return. Do not worry. I will watch over you."

"No way," she said, tugging on her panties and grabbing a pair of jeans that lay across a chair. "I'm coming with you."

She heard the pop before she could say "No," and ended up shouting the word to thin air. Alexander had gone. "Dammit," she said, racing around her room to find a bra and then dug up a sweatshirt from her dresser. She fumbled with her sneakers, swearing as she tried to unknot one of the laces. When finished dressing, she swore again. She had no idea where to go.

It took just a moment before she remembered the knife. She tossed socks all around, digging in her drawer for the chaos blade. Removing it from its t-shirt wrapping, Zoë slid it from its sheath, and held it in the air for a moment, looking at the cool glow of the alien metal. Tucking the sheath into the waistband of her jeans, she steeled herself to begin.

She had no idea if it would work. Sure, she'd seen into the celestial circle's waiting room at will, but Alexander hadn't told her where he planned to go or what had alarmed him so much. If she was the praying kind, she would have said a prayer for Henry. She hoped he was okay. The idea of him and Rose lost in blackness made her feel desperate and sick.

Focusing her mind on Henry, Zoë tried to see him and Rose, willing the blade to form the black archway she'd seen the night before. Nothing happened. Tears of frustration formed in her eyes, and she used all her effort and every ounce of strength she could muster. But it was as though they didn't exist.

It dawned on her that maybe the blade would not locate a dead human. The angels claimed chaos weapons had been crafted specifically to kill them and not demons or faeries or humans, so could the mordicite be attuned to their race? She couldn't be certain, but she shifted her thoughts to Thomas. She'd try anything at this point.

The black arch formed in front of her, groaning like a landslide. Again she saw nothing but blackness within. Striving to remember how she'd done it before, she recalled thinking about Thomas and their conversation before the trial. Instantly, she saw the empty gray waiting room on the other side of the arch. Not wanting to dwell on that place, in case someone showed up, she shifted her thoughts back to Thomas.

The inside of the archway went dark. "Come on, Thomas," she whispered. "Where are you?" Snatches of conversation came through the darkness. Her heart leapt. It sounded like Thomas and a few others, but their voices sounded distant. "Thomas," she shouted into the Void. "Thomas." She caught distorted glimpses of him, as though she was looking at him through waves of black water. The scene shifted and continually changed, and she could not get a lock on it. Trying to hold on to Thomas' voice was like grasping at water.

"Okay, Zoë, think." She sat down on the edge of her bed with the blade in her hand. The picture of the celestial waiting area had come in clearly. That could mean either the blade only showed places, not people, or maybe Thomas was out of reach. Taking a moment to breathe, she shifted her focus to the place beyond the portal where Thomas had led Henry and Rose.

The deep black in the arch turned gray, and not the bright gray of the celestial waiting room, but the swirling miasma of that strange in-between place where Henry had hidden. Zoë's stomach tightened. Without a doubt she could not just wander in there. That's exactly how Henry had died, and she doubted she'd fare any better.

No familiar voices came from this place. She stepped closer to peer into the mist. "Thomas?" she said quietly. "Henry?" A face coalesced in front of her, but it wasn't familiar. An insubstantial and contorting shape formed and then wavered. She couldn't tell if it belonged to a male or female, although it looked vaguely human. Its mouth opened and snapped closed as soon as Zoë caught its eye.

"Oh crap," she said, and the soul rushed toward her. As quickly as she could, she flung the knife away from her, and the archway slammed shut just as the soul reached the opening. Zoë let out a choked half-sob, heartbroken that the soul was lost and hungry. But self-preservation told her she shouldn't yank souls out of the ether.

Okay, she told herself, *no more other-worldly destinations*. That left the only place she could think of where Alexander might go when trouble brewed. After wiping her hands on her jeans, she picked up the knife and focused on Thomas' place. Although it was perhaps technically other-worldly, compared to the Void, it seemed a relatively harmless choice. The previous encounter told her anyone could see her through the other side of the arch, so she didn't focus on the public bar. Didn't seem wise to use an assassin's weapon to tumble into a room full of angels. Instead she thought about the office in the back.

In seconds the office appeared inside the archway. She saw Camille putting something into a cabinet at the rear of the room. Even with her back turned, Zoë recognized her long raven hair. When the angel turned around, her eyes widened in surprise. "Zoë?" she said.

"Camille." Zoë wanted to cry with relief. "Where is Thomas? Alexander took off, but wouldn't say what happened. Did something go wrong with Thomas and Henry? Is Rose okay?"

"Slow down, Zoë," Camille said, looking at the

archway uncertainly. "I heard from Thomas a moment ago. He's returning."

"Where is he right now? Could something have gone wrong?"

Even through the strange archway, she felt the pop of air as Thomas materialized in his office. He appeared with his back to Zoë, and stopped suddenly when he saw the look on Camille's face. Turning quickly, he stared through the archway at Zoë, and down at the blade in her hand.

"It's got to be Robert," Zoë said. "How could I be so dumb?"

She waved her arm in front of her, as though erasing the words on an invisible blackboard. When she did, Thomas and Camille disappeared. It only took seconds for the scene in the archway to shift to Robert Benson's living room.

Robert lay on the floor unconscious, with blood trickling from the corner of his mouth. Zoë immediately stepped through the archway and rushed toward him. She expected to feel cold or dizzy or something, but it was about as dramatic as stepping into the bathroom from the hallway. As soon as she passed through, the archway groaned closed behind her.

She ran forward and knelt beside him. "Robert? What's happened?" He didn't move. "Don't worry. I'll call an ambulance." As soon as she turned toward his desk and the phone, she found she wasn't alone.

"You," she said at the exact same moment the same word came from the mouth of Ren Jones, the necromancer she'd seen in Thomas' office, the very same one who had bound Jackson Burly. He was taking the last of the mordicite keys from Robert Benson's library wall, careful to leave them inside their protective glass cases. With the knife in her hand, she understood why.

He didn't feel to her senses like an angel, nor did he feel human, but the chaos blade vibrated intensely. "You're half angel," she said. She hadn't thought that possible. A half-angel necromancer?

"Stalker," he hissed.

A crash outside told her Ren had not come alone. A bird-like screech sounded. "Alexander," she whispered, feeling his presence somewhere nearby. She could sense other angels with him, as well as other presences that felt strange and unfamiliar to her.

"Don't worry about him. My friends will see to Alexander." His eyes never left the knife. "They'll be most interested in your blade. Demons do love mordicite."

"Demons?" Zoë said. "Ren, you're half angel. How can you side with demons?"

He barked a laugh at her. "You really are so human." He paused. "You know what? I don't think you know how to use that. I'm not interested in the mordicite for myself, but my friends perpetually seek it. And I have to confess, I don't mind the idea of the world losing a Stalker."

Ren moved around the desk and came at her. She had no idea what the half-angel part of his physiology would mean, but even if he were all human, she'd not want to take on a man his size. If demons were indeed outside, that made running away an unattractive prospect.

Ren hesitated when Robert Benson stirred behind her and moaned loudly. "Robert?" she said without taking her eyes off Ren, who had frozen in his tracks. "Are you okay, Robert?"

"Zoë?" he croaked. "Zoë, is that you?"

"Yeah, Robert. It's me. I came to help."

"Why are you glowing?"

She glanced down. The radiance started at her right hand, which held the chaos blade, but it covered her whole body now. She glanced up at Ren, who looked confused. Judging from the expression, she figured he couldn't see it, but Robert's words had given him pause.

Even without knowing what it meant, the strange glow on her skin filled her with confidence. Ren Jones would not hurt her or Robert Benson. She knew it in a way she couldn't explain. She could almost see the next few minutes play out in front of her in a whirling tableau. When Ren lunged, it happened exactly as she saw it. He grabbed for her wrist, but the foresight gave her just enough time to dodge and slip to the left, catching him off balance.

Then as though the knife had a mind of its own, it surged toward Ren's half-angel heart. She could almost hear it beating in her ears, and she watched herself act out a dance with graceful motions she knew by heart.

When the mordicite entered his body, Ren Jones screamed. He bucked against her fist. The blade pulsed, and primal energy coursed through her body. It exhilarated and repulsed her. She couldn't help but wonder what the chaos blade would do to Alexander or Thomas, if this was what it did to a half-angel.

Robert looked up at her. His dark skin had taken on an ashen color. "My guardian angel," he whispered.

"No," she said, fighting back tears. "I'm something else." Ren Jones' body fell to the ground beside her, black blood oozing from a cut in his torso. It smoked and burned, as though someone had poured acid into the wound.

"You moved like he did. So fast. You're not one of them?"

"No," she said.

An eerie howl came from somewhere nearby. The sound made her shudder.

"How many are out there?"

Robert coughed and tried to sit up. "Three more? I am not sure. He's the only one who came in. Did he get the keys?"

"No. Hey, don't sit up. The keys are still here. I'll gather them. Don't worry."

"An angel-killer. How scrumptious." The voice at the doorway sounded somehow more than human with subtle tones that overlapped each other. Zoë looked up to see a stunning man with blond hair down to his shoulders. His eyes shone too brightly for him to be human.

"Demon," Zoë said.

He smiled, leaning against the door jamb. "You make it sound so dirty."

Zoë listened for Alexander. The din of fighting had gotten louder, as though a zoo had emptied out and all the predators had decided to go to the gazelle enclosure at once.

"I'm afraid we didn't quite expect Dr. Benson to have so much protection. One Guardian we could have handled, but not four. Four, plus you. How wonderful. One Celestial Angel, three Fallen Angels, and one angel Stalker. You keep interesting company, Dr. Benson."

"Go to hell," Robert coughed.

The demon in the doorway threw his head back and laughed. "I'm on my way already," he said.

That's when Zoë noticed the darkness within him. She saw through him in her mind's eye, and a cloud filled the inside of his torso and one millimeter at a time, crept outward.

"What's wrong with you?" she asked. "It looks like cancer, but not."

"Fascinating," he said, looking closely at her. He shrugged, as though it was a matter of no consequence. "I'm dying," the demon said. "And so, I'm afraid, are you. You see, I need the mordicite in that blade. I could have gotten a tiny bit from the cores of each of those keys, enough to keep me alive for a few years. But that..." He shook his head in disbelief. "That, my dear, is priceless. I could keep five of us alive for an eternity with mordicite that pure. And since, as you know, a chaos blade cannot be stolen, we have two ways we can do this. You can give it to me, or..." He shrugged.

"Or you'll kill me." She hadn't actually known a chaos blade couldn't be stolen, but she filed that tidbit away, hoping she'd live long enough to make use of the information.

"With you dead, I can claim the blade by right. A shame, of course. I'm not violent by nature."

Zoë snorted her disbelief. "Apparently I am." She gestured down at Ren's still-smoking body. "I'm not giving you this knife." She crouched slightly, waiting for him to make his move.

"You must know that weapon will not hurt me in the least. If you cut me, I will heal, rip your delicate throat out, and take it."

She hesitated. If that were true, why didn't he just do it? Why stand around talking and posturing? "Come on then."

Unlike Ren, when the demon attacked her, he did not lunge, but drew back, hovering off the ground, and then he flew at her. He bared vicious, sharp teeth and let out a horrific sound. She tried to duck, but he quickly landed on top of her.

The knife did not respond to the demon as it had with angels, or even the half-angel, Ren. It didn't thrum in her hand or push itself toward the demon's heart, if he even had one. But even without its guidance, she managed to thrust it upward, clumsily once, and then again. Searing pain filled her shoulder where the demon bit her viciously.

Zoë struggled beneath the demon, terror ripping through her. Adrenaline surged, and the pain of the bite and the demon's claws digging into her shoulder receded. Screaming filled her ears, and it took a moment before she realized it was her own voice.

He held her so tight that when something behind the demon grabbed him and yanked him upward, Zoë flew forward with him. She cried out with relief when she recognized Alexander's blue wings stretched out behind the demon.

The demon's face changed. He was no longer handsome with a cultivated air. He looked as though he was being eaten alive from the inside out, and the extent of his illness showed in his sunken features. "I must have that mordicite!" he cried out. "The corruption is killing me."

Alexander restrained the demon from behind, but the creature struggled. Although Zoë felt weak, her heart pounded, and she did not hesitate to act. "No," she said. "I am." She plunged the chaos blade into the demon and thrust it upward, under his ribcage.

The demon had lied. Although the mordicite did not affect him the way it did the angels, he had no protection from the deep cut in his flesh. His eyes widened with shock, and he released her, dark blood gushing from the wound.

She yanked the blade out of the gash and staggered backward. With a thud, she fell onto her backside next to Robert. Alexander dug his claws into the demon's neck, finishing the task. Zoë turned away. After everything she'd seen that night, she couldn't bear to watch another death. With her foot, she shoved the body of Ren Jones over and laid her head on the ground next to Robert Benson.

Her voice thin, she said, "What kind of doctor are you anyway? I seem to be bleeding a bit." She fought the blackness that threatened to blot out her vision. The pure white ceiling above her was flawlessly smooth, like rolled fondant icing.

She closed her eyes and felt several hands on her. She recognized Thomas' voice as well as Alexander's. One of them, she wasn't sure which, said, "I've got her."

Although Zoë thought she'd only had her eyes closed long enough to blink slowly, when she opened them again, she found herself lying in a bedroom she didn't recognize. Part of her wanted to stay beneath the huge, fluffy comforter forever. She had to get up though, to find out if Robert Benson was all right.

It took her a few moments of stumbling through hallways, following familiar voices to find her way back to the front of the house. She saw Alexander first, now in his human form, looking unfairly immaculate as he leaned against Robert's desk in the library. As soon as she came to the doorway, he rushed toward her. "Little Zoë," he said. "You need rest."

"Robert," she said, leaning into Alexander as dizziness overtook her. "Is he injured badly?"

He led her to the couch, where Thomas sat, concern also showing on his face as he helped her sit. "Camille is with him now. She is an excellent healer," Alexander said. "She took care of your shoulder already."

Zoë hadn't realized someone had tended the deep bite-marks on her shoulder, partly because it hurt like hell. She pulled back the torn flaps of fabric on her sweatshirt and saw the red and rumpled skin where the demon had bitten her, but she could hardly complain about a few scars. The scratches had faded, although smears of dried blood covered her skin and clothing. "Angels can heal?"

"Camille can," Thomas said. "It's a rare and special gift. She cannot heal blood loss, however, which is why you should lie down. It looks ugly, but it will continue to improve."

Zoë looked about the room. Books and papers littered the floor, and Ren's bag of mordicite portal keys still lay on the floor near the desk. The bodies, both Ren's and the demon's, were gone.

"What happened?"

"When I arrived," Alexander said, "the demons had already ambushed Cesara, Robert's Guardian. Ren had led them here, having learned of the cache of mordicite keys. A human had accompanied them." He paused and looked at Zoë. "Peter Delancy."

"The guy that killed Kent." Zoë's mind reeled. "How did he find out about Robert?" It hit her with agonizing clarity. "He followed me here?"

Alexander nodded. "He took Henry's keys to Ren

and their demon masters, but those he had retrieved were not mordicite. Judging from the shape we found him in, his failure displeased them greatly. He followed you here, and that's when he discovered Robert's collection."

"Where is he now?"

"Dead," Thomas said.

Zoë nodded. She couldn't say she was exactly sorry to hear the news.

"He reported to Ren, who planned an attack."

"I don't understand Ren. With the blade in my hand, I knew what he was, a half-angel. How could he take up with demons and have become a necromancer?"

Thomas looked away, as though he held himself responsible. His voice was tight with anger. "Some angels, Zoë, fall further than others. We, Alexander and me, Camille and others, we are Free Angels. Ren had truly fallen. I thought I could save him."

Zoë reached over and gave Thomas' hand a squeeze. "You can't save everyone, Thomas."

Alexander looked at Zoë. "Apparently *you* can, my love. If you had not gone to get Thomas and Camille, I do not think I could have taken them alone."

It pleased her somewhat to know she'd rescued him, but she bit her lip when trying to decide whether to confess that she hadn't been quite as heroic as he thought. Summoning Thomas to their aid was more of an accident than a brilliant plan. She looked at Thomas, who shook his head subtly. She couldn't help but smile when she realized he wouldn't burst her bubble.

"You're going to have to tell me more about that archway, Zoë," Thomas said.

She nodded, weary. "I don't know. I can only do it when I'm touching the chaos blade. I discovered it quite by accident, yesterday, in fact. I have no idea what it means. My skin glowed earlier, when I held the knife." She looked down at her arm, and then panic gripped her. "Where is it?" She glanced around the room and peered under the couch. "Where is the chaos blade?"

"Here," Alexander said. He handed her a rolled up deep green bath towel. When she flipped the end of the bundle, it unfurled, and in the end she found the chaos blade. She picked it up quickly and inspected the edge. It was clean and wickedly sharp. She felt at her waistband and found the sheath still there. She slid the knife into the sheath, and covered it with her sweatshirt. She could tell by the looks on their faces that it made Alexander and Thomas uncomfortable, but they did not comment.

"The demon lied," she said. "He told me that the mordicite wouldn't hurt him."

Thomas chuckled. "Our cousins do that."

"Cousins?"

"They were the second created race after angels. Our creator found angels too static. We have little capacity for growth and change. When he created demonkind, he gave them the ability to lie and deceive. They know fear and desire in a way our kind does not. In the end, though, he went too far. Demons suffer from a corruption that eventually infects them all."

"He told me he was dying. I could see the blackness inside him."

Thomas nodded. "As much as this fact goes against human folklore, demons are not inherently evil any more than all angels are good. Our creator would not have intentionally made a race contrary to his own nature. But once the corruption takes root, they lose their hold on their basic good nature."

"And mordicite can cure them?"

Thomas shook his head. "Constant contact with mordicite will keep the corruption from spreading, but they've never found a cure for it."

"And what about healers like Camille? Can she not undo the damage?"

Alexander lifted Zoë's hand to his mouth and kissed her fingertips. "You are wonderful, to think of healing demonkind."

"No," Thomas said, "I don't think Camille could heal the corruption."

"I don't know if a demon would let me get close enough to try," Camille said from the doorway. Although still stunning, she looked weary.

"Not fans of angels then, huh?"

Camille smiled. "How are you feeling?"

"Tired," Zoë said. She looked down at the stains on the carpet. "I don't know why I don't feel worse. I killed two men. Well, one half-angel and one demon, but still. I should feel something, right?"

Alexander pulled Zoë close to him. "They would have killed you without a second thought, Zoë. The chaos blade is powerful in more ways than one. Some will want it for its more magical properties. Demonkind will desire the eternal metal."

Zoë swallowed hard. "I guess I am a Stalker after all. I mean that's what Stalkers are, right? Angel-killers?" After all the fierce denials, in the end, she had killed an angel. Granted he was a hateful, slimy, *truly* Fallen Angel, but she didn't know if that would make a difference to anyone hearing the story.

"Whatever you are, little Zoë, remember you also saved Robert Benson, and you saved me."

Thomas turned his head to the side, the way he did when he used telepathy. "I have to go. The celestial circle wants a report."

Zoë snorted. "Since when do you report to those windbags?"

Thomas laughed. "I'll be sure and give them your regards, young Stalker."

Camille smiled at Thomas. "I'll stay with Robert Benson. At least until he wakes."

"That's a good idea," Zoë said. "He'll probably have a million questions when he feels well enough to ask them. Wait, Thomas, before you go...is Henry all right?"

"Yes, I did get them to a refuge where they will be safe and Rose can perhaps begin to heal." He nodded to her before pulling his arms close to his body and popping out of the room.

Alexander helped Zoë to her feet. "Shall I take you back to your home, or do you wish to stay with me at mine?"

Zoë smiled, turned to Camille and gave her a hug. "Thanks for saving my life, Camille."

The beautiful angel smiled, her eyes looking happy and sad at the same time. "It was my pleasure, Zoë."

Zoë turned to Alexander and said, "First my place, so I can grab a couple of things and make a phone call. I think I'm going to call in sick tomorrow. Then, if it's okay with you, we'll stay at yours?"

"As you wish, little Zoë," he said. He kissed her gently on the forehead and drew her close.

She breathed in and out, enjoying the feeling of air filling her lungs: a simple thing, but one that made her immensely grateful. Life had gotten scary, and fast. She wasn't the same Zoë she had been a week ago. She didn't know if she could go back to work and act like nothing had changed. Before, she hadn't realized half-angels were real, much less plotting with demons. In her old life, corrupt humans wouldn't attack a man to steal his otherworldly keys, no one would gladly murder her, and she, ordinary Zoë Pendergraft, wouldn't kill anyone either. Now, she'd dispatched two powerful beings in one night.

For now she wanted to feel safe and normal. She buried her face in Alexander's chest and held on to him tightly. "I love you," she said and meant it with all the strength in her. Alexander had become her refuge in a scary world, even if she did have to save him once in a while.

A Note From The Author

I believe in angels, the power of pixie dust, and things that go bump in the night. When my son was small, I never, ever told him, 'Don't worry. It's just your imagination,' because I know the imagination is the most beautiful and terrifying thing a human being possess. The goal of every book is to spark the imagination. I hope very much this story has touched yours, and that you've enjoyed it. I'm honored that you chose to spend a little of your time immersed in my world. Thank you.

India Drummond

Be sure to watch for the second Zoë Pendergraft novel, Familiar Demons, in 2012!

If you enjoyed this, you may also enjoy my Caledonia Fae urban fantasies. The first novel in that series, Blood Faerie, is available now, and you can read the opening pages at the end of this book. Azuri Fae, the second in that series, has a planned release date in late 2011.

India's Website:

http://www.indiadrummond.com

Reader eMail:

author@indiadrummond.com

Also by India Drummond:

Blood Faerie

EILIDH DETECTED THE GREASY SCENT of evil moments before she heard the scream below. She perched in St Paul's steeple, watching Perth's late night pub-crawlers through rotting slats. The scurrying footfalls of humans did not hold her interest, nor did the seeping ruby blood that spread quickly over the flat, grey paving stones. Instead, her eyes turned north along Methven Street, seeking the source of that familiar smell.

Evil smelled like nothing else, worse than a rotting corpse, worse than sewage and disease, more vile than the fumes that billowed from modern machinery, more cloying than the shame of drunken whores. This particular evil was fresh, but not quite pure. It mixed with rage but was contained, refined, as though gestated in the belly of ancient hatred. This evil held promise, and for the first time in decades, Eilidh hesitated, slightly afraid.

The familiar magic that nestled in the subtle overtones of this particular wrong propelled her into action. She pulled back the shutter and leapt down to the roof below. Her feet made scarcely a sound as she landed on the mossy stone. She ensured that the black sweatshirt hood covered her short white hair and the other tell-tale signs of her race. Moving faster than any human could, she skipped down the side of the building, lightly touching window frames and door tops until she landed on the hidden south side of the dilapidated octagonal church.

The corpse at her feet stared at the full moon, glassy-eyed and empty. She crouched beside it and sniffed the air. The hole hacked in his chest left bone and organ exposed. Blood poured from it. He'd passed by the church only moments before. Eilidh had seen him with a human female who leaned against him, taking drunken steps, screeching too loudly, laughing at nothing. Eilidh had paid neither of them any attention. They were like scores of others who staggered down her street most nights.

Her senses caught the earliest whiff of decay. It began immediately upon death, as soon as the heart no longer thrust blood through mortal veins. Eilidh had to move before it masked the trace she hunted. She sprang forward and her feet carried her north just as someone behind her shouted, "Oi! You!"

The scent was not difficult to track. She darted past the small groupings of oblivious people, mostly gathering in the doorways of pubs, smoke wafting from their mouths. Various human smells: sweat, smoke, cars, and food all mingled together, but none could distract Eilidh from her quarry. She knew this smell because it was old and magical, and, like her, it was fae.

Read the novel now in print or on an eReader!

ISBN: 978-1-908436-01-6

e-ISBN: 978-1-908436-00-9